THE REAPER

MAC TIRE MAFIA

USA TODAY BESTSELLING AUTHOR

KALLY ASH

The Reaper
(Mac Tíre Mafia #2)

Copyright © 2022 by Kally ash
www.kallyash.com

The right of Kally Ash to be identified as the author of this work has been asserted by her under the Copyright Amendment (Moral Rights) Act 2000

E-book ISBN: 978-1-922353-54-2
Paperback ISBN: 978-1-922353-55-9

Cover design by Sly Fox Cover Design
Interior design by Sly Fox Cover Design
Editing by More Than Words Copyediting & Proofreading Services
Proofreading by Evermore Editing

CONTENT WARNING

This story contains explicit sexual content, profanity, graphic violence, and topics that may be sensitive to some readers. For a detailed list, please visit www.kallyash.com/ content-warnings/

For all the unashamed smut lovers out there.
Lap this shit up!

And for Leila ...
#teamleilaforlife

1

FALLON

I SHUT THE TEXTBOOK I'D BEEN FLIPPING THROUGH and glared at the cover. *The Fundamentals of Nursing Practice.* As far as I was concerned, those fundamentals could go suck a dick. Blowing out a breath, I ran my fingers through my unbound hair and dropped my head into my hands. Why the hell did I think I could do this? Studying full-time to become a freaking nurse?

Maybe Grayson was right, and I wasn't ready for this.

I'd barely been clean for a year when I started my nursing degree. I still had shit I had to work through, but my therapist had suggested focusing my thoughts on something other than my sobriety for a while. I didn't know what I wanted to do, but after talking to Grayson, he reminded me that there had been a time when I wanted to help people suffering from cancer like our ma had.

Nursing had seemed like the most logical choice.

But right now, it all seemed too difficult.

Maybe I just needed to take a break. I'd been studying for close to seven hours. The length of time had nothing to do with needing to study, but more to distract me from the quietness of the house. Grayson and Sloane had been gone for only two days, but it felt like a lifetime. For as long as I could remember, it was me and Grayson against the world. I didn't begrudge him finding happiness with Sloane—he deserved that—but I hadn't truly been prepared for what my life would be like without him in it every day.

Standing, I stretched my arms over my head and stumbled in the direction of the kitchen. I drew to a stop, however, when there was a thunderous knock on the front door. My whole body froze as fear overrode my senses, locking muscles down on bone and turning my blood to ice. The unease I was feeling expanded quickly until I could hardly breathe.

My world seemed to shrink down to just the door. Swiping my tongue over my bottom lip, I willed my body to break from the atrophy. To move. To do something. *It's only someone knocking on the door*, I tried to reason with myself. But that old fear—the one that crept up on me whenever I was alone—began to whisper in my ear.

What if it's him?

What if he came back?

Exhaling sharply, I forced my fingers to flex, telling myself that Owen Ward didn't know where I lived. That he wouldn't come back for me—not after Grayson made such a display of the other four men's bodies. Besides, he'd gone into hiding and Grayson hadn't been able to find hide nor hair of him no matter how much he looked.

Biting my lip, I started toward the door. Reaching up onto my toes, I peered through the peephole and looked out onto the street beyond the porch. It was dark outside, the streetlights barely breaking through the heavy rain that hadn't stopped falling since I'd started studying this morning. It had worsened though when a storm rolled through about two hours ago.

Orange lights flashed somewhere on my right, and I opened the door to find a black Range Rover parked haphazardly in front of my house. I frowned. Whoever it was, had half mounted the curb, and … was the driver's side door open? Squinting, I stepped forward to get a better look, only to nudge something with my foot on the front step.

My gaze dropped, my brain trying to make sense of what I was seeing. There was a dark mass—the shape indiscernible to my adrenalin-addled mind. Blindly, I reached behind me to flip the porch light switch beside the door. Yellow-gold light illuminated the doorstep, and I gasped when I saw what was lying there.

"Help." The word was breathless—a rasping baritone that simultaneously sped up and slowed down my heart. Whatever fear had been pinging through my body not more than a minute ago dissolved as I kicked into motion. My instincts took over—the same ones that were able to help Grayson after Sloane had brought him home beaten to within an inch of his life.

Crouching, I pushed the dark, rain-soaked hair away from the face of the man who had collapsed on my doorstep. I scanned his features, taking in the square jaw and dark stubble spread over it. A flicker of recognition shot through me. This was Orin Lynch, the clan's Reaper. Grayson had always warned me away from him—saying he was unstable and a danger to women.

But why the hell was he on my doorstep?

Injured. He must be injured. I surveyed his body for wounds, skimming my hands along his soaked clothes.

His skin was like ice against my palms.

I found the first injury on the left side of his ribs. My hands were coated in his blood, so I continued quickly to see if there was anything more serious. I felt all the way down his body and legs, not finding anything else, but I needed to get a better look at the wound in his side.

The sound of a roaring engine reached my ears over a rumble of thunder. A black SUV had turned into the street and was slowly driving down the road. I squinted against its bright headlights, wondering briefly whether it was someone from the clan to pick up Orin before I saw a bright flash coming from the dark interior.

Something *thwacked* into the wall beside me, and I turned in slow motion to see a hole in the white cement render.

Jesus, fuck, that was a bullet!

Throwing myself to the ground, I draped myself over Orin and squeezed my eyes shut as I waited for the volley of suppressed gunfire to stop. My heart wasn't interested in waiting it out, deciding to leap into my mouth. My pulse raced. My palms were sweating despite the rain. For a few long seconds, near-silent bullets pelted the Rover and the front of my house, shattering the small window in the front door.

Then, just as quickly as they'd started, the bullets stopped, and the SUV sped off in a squeal of tires, leaving the acrid smell of burned rubber mixed with cleansing rain in its wake. My pulse was still thundering when I straightened and checked Orin. He didn't appear to have been hit, but if we stayed out here, they might come back to finish the job.

Rising on wobbly legs, I hooked my hands under Orin's arms and attempted to lift him. A couple of inches was all the ground I could manage, so I tried again. He was deadweight—probably more than double my own. I tried again, grunting with the effort. Each time I managed to drag him only an inch or two, but I finally had him inside.

Once his legs were in, I hustled around to shut and lock the front door. Broken glass crunched under my feet. Grabbing a magazine and some duct tape, I shoved it over the window casement and secured it, then shut off the porch lights and turned around. Outside the windows, lightning illuminated the sky, sending shadows and light dancing along Orin's body sprawled on the hallway floor.

Hurrying to his side, I lifted his shirt to get a better look at the wound, but the soaked fabric stuck to his clammy skin. I was going to have to remove it. In the kitchen, I found the scissors in the top drawer, washed my hands, then snagged the first aid kit from under the sink. From the laundry, I grabbed a clean towel and ran back to Orin.

Balling up the towel, I put it under Orin's head, then got to work removing his shirt. Sliding the scissors under the hem, I sliced through the cotton quickly and peeled away the sides. Blood coated the left side of his body from under his arm to his waist. Blood was still pouring from the wound over his ribs, and I slapped my hand over it while unzipping the first aid kit with my teeth. The kit's contents spilled out over the ground, and I searched for a packet of gauze.

Pressing it to his side, I applied pressure for a minute before swapping it over for another clean wad. I had no idea whether this was a gunshot or knife wound, but the one thing that was apparent was that he would die if I couldn't figure out how to stop the bleeding. Pulling the soaked gauze from his side, I irrigated the wound to clear some of the blood away. Now that I could see better, it was clear it was an exit wound—a bullet wound—but how in the hell had it missed his lung? He should be struggling to breathe right now.

However it had happened, he was a lucky fucking bastard.

When I was satisfied that he wouldn't die in my hallway, I put in some hasty sutures. They weren't pretty, but they would hold for now. I'd taught myself a crude and rudimentary way to suture when Grayson started coming home with wide gashes on his forehead.

Turning Orin onto his side, I searched for the entry wound. A small hole marked his left side, coming in at an angle under his ribs. After irrigating the site, some more sutures, and bandaging him up, I wrapped another bandage all the way around, then dragged him into the living room.

I was panting and sweating by the time I got him in there, and I eyed the distance from the floor to the couch. There was no way I would be able to lift him, so I set the towel back under his head and then grabbed the blanket from the back of the couch. Kneeling beside him, I draped the thick blue fabric over his body. One edge had folded under, so I leaned forward to fix it, but the shift in position left me with my face hovering close to his upper body.

His chest was covered in tattoos, and a thrill of ... *something* went through me. It was a foreign feeling, although I *thought* I recognized the echo of it. As if without thought, my hand moved to one of the largest designs, hovering over the outline of the Mac Tíre tattoo in the center of his chest. I traced the edge of the proud head and elegant back of the wolf, the pads of my fingers running over the curling tail and the Celtic whirls. Grayson had the same design on the back of his hand, but I had never found it appealing. On Orin, though, there was a certain attraction to it.

Dragging my hands down further, I touched each tattoo, willing the heat from my body to transfer into his. His skin was still too cold. I needed to warm him more. I was startled, however, when a stronger-than-it-should-have-been hand wrapped around my wrist where it rested against Orin's chest. My frantic pulse matched my frantic gaze as it darted to his face. Irises the color of midnight stared back at me. Surprise danced through his features for the briefest second before his eyes rolled back in his head and he slipped back into unconsciousness.

Rising from my crouch, I turned up the heater in the living room, then wrapped my arms around myself. What was I supposed to do now? I didn't want to leave him alone—not when his injuries could turn dire. I also didn't know whether someone would be shooting at us again. I couldn't leave.

So, I settled onto the couch and began my vigil.

I WOKE TO SAVAGE CURSING. MY EYES FLUTTERED briefly before fully opening to find Orin sitting up, clutching his ribs, and taking in the room. When he removed his hand, I saw the fresh blood decorating his palm and the bandage.

Leaping from the couch, I shouted, "Stop moving, you daft prick!" Slapping his hand back over the wound, I pressed, eliciting a sharp hiss from his mouth. He gave me a venomous look from the corner of his eye, which I studiously ignored. "You'll open your stitches if you keep moving around like that."

I thought I heard him mutter, "I didn't imagine you," before saying in a much louder, much more commanding voice, "What the hell happened?"

Fixing him with a glare, I pulled the first aid kit closer and rummaged through it until I found the gauze. Ripping open the packaging, I motioned for him to move his hand away, unwound the bandages, and removed the newly soaked gauze pad. The wound—although bleeding freely—wasn't any wider than it had been before. It looked like my sutures were holding, too.

Quickly covering it with fresh gauze, I applied pressure as I reached for a sterile bandage, my eyes darting to his face when he hissed in another breath. His eyes flashed with rage … rage and *pain*.

Pain he tried to hide behind a snarl.

He barked, "Watch it."

Ignoring the hostility, I wrapped the bandage around his torso, my arms reaching behind his back with effort. When my arm brushed against his skin, he recoiled.

"Don't touch me." His voice was hoarse.

Tension radiated from those three words, and I paused.

"How am I supposed to bandage you up if I don't touch you?"

For a long minute, he stared at me, clearly thinking it through and coming up with the same conclusion I had.

With a dismissive grunt, he replied, "Just hurry the fuck up."

"Don't go raging at me, you langer."

Despite the pain still etched on his features, one of his dark brows winged up—as if he couldn't believe I'd call him on his bullshit. Darkly, he replied, "If you knew who I was, you wouldn't be saying that."

Even though I didn't want to, I looked him in his cold eyes and said, "I know exactly who you are and what you do."

"Then you'd do well to remember that I don't let those who hurt me remain breathing."

My chest squeezed with the threat not just of his words, but also the razor-sharp weight of his gaze. He was the Reaper, and I had no doubt he would do whatever he had to do to ensure his survival. But I had grown up with Grayson, who could be just as prickly if I caught him on a bad day, so I decided to deal with Orin like I dealt with my brother when he was being an ass.

With bravado and a take-no-shit attitude.

"And you'd do well to remember that I saved your life." I glared at him from beneath my lashes. "You would've died on my doorstep if I hadn't dragged your arse inside."

He dismissed me with a grunt. *Again!*

"Not to mention, I could've been *shot* while saving you."

His eyes widened a fraction while the muscle in his jaw

ticked. Rage flowed off his body as he demanded, "*Shot?* Who the *fuck* shot at you?"

2

ORIN

MY MURDEROUS RAGE—THE SAME ONE THAT had been simmering in the background for all my life—flared to life almost violently. "*Shot*? Who the fuck shot at you?" And why the fuck did I see red just thinking about someone harming this woman?

I told myself it was because she was Grayson's sister, and that made her friend to the clan, but an insidious part of my fucked-up brain screamed that it was something else, something I didn't want to consider right now.

"Fallon?" I asked forcefully, trying again. "Who the fuck shot at you? When did this happen?"

Securing the bandage, she avoided my eyes as she said, "I don't know. It was dark. And last night."

The neck of her oversized shirt fell off her shoulder, and my gaze dropped to the small birthmark that had been hidden beneath the fabric. Tearing my eyes off the smooth expanse of her skin, I asked, "What kind of car was it?"

"A black Rover just like all the clan cars."

Fuck. She had no idea how fucking lucky she was—how lucky we both were. I ran a hand through my hair, clenching my fingers tightly and tugging. I turned back to her, searching her face before dropping lower. I scanned her body for any signs of injury, taking in how her yoga pants hugged her curves and her t-shirt clung to her breasts.

"Tell me what happened."

She arched a brow at my sharp tone. "You knocked. I answered. You passed out. A Rover came around the corner and slowed in front of the house. The next thing I knew, I was covering your body with mine and waiting for the hail of gunfire to stop."

I nearly swallowed my own tongue. This woman had protected me with her body, without a second thought about her own safety. Shockingly, my anger was placated by her response. Clearing my throat, I asked, "You didn't get hurt?"

"Why do you care if I got hurt or not?"

"Fuck, Fallon, you're a fellow clan member's sister." It was a partial truth and one I had no interest in exploring further right now. Besides, she had saved my life at the risk of hers. The least I could do now was protect hers since it seemed I'd brought violence to her doorstep.

Literally.

I stared into her blue eyes, feeling like I was falling into the bluest ocean.

Then I shook my head and told myself to stop being such

a fucking pussy.

A woman in my life would only ever be seen as a target for my and the clan's enemies.

Besides, I was thirty-six years old. Fallon had to be at least fifteen years younger than me.

Too young. Too fucking innocent.

"So, do me a fucking favor, and tell me—" *Too close.* She was too close, the scent of ylang-ylang growing stronger. I shifted my body away from hers, sucking back a nasty curse when my side let me know in no uncertain terms that it did *not* enjoy the movement. After a few deep breaths through my nose, I finished, "Did you get hurt?"

She sat back on her heels, her mouth twisted into a frown for a split second. "No. I didn't."

With a grimace that I tried to hide, I slid backward until my shoulders hit the wall. Getting to her feet, Fallon retreated to the couch, falling into the cushions without taking her eyes off me.

"How long have I been unconscious?"

She shifted her eyes to something on the wall above my head. "At least twelve hours."

I licked my lips, drawing her gaze for a brief second before she looked away, a flush creeping up her delicate throat …

A throat I wouldn't mind seeing peeking through my fingers as I wrapped my palm around it …

Fuck. Dangerous thought. Dangerous *fucking* thoughts.

She cleared her throat. "You should go to the hospital to get that wound checked out."

I shook my head. "Not going to happen."

My response elicited a frown. When she finally spoke, her

tone was bland. "The bullet only missed your lung by a millimeter. I honestly don't know why you aren't in worse shape. I'm about three and a half years away from being a fully qualified nurse." She jabbed her finger in the direction of my ribs. "And my suturing skills aren't great, so there's a high chance of them snapping before your body can fully heal. You need to go to the hospital and get checked out properly."

I stared at her for a solid minute, waiting for her to back down. Most people did when they felt the full force of my black gaze. When it was clear she wasn't going to break, I said firmly, "No."

She blinked like she was having trouble processing what I'd just said. "No? What do you mean, *no?* You're putting your life in danger by not going."

"My life is always in danger." And now, thanks to me, so was hers. "Have there been any other shots fired into the house while I was unconscious?"

She held onto her upper body tightly, her throat bobbing with nerves. "No."

Maybe there hadn't, but that didn't mean there wouldn't. I got to my feet, pain stabbing at me like a relentless dagger. Fallon's eyes narrowed on the savage twist of my mouth as I breathed through the pain.

Leaping up, she tried to urge me back down. "You shouldn't be pushing yourself right now."

My stomach turned as if it agreed with her. Well, too fucking bad. I brushed past her—or attempted to, at least. My knees buckled, making me throw my arm out to the wall to keep myself from going all the way down. Fallon was there a moment later, arm around my back and taking my weight.

"You need to sit down."

"No." I blinked, my vision fuzzing out to black. Shaking my head, I repeated, "No. I need to go …"

It turned out I wasn't going anywhere.

The next thing I knew, I was staring at the ceiling while Fallon tried to disentangle her arm from behind my back.

"Jesus, you weigh a lot," she muttered angrily. Her eyes returned to my face, her brows rising in alarm. "Orin? Orin, can you hear me?"

"ORIN? ORIN, WAKE UP!"

The words were hissed and laced with fear.

I was instantly alert, my eyes opening wide to search for danger. They shifted over to Fallon who was looking at something behind us. When her blue eyes returned to my face, they were wide—terrified.

"What is it?" I asked, my voice rasping over my rough vocal cords.

Her voice dropped even lower. "Someone's trying to get in the house."

My first instinct was to sit up, but my ribs still screamed at me. How long had I been unconscious this time around? With a groan, I attempted to get upright again, only to lose the battle to get vertical. If it wasn't for Fallon's hand under my arm, nothing would've stopped me from collapsing backward.

"What happened?"

"I fell asleep on the couch. I woke up a few minutes ago when I heard the front door handle jiggle. Then I saw shadows pass by the windows."

She pointed at the living room windows opposite us with a shaking finger. I waited—tense and wound tight—to see whether the shadows would reappear. It only took a few minutes, but two men walked past the windows, trying to peer past the sheer curtains.

Turning to look at Fallon, I demanded in a low voice, "Tell me you have a gun in the house."

Her whole body stiffened, but she nodded.

"Where is it?"

She bit her bottom lip. "Grayson has a safe in his room."

"Where is that?"

"Upstairs. Second room on the left."

More shadows continued to fall across the floor, and as much as I hated to send her up there on her own, it was better that she went. She knew exactly where to go.

"Go. Now."

Without argument, Fallon took off out of the room, the creak of the stairs the only indication of where she was in the house. The handle on the front door rattled again before it shuddered as someone attempted to kick it open.

I hauled myself onto my feet and stood behind the living room door, where I could remain hidden from view for as long as possible.

A loud *crack!* thundered through the room as the wood finally yielded to the force being exerted on it.

I heard only one set of boots on the floor, kicking through

the debris, moving toward the living room. Fallon would've had to have heard that. I hoped to God that she was smart enough to stay out of sight. She was already collateral damage in this. Having her blood on my hands would make this already fucked-up situation ten times worse.

The sound of the boots stopped suddenly, muffled by the carpet as they stepped into the living room. First, my gaze zeroed in on the muzzle of a gun, then the leather-clad hand holding it. Despite my injuries, anticipation drilled through me, the monster lurking in the back of my subconscious already salivating with the knowledge that blood would be spilled in the very near future.

He stepped fully into the room, and I saw the clan tattoo on the side of his neck.

Motherfucker.

"Where the fuck are you, cocksucker?" the Bèar Clan member asked the empty room in a bass growl.

Glancing down to my left, I saw a horse-shaped stone paperweight on the mantle. Picking it up, I tested the weight in my palm.

A floorboard creaked on the stairs.

The guy spun around, his gun raised, but he was aiming at the door, while I was standing a few feet to the left. Adrenalin hit my bloodstream like high-octane fuel, making me forget about the pain that was pumping through my body.

I lunged for him, swinging my fist, and the paperweight clutched tightly in my hand, into the side of his head. It made a heavy thudding sound as it connected—the blow and my momentum sending us both to the floor. The gun fell out of his hand, and I crawled over his body to snatch it up before he could. The hit must've stunned him for only a moment because the next thing I knew, we were wrestling for control of the weapon.

I didn't hear the heavy footsteps of the other guy coming to help, but I did feel the cold bite of metal against the back of my skull.

"Ease off, arsehole," the other man told me, pressing the weapon in a little tighter. I recognized his voice immediately. It was Brian Farrell. The fucking Bèar Clan's Reaper. "Let Will go. Nice and easy now."

Pulling back, I released my hold on Will and sat back on my heels. The gun muzzle followed my movement, the same amount of pressure applied the whole time.

Farrell laughed. "Orin Lynch, on his knees. You know, if I did men, I'd get you to suck my cock right now. Hell, I should get you to do it anyway. A little degradation and humiliation before death never goes astray. Right, Orin?"

I didn't dignify that statement with an answer. Instead, I kept my mouth shut because there was a chance they would leave with me now, and they wouldn't have to know that Fallon was in the house. She would be safe.

"Where's the bitch who lives here?" Will asked, getting to his feet.

Since I'd been brawling with the bastard, I hadn't been able to get a good look at him, but now that I could see his face properly, I realized it was Brian's brother, Will.

I bared my teeth in the parody of a smile when I saw the blood trickling from his lip. That little show of defiance earned me a strike to the head with the butt of his gun. My ears rang from the force of the blow, and that paired with my already damaged body, left me feeling like I was going to be sick.

My defiance earned me another strike—this time from Brian. "Where's the woman?" he hissed.

"I don't know anything about any woman." My words were surprisingly steady.

"Bullshit. We know she lives here." There was a brief pause before he said, "Did you put a bullet in her head? Get her out of the way? I heard you were ruthless like that."

"There is no woman. She left a couple of hours ago." The lie came out as smooth as butter.

Brian growled in frustration. "Will, go and check upstairs."

It took everything in me to stay perfectly still and not react. I'd been speaking loud enough that Fallon would've been able to hear the entire conversation. All she had to do was hide somewhere until Will was gone, but my heart stuttered to a stop when I heard the creak on the stairs behind us.

Will glanced up at the open door. With his gun raised, he moved into the kitchen and down the short hall to the base of the stairs. The bottom tread creaked again when he stepped on it, and I braced for Fallon's scream …

But it never came.

Instead, it was a gunshot—so loud in this quiet house, on this quiet street that I knew someone would be calling the cops soon.

"Will, is she dead?" Brian called. When there was no answer, he tried again.

The pressure of the muzzle on the back of my skull was suddenly gone as Brian stepped from the living room and followed in the direction his brother had gone. I was on my feet a moment later, a clawing sense of urgency rushing over me.

Rounding the corner, time seemed to slow down to a crawl.

I took in the scene.

Will's forehead had a neat hole dead in the center.

The wall was painted with gray matter and fragments of bone.

The force of the shot had knocked him backward, so he was draped over the railing behind him, blood leaking from the massive wound to the back of his skull.

Brian had crouched down at his brother's side, talking to him in a low voice that would never be able to rouse the dead. Movement from my peripheral vision caught my attention.

It was Fallon, peering out a broom closet opposite the stairs. Her ocean-blue eyes were wide with a fear I felt trickling down my own skin. She had killed a rival clan member, and I knew what that meant.

Holding out my hand to her, I expected her to take it, but she shook her head and pointed behind her. That was when I realized it wasn't a broom closet but an attached garage. Fuck, it was our way out. We had to move quickly—before Brian pulled himself out of his grief. I moved toward the door quietly, sliding inside the darkened garage.

"Tell me you have the keys," I asked in a low voice.

She nodded and pointed at the car. I moved over to it. It was a Ford Mustang Mach 1—something fast enough to put enough miles between us and this clusterfuck of a situation. Sliding into the driver's seat, I waited for Fallon to get in too.

"The garage door control is on the visor," she said so softly I could barely hear her. She pointed at the visor with a shaking hand. Shock. She was going into shock, and I couldn't blame her. She had shot a man in the head.

I hit the button to open the door, then waited until it was just high enough for the Mustang to slide out. Gunning the engine and throwing it into reverse, I got us the fuck out of there. The tires squealed as they dropped off the driveway and over the gutter. But it was the sound of gunfire that made my head jerk around.

Brian stood spotlit in the house's doorway with his gun raised. The slash of blood arcing across his forehead looked black in the fading light. He took aim again, and I shifted the car into gear. I hit the accelerator, the force of the V8 engine catapulting us forward. Brian continued to shoot at us, but the bullets glanced off the car's body.

Fuck, did Kent get fucking body armor on this thing?

I got a look at Fallon's face which had drained of color. She also had a hand wrapped around the door handle, her knuckles turning white from her grip. Driving as fast as I could without drawing attention to what was going on, I got us onto the freeway and started heading south. There was no way I was going to drive us straight to the safe house—not with Brian Farrell on our asses.

Movement in the rearview mirror caught my attention.

Farrell was in his car and catching up fast.

"Hang on," I told Fallon, then put my foot down.

3

FALLON

I WAS SHAKING. COLD. BREATHING SO QUICKLY that I was getting light-headed, and my stomach was beginning to cramp. I knew the signs of shock when I saw them. Glancing down, I found the gun still clutched tightly in my hand—my fingertips starting to get a bluish tinge to them.

Orin was driving too fast down the freeway, blowing past cars and lorries that happened to get in our way. Ducking down, I peered through the side mirror and saw a black Rover a couple of hundred yards away. Were we being followed?

"Farrell isn't going to let us go without a fight," Orin said, his voice surprisingly gentle. "I'll lose him though."

"Who's F-F-Farrell? Someone from another c-c-clan?" My teeth were chattering so badly I barely got the words out.

Orin's dead-of-midnight eyes raked over me for a brief

second before returning to the road. Apparently, that was all the answer I was going to get.

Then, he murmured, "You can let go of the gun now."

My gaze skittered down to my lap. My fingers were aching. Taking in a shallow breath, I tried to relax them, but I couldn't seem to get my brain and hand to communicate.

"Fallon?" Orin's voice was gentle. "Look at me, Filly."

I turned to look at him, and my question was a whispered, "What did you call me?"

He glanced away, suddenly intent on looking anywhere but at me. Holding out his hand, he waited for me to do as he demanded. When it was clear he wasn't going to answer my question, I forced myself to relax and released the gun into Orin's large, waiting hand.

Without taking his eyes off the road, he popped open the lid of the center console, slid the weapon inside, and closed it.

Orin continued to guide my car across the lanes of increasing traffic, weaving through impossible spaces all in the hopes of losing our tail. Christ, I never thought I'd say those words. This wasn't my world. This was my brother's world, although now that I had shot a man in the head, I supposed it was mine now, too. My eyes darted to the center console.

"Fuck." Orin's dark eyes cut to the rearview mirror, his brows dipping low.

"What is it?"

"The fucker is still behind us." He cut the headlights on the Mustang, making the road in front of us disappear for a moment.

Panic clawed at me almost immediately until I realized that the night blindness was wearing off and I could see the freeway just fine with the intermittent lighting alongside the stretch of road.

We eased off the road at an exit, and I watched to see whether the Rover would follow us. It did, Farrell pulling in hard to the exit and speeding up. We were spat out into an industrial area, but soon, the two-lane stretch of asphalt became narrower … and darker until finally, we were heading out of whichever town we'd driven through and out onto a regional road. Orin flicked the lights back on to illuminate the road in front of us—although road was a generous term for it. It was more like a lane, with intermittent stacked stone walls on either side of the shoulder, along with overgrown grass and bramble bushes.

It was barely wide enough for one car, let alone two.

Up ahead, there were a set of red taillights, which were moving a hell of a lot more slowly than we were. Orin saw the slower-moving vehicle ahead before his attention returned to the rearview mirror.

"Motherfucker."

I peered over my shoulder to see that Farrell was still there. The Rover's high beams were spotlighting us. As Orin swerved across the road, I blinked away the glare and saw a hand stick out the window, and in that hand was a …

"Get down!" Orin grabbed the back of my neck and forced my upper body to fold down. The side mirror disappeared in a spray of glass, and my heart thought it was a good time to start pounding extra hard. Orin hit the gas, sending my Mustang hurtling forward until we were practically kissing the car in front's ass.

More shots were fired, and the car in front nearly made us smash into him when he suddenly swerved off the road and onto the narrow shoulder that couldn't have been more than a foot wide. Of course, given the width of the road, we were forced to swerve onto the other side to avoid hitting him.

Another shot pinged against the rear of the car, and I was never so glad that Grayson had insisted on making my car bulletproof. I had no idea it was even possible, but he'd apparently made it happen.

Up ahead, another car appeared on the other side of the R-road. Orin put his foot down and accelerated toward it. I clutched at the edge of my seat and watched in wide-eyed terror as he played chicken with the oncoming traffic.

I licked my lips. "Orin?" I asked.

"Trust me."

We were probably only a couple of hundred yards away now, and it didn't look like he was going to move in time. With one yank on the wheel, he slid over enough to be able to pass safely, but so did Farrell.

Orin growled, dark eyes bouncing between the road and the rearview mirror.

For miles, we zigzagged between oncoming cars, always pulling onto the correct side of the road at the last minute.

"Come on, you bastard, make a mistake," he muttered under his breath. He suddenly smiled, and I looked ahead to see what had caught his attention. An articulated lorry was heading right toward us. There was barely enough room for us to pass one another, so Orin stayed in the middle of the road.

"Orin," I repeated, this time clutching his forearm. He hissed at the contact, his dark eyes swinging to mine. I swallowed. "Please."

"Do you trust me?"

I answered him honestly. "I don't know you."

"You're part of this clan now, Fallon. You should know that you can trust me with your life now."

Part of the clan? I shook my head. "I'm not part of the clan. I made a mistake."

"A mistake that saved my life."

Startling yellow-white lights began to cover his features, and I turned my face back toward the road. The truck was maybe a hundred yards away now—close enough for his headlights to wash over the car's interior.

The lorry driver blew the horn in warning, flashing his high beams at us, but Orin kept us steady. My pulse was beginning to crawl out of my throat, and I clutched the door release, wondering if I could survive rolling out at this speed—although, to be honest, there was nowhere for me to roll. If I opened this door, I would be slamming into a stacked stone wall and either sustaining a head injury or internal injuries—both of which could kill me.

If Orin didn't do it first in a fiery crash.

Orin's eyes cut to where my hand rested. "Trust me, Filly."

I froze, the use of my nickname jarring coming out of his mouth. I wanted to know how he knew that was what my mom had called me, but clearly now was not the time. The truck was less than fifty yards away now, and no matter how badly I wanted to shut my eyes and not watch what was about to happen, I knew I had to. If I was going to die, I had to do it with my eyes wide open.

Thirty yards.

Twenty.

Ten.

The whole car was awash with flashing lights and a blaring horn. Orin looked behind us, an evil grin spreading across his mouth. He yanked hard on the wheel, sending my car into the small space between the side of the lorry and the wall. Sparks flew when metal and stone met, showering the night with a riot of fireworks. I spun around in my seat to peer out the rear window just in time to see the Rover slam into the wall and go through it—his momentum carrying him into the field beyond.

The lorry driver was still hitting the horn as he passed but didn't slow down.

"…you okay?"

I turned to find Orin's gaze zeroed in on me. It looked like he was waiting for something. Waiting for me to say something. "What?"

"I asked if you were okay."

Running a shaking hand through my hair, I nodded. "Yeah, I think so. Orin, that was fucking terrifying."

He grunted. "We lost him. For now, at least."

Suddenly, all I wanted was to crawl into bed and pretend it was all a dream. Or better yet, crawl into a bottle and never come back out. I shook my head at that last thought. That wasn't my sobriety talking—that was my trauma—and I'd worked too damn hard to backslide now.

"I want to go home." I'd accidentally let the words out, and they were a pitiful whimper. I felt Orin's eyes on me but couldn't bear to look at him.

"You can't go home."

Flickering my eyes to him briefly, I found that even though his dark eyes were on the road, they somehow felt like they were all over me at the same time. "What?"

"You can't go home. You killed a rival clan member. You're public enemy number one to them now. You can't go home."

My eyes dropped to the center console, and I licked my suddenly dry lips. "Ever?"

His jaw tightened. "Once the threat has been taken care of, I'm sure you'll be able to."

"How long will that take?"

"However long it takes."

We fell into silence, and I stared at everything and nothing as we drove through the night. I didn't even know where we were.

"Not far from Ballymahon."

Shit, my mind must've spat the words out unconsciously. "Ballymahon? That's at least sixty miles from Galway. Are we going back to the safe house or something?"

Orin pulled his phone from his pocket and made a phone call, ignoring my question completely. "Finnan, work has forced me into hiding. I'll be gone a few days … Can't. Mannix will have his clan looking for me … I don't want to draw attention to the location of the safe house … I'll check in in a few days." He hung up.

"Where are we going?"

"Somewhere that'll be safe for now, but not before we dump your car and get another one."

Dump my car? "Dump it where?"

He shrugged. "Don't care, but it's too conspicuous."

TWENTY MINUTES LATER, ORIN PULLED INTO THE parking lot of a 24-hour Tesco and turned off the engine. Getting out, he said, "Take what you need from the car, including the gun," then began walking away toward the store's entry.

I wound down the window. "Wait!" I called out. "Where are you going?"

"To get supplies," he called back over his shoulder.

"You don't even have a shirt on!"

He waved off my concerns.

Infuriating man. I did as he asked though, getting out and opening the trunk to find the first aid kit I kept there, as well as a blanket and a towel. Popping open the lid of the first aid kit, I took a quick inventory, then retrieved the gun.

Touching it a second time wasn't a comforting experience, and I grappled with the fact that I had killed a man. I was studying to be a nurse. Sure, I hadn't taken the Hippocratic oath, but I would have to recite the nurse's pledge when I graduated nursing school. I would swear to serve humanity. I would promise that my patient's health came first—always.

And now, I felt like a complete and utter hypocrite for what I did tonight.

I blinked rapidly when a man started walking my way, and my fear—the one that seemed to lurk in my brain's subconscious—began to stretch out. He was backlit by the store's bright lights, so all I could see was his silhouette, but he cut an imposing figure.

Instinctively, I retreated a step.

"Fallon?"

I relaxed at the sound of Orin's rough voice, even though he was the antithesis of what would be considered safe.

"Are you okay?" he asked, stopping in front of me. Now dressed in a black t-shirt, he had an armful of protein bars, fruit, bottled water, and frozen meals. "Did someone say something to you?"

I shook my head, still unable to speak.

"What's wrong then?"

I blew out a breath and shook my head. "Nothing. I just … it was nothing."

He studied me for a full minute before placing the groceries onto the hood of the car. "I'm going to get us another ride. Stay here."

I glanced around the lot. There were maybe two dozen cars parked throughout, and I knew he wasn't going to try to hail a cab. When Orin said he'd get us another ride, he really meant he was going to steal us another ride. I watched him stalk through the lot, bypassing cars I thought he would choose until he stopped at a small hatchback. Glancing around to make sure the coast was clear, he pulled out a wire coat hanger that I hadn't even noticed he'd had and began to break into the car.

When he popped open the handle, he got in and started it, backing out of the spot and driving my way. He pulled to a stop beside me and opened the passenger door.

"Grab our stuff and get in."

I did. Once we were out of the supermarket parking lot, he headed northeast.

"Where are we going?"

"There's somewhere we can lay low tonight. In the morning, we'll go to my safe house."

"Why not go now?"

"Because you look like you're about to fall over."

He was right. With the adrenalin wearing off, I felt the exhaustion roll over me.

"Where are you planning on stopping?"

"Rathowen. I have a … friend who runs a bed and breakfast. We can stay there tonight."

I didn't know why, but the fact that he hesitated over the word *friend* gave me pause.

"Who's your friend?"

Orin cast his eyes over me, then returned his attention to the road.

Only a few minutes later, we were passing through a low sandstone wall and driving down a stone driveway. The house we pulled to a stop in front of was white with gabled windows and a covered porch. The lights were on like we were expected.

Orin put the car into park and got out. I expected him to leave me to get out on my own, but he opened my door and helped me from the car.

"Where are we?" I asked, eyeing the quaint cottage.

"It's called Inny River Cottage. We'll be safe here."

Before I could dig for more information, the house's front door opened. A tall, willowy woman with green eyes and long mahogany hair stepped outside, smiling openly at Orin.

"Blakely," Orin said in that rough way he had.

"Orin," she replied, wrapping him in a hug. I noticed he was stiff in her embrace like the touch wasn't welcome. I found it strange considering he called her a friend. The woman—Blakely—turned her green eyes on me. "Who's your friend?"

"It doesn't matter," he replied matter-of-factly, stepping away. "Thanks for letting us stay."

She took the hint and didn't pry any further. "Of course," Blakely replied, folding her arms over her chest. "You know which room is yours. Do you have a lot of luggage?"

Orin flicked me a look, then said, "We left in a hurry."

Blakely licked her lips. "Because you couldn't wait to see me, Orin?"

He shook his head. "Something like that. I promise it'll only be one night. We'll be gone before the sun comes up tomorrow."

Blakely's gaze darted between Orin and me, her jaw tight. "Fine. I won't ask questions. I just hope it's not something illegal you're running from."

Then Orin did something I had never seen him do.

He smiled.

Disarmingly.

And it looked good on him.

Clasping her gently by the arm, he leaned in and kissed her briefly on the cheek. "I swear on Dee's life it's not illegal."

The lie rolled off his tongue so easily, I wondered whether it was a regular occurrence for him.

"Once you're settled, come downstairs for a cup of tea

and something to eat," Blakely called out as we stepped inside.

I climbed up to the second level of the house, hanging back while Orin opened the second door on the left and entered it. I hesitated in the hallway, biting my bottom lip as I waited for the fear to surface. To take over. The one that screamed that being alone with a man would lead to something bad.

But it never came, and I realized I hadn't felt that way with Orin earlier either.

"Are you coming?" he asked, setting the bag of supplies on top of the dresser.

I stepped into the bedroom. There was a bed with a chunky, wooden bedframe. The linens were cream and pale blue, and I eyed them with trepidation. Oblivious to my inner turmoil, Orin shut the door behind us, locking it.

I spun around to face him, bracing for the fear to roll over me, but it was still curiously absent.

"Are you hungry?"

"No."

He narrowed his eyes on my face. "When was the last time you ate?"

"I'm not sure. Maybe last night after I treated your wounds." Speaking of wounds, I stared at his side and then stepped toward him. "How is it feeling?"

"Fine." He brushed past me and opened the door into an en suite shower room. Turning on the faucet, he began washing his hands. "You're going to come downstairs for some food," he announced, his tone telling me more than his actual words. What he meant to say was that *You're coming downstairs for food, and you'll damn well eat.*

"And what should I tell Blakely if she asks me any questions?"

"Lie."

That got my hackles up. "I know lying is second nature to you, but I find it a little more difficult."

He turned those cold eyes on me. "Would you rather tell her we're on the run from a rival clan because you shot one of them in the head?" He was getting irritated with me, but then that made two of us.

I folded my arms. "Fine. I'll lie."

Dropping the hand towel he'd been using, he stepped toward me, standing toe-to-toe. My folded arms brushed against his firm abdominals, and I tilted my head back so I could see him properly.

Leaning closer, he said, "Good," then stalked from the bedroom.

I huffed out a breath, the desire to push him a little further niggling at me. After a minute, I followed him. When I stepped into the entryway, I heard the low rumble of his voice coming from deeper inside the house. I found him in the kitchen with Blakely, who was pouring tea from an ancient-looking teapot into three awaiting cups. She looked up when I stepped into the room.

"Do you take sugar, Mysterious Woman who Came with Orin?" she asked, a small smile playing on her lips.

"No. Thank you. Just a little milk. And my name is Fallon."

Blakely's smile grew. "I told you she'd tell me her name."

"It could be fake," he replied, acting nonplussed as he

shoved a sandwich into his mouth and chewed slowly.

"It's not," I replied, keeping my eyes locked on Orin. I turned my attention back to Blakely, though, when Orin brushed off his hands and went to the fridge. There was an element of familiarity between them, and he moved around the house like he'd been here before. It would stand to reason that he had been given he said it was safe here.

Blakely handed me my cup, and I took a large gulp.

"How do you know each other then?"

I could feel Orin's raking gaze on me, but I ignored his warning stare. "He's a friend of my brother's."

Her green eyes flickered to Orin, then back to me. "Brother's best friend, huh?"

"What?"

She gave me a small smile. "Forbidden fruit is the best." She leaned to the side to get a better look at Orin, who had sat himself down at the kitchen table. "I can't imagine this bastard being sweet enough to attract any woman though."

She thinks Orin and I are a couple? I opened my mouth to set her straight, when Orin spoke over me.

"Her brother doesn't know. He'd have my arse if he did."

Whipping around, I shot him a look, which he ignored.

Blakely leaned her hip against the kitchen counter and took a sip of her own tea. "Are you two eloping?"

I was still facing Orin, so I saw that same smile as before. "No. I'm just taking her to see some of my favorite places while her brother is away. We don't often have the freedom to see each other without keeping it secret."

"Hmm," Blakely agreed, then asked, "Fallon, would you like a sandwich? Best to have one now before Orin eats them all."

I was still trying to process the lie Orin was spinning, so I wordlessly accepted the plate she was holding out to me and took a seat at the table opposite him. I ate my sandwich, chewing and swallowing without taking my eyes off him while he spoke to Blakely. After eating, I drank the rest of my tea and set the dishes into the sink.

"I'm going to head up to bed," I announced.

"Sleep well, and it was nice to meet you," Blakely said, putting her cup into the sink too. "You'd better hug me now before you disappear from my life again, Orin." She held out her arms, and although he rolled his eyes, he did step closer and let her hug him. Once again, he was stiff in her embrace. When they broke apart, Orin caught me watching.

He approached me, reaching out to rest his hand on the small of my back. "Let's go to bed," he said, giving my ass a playful slap.

I glared at him over my shoulder but walked back the way I'd come. As soon as we were out of Blakely's sight, he dropped his hand and put a good foot between us. In the bedroom, he shut and locked the door behind us and then sat on the edge of the bed, his hand wrapping protectively around his side.

"You're in pain."

He looked at me from under his lashes. "I'm fine."

"You're not fine. Let me take a look." I stepped toward him, pushing his hand out of the way. I was shocked when he let me do it but didn't dwell on it for too long. Lifting up his shirt, I pulled away the gauze. There was a bit of fresh blood, but otherwise it looked fine.

"I might as well change the dressing while I'm here, too. Here, hold this up." I transferred the end of the shirt to him, then stopped when a thought dawned on me.

"What's wrong?"

"Left the first aid kit in the car."

With a grunt, he jerked his chin in the direction of the bathroom. "Check under the sink. Blakely started keeping one in there after my first visit."

I raised my brows at his statement, but he ignored my unspoken question. In the bathroom, I found the first aid kit that was packed with fresh gauze and new bandages. Bringing it back into the room, I drew to a stop when I saw that Orin had removed his shirt completely. Even though I'd seen his body before, it didn't stop me from gawking at it for a moment. His muscles were chiseled, and I wanted to ask about his tattoos. I realized with a jolt that I wouldn't mind doing other things to those tattoos, too, and the thought pushed me back into motion.

Since he was sitting on the edge of the bed, I kneeled in front of him, placing the first aid kit beside me on the floor.

"What are you doing?" he suddenly croaked. My head jerked up to see why his voice had sounded so strange, and what I saw both thrilled and scared me.

Orin's already dark eyes had swelled—his pupils blown out. He looked as if he was in pain. His jaw was tight. His mouth pinched into a firm line.

"Does it hurt worse than before?" I asked, reaching for the gauze to see if I could see anything, but he reared back.

"Don't touch me right now, Fallon."

I sat back on my heels. "Why not?"

He stared at me like he was a hungry lion. "Because I told you not to."

Brushing off his comment, I leaned in to peel the gauze all the way off when I noticed a large bulge behind his pants zipper. He was hard and thick, and my gaze darted to his. I was so close to his body that the scent of his body grew thicker. I swallowed.

"You're … you're …"

He shut his eyes. "Don't say it. And for fuck's sake will you get up off your knees?"

Frowning, I did as he asked, dragging a chair over to the side of the bed instead. "Happy now?" I asked him with venom in my voice.

"Very," he snipped back. "Just change the fucking dressing, then we can get some sleep. We have to be out of here in five hours."

4

ORIN

I STAYED UP LONG AFTER FALLON HAD GONE TO sleep, knowing that the hours were dripping away from us. I should've rested, but the truth was, I was terrified of the reaction she had stirred in me. When she'd been kneeling in front of me like that, all I could think about was her bare skin, creamy and warm, begging for my touch. I'd often wondered what she looked like naked, and I shouldn't have because the fact of the matter was, she was off-limits to me and my fucked-up version of sex.

Christ, even hugging Blakely had been torture. Touching anyone caused this horrible nausea to roll through me … no, not *everyone*. Touching Fallon didn't elicit the same response, and perhaps that was the biggest and best reason of all not to inspect that too hard.

So, yeah, I watched her while she slept and tried to tell myself again all the reasons why thinking about her sexually was a bad idea—the biggest being that she was Grayson's sister. But no matter how many times I told myself that, my dick conjured up thoughts of her on her knees again, only this time she was compliant and waiting for my command.

"Fuuuck." I drew the word out, running a hand through my hair. This was so fucking messed up. Fallon sighed softly in her sleep, rolling from her back to her side so she was facing me. There was a large part of me that wanted to crawl in between those sheets and wrap my arms around her, but there was an even bigger part of me that refused to let another woman get their hands on me. The only reason Blakely was allowed a hug was because I knew her before that fucked-up bitch had torn my innocence apart. Even though I knew she was safe to me, I still didn't enjoy the feel of someone else's skin on mine unless it was my hands wrapped around the throat of an enemy.

I wanted to touch Fallon though. I wanted to see how long it would take me to make her pant, then scream my name in pleasure. I didn't think she was the submissive kind, no matter how much I wanted her to be.

As if my thoughts woke her, Fallon's eyes fluttered open. She seemed to lay there a moment before her reality snapped violently back into place. Tilting her head back, she fixed her blue eyes on me. "What time is it?"

"Too early. Go back to sleep."

"Have you slept?"

"Don't worry about me." Jesus, I hope she took my gruffness as the warning I wanted it to be. I pinched the bridge of my nose with my thumb and forefinger because I suddenly had a pounding headache.

Her eyes drifted shut, but she reached out and patted the mattress beside her. "You need to rest properly. Doctor's orders."

I felt my mouth pull into a rare, real smile. "You're not a doctor," I told her in a soft voice.

Her brows drew together, but she still didn't open her eyes. "Nurse."

"By your own admission, you're only a nursing student."

That statement earned me a glare. "I'm cold, okay."

I stared at her for a heartbeat, my memories of the past warring with my present desires. I wanted to lay with her, but I couldn't bring myself to give her the trust she needed.

"Go back to sleep. I'll watch over you."

I WAS ROUSED SOMETIME LATER BY FALLON SLIDING out of the bed. I pretended to still be asleep, only opening my eyelids a hair to see her in nothing but her underwear and the shirt she'd been wearing for the past who knew how many hours. I tried not to stare at the perfect globes of her ass, but it was just as difficult as ignoring the urge to slide into bed beside her had been.

Once she was safely locked behind the bathroom door, I rose from my position in the armchair, stretching out the best I could. My side throbbed back to life just as I knew it would as soon as I stood, but when a sharp pain lanced through me, I let out a sharp hiss.

Fallon popped her head out, her eyes narrowing on me.

"Are you okay?"

"Fine," I snapped back, hoping to deter her from trying to look after me anymore. I should've known better than that.

She stepped from the bathroom fully, and I turned my head away. Fuck.

"What's wrong now?"

I gestured in the vague direction of her chest. "You're not wearing a bra and that shirt is fucking see-through."

She cursed softly, and when I looked back, she had her arms folded across her chest. With her chin, she gestured to my side. "Does it hurt?"

"It's fine. Do what you need to do then we can leave."

"I heard you hissing."

Jesus *fuck*. "I was just stiff from sleeping in the chair."

"Are you sure?"

I turned my steely gaze on her, hoping to cow her. When all she did was arch her brow at me, I added, "You don't need to worry about me, Fallon. Are you finished in the bathroom?"

I brushed past her, feeling every single one of my nerve endings catch alight, but I shoved all that longing deep down and shut the door behind me. After washing my face, I lifted my shirt and looked at the wound. The skin around it was beginning to bruise, and as I touched the edge of the puncture, I winced. There was some swelling there—the tissue raised and red. Retaping the gauze back into place, I stepped out to find Fallon sitting on the bed, fully dressed.

"I need some more clothes."

I nodded. "We can pick some up on the way to my place."

"And a toothbrush."

I grunted. "I'll get you whatever you need, Fallon." I ignored the way that statement made me feel. I didn't need to start having territorial urges with this woman, but it felt fucking good to provide for her. "Are you ready to get on the road?"

"Yeah, I guess."

It was dark outside when I opened the front door of the house, but the sun was starting to warm the sky on the horizon. Once we were safely inside the car, I started the engine and turned around in the driveway.

"How many times have you done this?" Fallon's question broke the silence.

I looked at her. "What?"

"Left your friend's place before the sun has even come up."

My hands squeezed the wheel. The truth was, it had happened more times than I wanted to admit. So many times I'd stayed here while dodging other clan's Reapers or watching targets.

Instead of saying all that, I said, "I don't know."

Before we made it too far from civilization, I stopped at a mall where she would be able to get everything she needed. I trailed her around as she swept through the racks of Primark, pulling off t-shirts and yoga pants as she went.

"I need to try these on," she said, lifting her full hands up to show me.

I gestured to the fitting room. "I'll wait out here for you."

She eyed me speculatively. "Are you armed?"

"I'm always armed."

She pressed her lips together in thought for a moment before disappearing into the fitting room. Was I happy to let her out of my sight even for a moment? No, I wasn't, but in the interest of expediting this whole process, I let her go. We were far enough away from Galway now that the Bèar Clan wouldn't even think to look this far afield.

While I waited for Fallon, I grabbed a few t-shirts and jeans for myself, not bothering to try them on. By the time I circled back to the women's section, Fallon was emerging. I eyed the bundle of clothes like it was a bomb.

"Get everything you needed?"

"Yes, but I still need to find some …" She drifted off, and my eyes zeroed in on her face.

"What?" I barked.

She lifted her chin, her expression steely. "Panties. Bras and panties."

Fuck, I wished I hadn't asked. I followed her to the store's lingerie section, trying to stop myself from picturing her in some of the sets we passed. She stopped in front of a rack of lace panties and began flicking through the sizes. I watched her with greedy intent, cataloging everything. Once she had enough panties, she selected the matching bras, and we were on our way.

I paid for her purchases in cash, then snagged the bags before she could. I kept them all in my left hand in case I needed to draw my gun. We stopped at the chemist for some toiletries for her, and then I hustled her out of the mall. We'd already been there for too long.

Back in the car, we headed northwest toward Derrycarne Wood.

"How long until we get to your place?" Fallon asked from beside me.

"Not long. Maybe another thirty minutes."

She nodded and looked out the window. For some reason, I wanted her to keep talking to me.

"Are you hungry? I can stop at a fast-food place and get you something."

She began shaking her head, but then her stomach let out a loud rumble. Right, it was settled, then. I pulled off the road when I saw a burger place that served breakfast.

"What would you like?"

She scrunched her nose up in thought, and I tried to *not* be that fucking pussy sap that thought it was adorable.

Adorable? What the fuck was I thinking?

"Surprise me," she eventually said, and I got out of the car.

I entered the store, and every set of eyes turned to me. As I approached the counter, the man in front who had been ordering saw me coming and quickly stepped to the side.

"You can go ahead of me," he said in an unsteady voice, gesturing to the cashier, who looked stunned. I didn't think they were being so accommodating because they knew who I was. Just as the Grim Reaper is never seen, neither am I when I come to collect a soul. Perhaps the look on my face was making people shit themselves.

I stepped toward the cashier—a young girl who had gone sheet white. "Can I help you?" she asked in a squeak.

"Yeah." I placed my order, pulled out some cash to pay, then peered over my shoulder at the guy who had given up his place for me. Peeling a few more bills from the roll, I slid them across the counter. "I'll pay for the guy behind me, too."

The little mouse took my money, then my order was suddenly there in a brown paper sack. She handed it to me. "H-h-have a nice d-d-day."

Grabbing the bag, I walked from the restaurant and back to the car. When I got back in, I handed the bag straight to Fallon.

"Take whatever you want. I'll eat whatever's left over."

She peeled open the top and looked inside. The scent of bacon, eggs, and sausage wafted out, reminding me that the sandwich I'd eaten at Blakely's hadn't been close to enough. She reached in, pulled out one of the breakfast sandwiches, and began to eat. As I reversed from the spot, I caught a glimpse of the happy look on her face.

Once again, that feeling of pride in providing for her filled my chest, making it thaw, if only a little bit. It was stupid. After I got her to the safety of the clan, and after things had died down, I wouldn't be spending any more time with her. I would be dropping her off and speeding away in the other direction because life as the clan's Reaper was inherently lonely.

Which was what I wanted.

All I'd learned was that people hurt other people.

And I had no interest in being the victim ever again.

Fallon finished off her sandwich, screwed up the wax paper wrapper, and dumped it back into the bag. I eyed her.

"You haven't eaten enough. Have more."

She blinked at me. "I'm fine."

"Eat," I commanded.

"No."

I ground my molars and snatched the bag off her lap, pulling it into mine. Without taking my eyes off the road, I reached inside and pulled out a sandwich. I attempted to unwrap it one-handed when Fallon plucked it from my fingers, unwrapped it, then handed it back.

"You could just ask for help," she muttered under her breath.

I ignored her and bit into the sandwich. My hunger took over civility at that point, and I finished it in five bites. Fallon reached into the bag again, pulled out the last sandwich, and unwrapped it.

Before she could give it to me, though, I told her, "We'll go bite for bite."

She frowned. "What?"

I took my eyes off the road for a moment. "You haven't eaten enough."

"I told you I have."

"You've been through some traumatic shit. Your body needs food to fuel it now more than ever. Now take a goddamn bite and stop arguing with me."

She scowled. "You're not a morning person, are you?"

Baring my teeth at her, she sighed and took a bite.

"Happy?"

I snatched the sandwich from her. "Never," I muttered under my breath.

Within two minutes, the sandwich was finished, and my territorial urges to feed and protect Fallon had been somewhat sated. I didn't even know I had this in me. I thought any compassion had been long since fucked out of me.

"So, where is this safe house of yours?"

"Why do you need to know?"

She rolled her eyes. "So, when I get to a phone, I can call for help." Sarcasm laced her voice thickly.

"Keep hold of that attitude, and I'll have to take you over my knee."

The words had come out before I could stop them, and I instantly regretted them. One look at Fallon's mortified face, and I wished I could've gone back in time and not said a goddamned word.

She turned her face toward the window, crossing her legs away from my body, and that was all I needed to know. She was disgusted by the thought of me touching her.

Good, I thought darkly. I shouldn't encourage any more than platonic thoughts from her anyway. I was older than her by more than a decade, and my past had made my sexual tastes very … *particular*. A girl like Fallon wouldn't be into the kinky shit I called normal.

That didn't stop me from wondering though …

5

FALLON

ORIN'S WORDS WERE STILL BUMPING AND JOST-ling around in my head.

Keep hold of that attitude, and I'll have to take you over my knee.

Ugh, why did my body react like that was the best plan ever? It had gotten to the point where my face had flushed so bright and hot that I'd had to turn away, but my impulsive body had latched onto the idea of his large palm spanking my ass that it had sent a wave of moisture between my legs. Crossing them had only intensified that sensation, so here I was, sitting next to a man whose very presence should've scared me, but I found myself turned on by him instead.

I tried to remember the last man who I was vaguely interested in, but I couldn't seem to recall a single face. The debilitating fear I was going to therapy for seemed to keep thoughts of men at bay, but Orin was different.

I cleared my throat, feeling his dark eyes land on me briefly before returning to the road. We remained in stilted silence until we turned off the N-road and onto a boreen. The rural lane was a single car-width in diameter, and as we continued down it, the stacked stone walls disappeared and were replaced by soaring oaks, pines, willow, and birch. The forest seemed to spring up around us the farther we went, and I wondered exactly where we were.

"It's just a little farther up here," Orin said.

I swallowed and watched as the road slowly began to widen. The dirt became gravel, and a small wood cabin emerged from the greenery. Everything about it was rough-hewn, from the shingles to the roof. There was a shallow porch on the front, with a railing that looked like it had been sourced from the forest and nailed into place.

I stared at the little structure, thinking it was the most beautiful thing I'd ever seen.

"It's not much." Orin's voice held a note of joy. "But it's mine." Pulling to a stop, he cut the engine, and we both sat there a moment longer.

"Yours? Not the clan's?"

"The clan doesn't know about it." He turned to face me. "And that's how I want it to stay."

"And if I did tell someone about it? Would you hunt me down and put a bullet in my head?" I'd only meant it as a joke, but Orin was serious when he nodded.

"If I had to." Although the words were threatening, the tone of his voice said the opposite. He might do it, but he wouldn't *like* doing it.

I swallowed again, then let out a deep breath. "Shall we

go inside?"

We got out at the same time, each of our doors slamming in unison. The forest was alive with the sounds of birds. The sweet songs of blackbirds, willow warblers, and robins filled the air while the wind itself whistled through the leafy canopy. I turned my face up, shut my eyes, and listened.

"It's so peaceful here," I said.

"It is." Orin's voice was close, and when I opened my eyes, I found him only a few feet away, watching me. "Come on."

We walked into the cabin, it smelled of Orin—of cedar and something else spicy and masculine.

"How much time do you spend here?"

"Not enough." He strode into the small kitchen with the groceries we'd picked up the day before. I followed him, touching the live edge counter and marveling at the rustic design. I watched as he placed the groceries on the counter, then placed his palms on the edge. He bowed his head as if he were exhausted.

That was when I noticed his slightly pale skin and the sheen of sweat dotting his brow.

I attempted to touch his forehead, but he jerked away before I could. For a moment, he only stared at me before mumbling, "Sorry. Habit."

I didn't know what that meant, but when he leaned forward for me to touch him again, he didn't flinch, although he did grimace a little.

"You have a fever."

He brushed past me. "I'm fine."

"You're not *fine*." Following him out to the car, he opened the rear door to grab the shopping bags with my clothes in them. I motioned for him to give them to me, but he pulled them out of my reach.

"You need to rest," I insisted, trailing him back into the cabin.

"I said I'm fine."

Stubborn man.

He walked into a bedroom where there was a single bed under the window and a chest of drawers on the opposite wall. He paused as his gaze swept over the space. "It's small," he announced finally.

"It's great. I think it's cozy." I sat on the bed, and he stared at me—his eyes becoming more and more unfocused by the second. He weaved on his feet. I jumped up and caught his arm just as he fell against the wall. Leading him over to the bed, I managed to get him laid out before running my hand over his forehead once again.

"Shit." He was burning up. It may have been a low-grade fever before, but it wasn't now. "Stay there," I told him, even though there was every chance he'd be unconscious when I returned with the first aid kit.

I found it in the kitchen with all the groceries and hurried back to the room. Sitting beside him on the bed, I opened the kit and pulled out the oral thermometer.

"Open," I said, pushing the cylindrical tube under his tongue.

Orin laid back with a groan. "I feel fine."

"Like hell you do. How long have you known about this fever?"

"I didn't know I had one," he replied.

Shit. Shit. Shit. He probably had an infection from the

wound. "I need to check your side. I'm going to help you sit up."

Tugging on his arm, I got him vertical before lifting off his shirt. As before, the sight of his bare chest and tattoos made my stomach dip, but I shoved those feeling aside and helped lay his head back against the pillow. His skin was hot to the touch, like he'd spent all day in the sun and it had retained that warmth. Lifting the edge of the gauze, I checked his wound. The edges were red—angry and puffy.

"It's infected," I announced, leaving the dressing off. "I'm going to try and clean it the best I can. Do you have any antibiotics here?"

He remained quiet, and I peered at his face. His mouth had gone slack, but his breathing was uneven. He was unconscious. Damn it, why hadn't I noticed he was running a fever? I should've seen the signs.

Rummaging through the first aid kit, I found some aspirin and put the bottle aside. They would help with the fever, but the infection was another matter altogether. Leaving the kit on the bed, I went in search of the bathroom, finding it across the hall. I tore open every drawer and cupboard looking for more drugs, but all I could find was an expired bottle of cough syrup on the highest shelf.

I shoved it out of the way in my frustration and noticed it didn't go very far. Something was blocking it. Pulling the bottle down, I patted my hand around on the shelf to see what else was there, the pads of my fingers grazing against a box. Inching it forward, I brought it down so I could see what it was.

I shook my head. It was a box of amoxicillin. A year past

its expiration date, but amoxicillin all the same. Yanking open the top of the box, I couldn't believe my luck that only one of the trays had a few capsules missing, leaving me with sixteen capsules. It was enough to stave off the infection.

Racing back into the kitchen, I grabbed a glass from the cupboard, filled it with water, then hurried back to the bedroom. I had to get the drugs into him as soon as I could. Perching beside him on the bed, I touched his shoulder, finding him uncomfortably hot.

"Orin? Orin, wake up for me," I said. His black eyes found my face, and he reached for me. His strong fingers ran along my jaw, his large, warm hand cupping my cheek.

"Fallon?" he asked.

I cupped my hand around his briefly—his eyes flaring at the contact. I'd learned he didn't like unsolicited touches, so I pulled his palm away from my face, severing the connection. "I'm here. Your wound is infected. That's why you have a high-grade fever right now. I'm going to give you something to help you fight the infection."

His eyes flared so wide that I could see the whites all the way around. He began shaking his head, his lips pressing into a hard line.

"Orin? Please. These will help."

He looked at me as if I was asking if he wanted me to put a bullet in his skull. His terror was on every strained line on his face.

"You have to take something. What about an aspirin? That'll help with the fever."

Again, he shook his head. If he had the drugs in his

cupboard, I didn't think it was a fear of swallowing the pill that was the issue. There was something more to it.

I licked my lips. "What if you took them? You could take them out of the packaging yourself?"

His eyes suddenly rolled back in his head, and he grew still. I felt so helpless that I wanted to cry. I wasn't going to force him to take the medicine—that wasn't what being a nurse was about. Orin had to *want* to take them, but he couldn't do that until he was awake again.

So, I did the only thing I could do. I made him comfortable. In the hall cupboard, I found the extra bed sheets. Unfolding one, I draped it over his body, leaving it folded at the waist, then went into the bathroom to wet a rag to put on his brow.

By the time I returned to the bedroom, he had kicked off the sheet in his restlessness. His body was glistening with sweat, his wound pulling the edges of his exposed skin. Folding the cool rag over on itself, I placed it on his brow and tried to soothe him. I didn't know what would work, so I started to sing a song my mother had sung to me when I was unwell. At first, the song was halting and unsure, but as more and more of the words came back to me, the melody revealed itself. Leaving the rag on his forehead, I started to stroke his shoulder, running my fingers over his tattoos and tracing the lines of the clan wolf.

Orin's restlessness seemed to settle with each passing second until he was sleeping peacefully. I rose from the edge of the mattress to leave him to sleep, but he reached for me—his fingers and grip surprisingly strong. When I felt eyes on me, I looked at his face.

"Don't leave …" He couldn't finish his sentence before he was asleep once more.

His arm dropped, and I stepped away from the bed. I let him rest, retreating from the room and closing the door behind me. In the kitchen, I opened all the cupboards to find out what was in each, then put away the meager groceries he had bought. I wasn't sure we could survive on protein bars and fruit for long, but it was a start.

Once the counter was clear, I made myself a cup of tea, then realized there was no milk. I remembered passing a small corner store on the way here and wondered whether I could make it back there on my own. The keys along with a few coins were on the counter, and I swiped them up on my way to the door.

Getting into the car, I turned it around so I wouldn't have to reverse down the drive, then headed back the way we'd come in. Once I was on a sealed road surface again, it was only a few miles before I saw the shop. Pulling up to the curb, I got out and entered the store.

An elderly man was busy stacking shelves, while an equally elderly woman stood at the ready behind the counter. She gave me a smile when I walked past her on the way to the fridges at the back of the store.

"You're a new face," she called out, still smiling.

I pulled open the glass door, snagged a bottle of milk, then turned around. "Yeah. Just visiting a friend."

"Anyone we might know?" she asked, punching the price of the milk into the ancient-looking cash register.

"No, I don't think so." I handed over the two Euro coin and placed whatever was left into the small ceramic bowl near my elbow. "Thanks for the milk."

"No problem, dear. We hope to see you in here again soon."

By the time I made it back to the cabin, my stomach was growling. I put the milk into the

small fridge, then pulled out one of the frozen meals Orin had bought.

After popping it into the microwave, I hit a couple of buttons and got things started. The hum of the microwave filled the space, and while it heated up my lunch, I went to check on Orin. He was shivering, and I picked up the kicked-off sheet and laid it over the bottom of the bed. His forehead still felt terribly hot against the backs of my fingers, and my gaze slid down to the wound. It was redder than it had been—angrier looking—and I knew the infection was taking hold.

If I couldn't bring his temperature down and treat the infection, I would have to take him to hospital. Out in the kitchen, the microwave *dinged* happily, and I went to retrieve my lunch. Curling up on the couch, I ate straight out of the container, shoveling the food in as soon as I swallowed the last mouthful. It tasted bland, but somehow, I couldn't bring myself to care.

Once I was done eating, I dumped the container into the trash and washed up my fork. It was a little after one in the afternoon, and I had no idea what to do with myself. There wasn't a TV that I could see—only a couple of board games and three one-thousand-piece puzzles. I decided on one of the puzzles. It was a pastel-colored, upside-down cityscape that reminded me a little bit of Escher's *Relativity*.

I sat at the small, round wooden table, upended the contents of the box, and began.

6
ORIN

I WOKE UP FEELING AS IF I'D RUN A MARATHON. I was drenched in sweat. I felt something—a presence, I guess you'd call it. I wondered whether I was dead and this was my version of hell. Knowing that someone was standing over me—watching me—but being unable to see them.

They touched me on the shoulder.

I wanted to move away, but I couldn't.

It was then that I realized they weren't here to cause me pain.

They were here to heal …

Fallon …

7
FALLON

ORIN HAD BEEN RESTLESS FOR THE PAST FIFTEEN minutes—his legs jerking spasmodically, his arms and fingers twitching like he was wrestling with an invisible opponent. At first—when I touched his shoulder to soothe him—his jaw had locked, his lips peeling back from his teeth in a snarl. Stunned by the aggression, I began talking to him softly. Telling him things like it's me, I'm here to help. His fever hadn't broken yet, and I was terrified. I wasn't equipped to deal with this, but I remembered Orin's insistence that he not go to a hospital. I'm not sure why he was so against it, but perhaps he—like a lot of other people in the world—had a fear of hospitals.

Lord knew I wasn't so fond of them. But was it any wonder? My memories attached to hospitals were of my ma going in for cancer treatments. Even setting foot into one now evoked flashes of waiting on plastic seats, of babies screaming as their parents tried to calm them in the waiting room.

"Shhh," I soothed, stroking back Orin's hair before placing the cold rag back to his scorching skin. I looked down at the man I had saved—twice—and who had saved me in return and wondered how long I could let this go on. There had to be a point where Orin's wishes weren't a good enough reason anymore. There had to be a point where his life was bigger than his ire.

I decided that in another twenty-four hours, that would be my point.

I would take him to a hospital where he could have IV antibiotics and be under the care of a professional—not just a studying nurse. Heaving a sigh, I rose from my chair. He was back to shivering, his teeth chattering ever so slightly. His eyes are still closed, his dark lashes like angry exclamation marks over his lids. Even in his sleep, he was threatening to harm people …

Everyone except me, it seemed.

I retreated from the room, keeping my gaze locked on him, willing him to open his eyes. But he didn't, so I shut the door and returned to my puzzle.

AN HOUR LATER, I WAS HUNGRY AGAIN, AND I shuffled into the kitchen to see what was left to eat. Opening the freezer, I found there was only one frozen meal left, along with a couple of protein bars in the cupboard. All the apples were gone. I needed to go back to the store, but the little issue of money was a problem. Orin seemed to carry cash in his front pants pocket, and as much as I didn't want to go and disturb a fever-riddled man, necessity was calling.

Creeping back into the room, I kneeled beside the bed and lifted the sheet at Orin's hip. I may have been in luck because the pocket closest to me had a slight bulge in it. Being as careful as I could, I slid my hand inside until my fingers closed around the notes and I pulled them out.

I drove back to the same corner store as before, pulling the car up to the curb. Rain began to splatter on the windscreen as I got out, then became a full-blown assault as I walked around the hood. The deluge hit, and by the time I made it inside the shop, I was soaked to the bone. The old man, who had been packing the shelves the last time I was there, was behind the front counter.

"Got caught in it, lass?" he asked kindly.

I pulled my soaked shirt away from my body, a shiver wracking me. "Yeah, it looks like it."

He gave me a friendly smile and returned his attention to whatever he was reading. Picking up a basket from beside the door, I started grabbing non-perishable things off the shelves. I also picked up a fresh loaf of bread, and another bottle of milk, then took everything to the counter.

The old man put everything through the register, then asked, "Anything else I can help you with?"

I licked my lips, hesitation clawing at me. "Just curious whether there was a hospital around here?" If Orin didn't improve, I had to know what my next move was going to be.

Bushy brows rose over rheumy blue eyes. "A hospital?" he asked. "Is everything okay?"

"Fine. Yes, absolutely fine. I just …" What? "I … I'm studying to be a nurse, and since I might be staying here a while, I just wanted to know which hospital you recommended. I wanted to see if I could do some practical work with them."

He studied me before saying, "There's St. Patrick's Community Hospital in Carrick-on-Shannon."

"How far away is that?"

"Oh, I'd say around eight miles or so."

I nodded my thanks and slipped the roll of notes from my pocket. "How much do I owe you?"

"That's a lot of money for a young woman to be carrying around," he said in a grave voice.

I met him in the eye. More firmly, I repeated my previous question. "How much do I owe you?"

He told me the total, and I counted off what I needed. Placing more than enough for the amount he said, I picked up the paper bag he'd put my groceries in and started out of the shop.

"What about your change, young lady?" he called after me.

"Keep it."

Running to the car, I threw open the door and sat the bag of groceries on the seat beside me. Slicking rain off my face with my hand, I started the engine and stared out at the water-clogged landscape. The storm drains were already overflowing with the sheer volume of water falling, and I knew driving back to the cabin was going to be difficult. Still, I couldn't sit here all day. Pulling out, I turned around at the next street and navigated back to Orin's cabin.

The rain intensified, and in the end, the wipers couldn't keep up with the amount of water. Barely able to see out the windshield, I slowed to a crawl, thankful that nobody else seemed to be out in this weather. I squinted through the downpour, looking for the turnoff.

I had to shield my eyes when headlights suddenly appeared behind me.

"Shit."

The lane was too narrow for them to move around me. I did my best to pull all the way over onto the shoulder so they could pass. When they made no move to go around me, I put the hazards on and stopped the car completely.

With my eyes on the wing mirror, I watched as a big black SUV pulled alongside my car. They paused there a moment, but I refused to look at them. My heart slammed into my throat as my mind went wild. Who the hell was this person driving around in the middle of torrential rain? Why in the hell were they stopping?

They were probably wondering whether I needed help, but I wasn't going to engage with them. After a full minute of idling beside me, and me ignoring them, the car pulled away, speeding off up the lane. I felt my pulse hammering through me, my blood soaked in adrenalin.

"It's fine," I told myself. "It's fine. Just … get back to the cabin."

Shifting the car back into gear, I returned to the cabin, grabbing the bag of food and bolting to the porch. Once the groceries were put away, I went to check on Orin. He looked worse than before I left. A rash had started to develop over his chest, and his legs still moved restlessly every minute or so. I was still going to respect his wishes and leave his body to work through it until he seized.

His whole body went stiff, and my nurse's training kicked in. Taking hold of his arm, I dragged his hulking frame onto the floor so he would be safer. The bed was already too small for him, and the risk of him rolling right out of it and hitting his head were too great. Once he was on the floor, I lifted his head and put the pillow underneath it.

When I cleared the area around him, I sat back on my heels and timed it. His arms and legs twitched uncontrollably, his skin shivering like a horse's when a fly lands on it. I kept an eye on his breathing, becoming alarmed when he seemed to labor. But it was when his lips started to turn a shade of blue that I became really concerned.

I had to remind myself that this was only a febrile seizure. I'd read about them only a couple of weeks ago. They were caused by high fevers, but usually only young children suffered from them. That wasn't to say that adults couldn't have them, but it was rarer.

Glancing down at my watch, I saw that we were in the second minute of the episode, and each second that passed made the knot in my stomach twist.

I let go of the breath I'd been holding when his arms and legs stopped jerking as much as they had, and his lips returned to their normal color. Orin's eyes flickered open, but he wasn't awake yet. Still, I had to try.

"Orin? Are you with me?"

His lids closed, and he dropped into unconsciousness once more.

I had to get him to a hospital, but how? I didn't have a phone so I couldn't call an ambulance, and after a quick search for his, I found that the battery had gone flat. The only way to get him to the car would be to haul him there myself. It would be difficult, but not impossible and I had to try. After all, I'd done it once before. I could do it again.

Yanking the blanket from the bed, I laid it out on the floor and then dragged Orin's deadweight onto it. At least, that's what I attempted to do. He had to weigh at least two hundred pounds, so I only managed to get one shoulder onto the blanket before I was sweating. Bracing my legs, I yanked again, gaining another few inches, but I was winded and had to take a break. I pulled again, gaining another inch.

In the end, it took me a full fifteen minutes to get most of his body onto the blanket. He hadn't roused once—not even when I started dragging him down the hall and accidentally clipped his elbow on the wall. When I made it into the living room, I released the blanket and bent in two—breathing hard. Resting my hands on my knees, I waited for my heart to stop racing and then straightened.

I hated to admit that what I'd just done was the easy part of the plan. Now, I had to get him in the car somehow. Walking to the front door, I opened it wide and stared at the torrential rain, which was now coming in sideways. The car was at least thirty feet from the door. Getting wet was inevitable. I glanced around, hoping an awning would magically appear. When it was clear that wasn't going to happen, I went back to Orin. There was absolutely no way I could carry him while he was unconscious.

Leaning over his body, I squeezed his shoulder and got in close to his face. "Orin," I said in a firm voice. "Wake up. I need you to wake up." His eyes moved beneath his lids. "Orin?" I called again, making my voice a command. "Wake up. On your feet."

Black eyes stared up at me, a small crease forming between his brows. "My beautiful Filly," he murmured, reaching out a hand to touch my cheek. "Don't leave me." His eyelids fluttered shut once more, and I wanted to scream.

"Orin!" I yelled it this time. His eyes opened more quickly, and I could see he was trying to focus. "I need you to get up. I need you to help me."

His gaze darted to the side, his disorientation clear on his face. "Where am I?"

"It doesn't matter. I need you to stand up. I need you to help me. Okay?"

He nodded slowly, easing himself upright in such small movements that I expected him to topple backward at any moment. Once he was sitting, I tugged at his arm, getting him onto his feet. He stood, swaying until I drew his arm over my shoulder and led him outside. The rain was cold, drawing a surprised gasp from me, and a pained groan from him. We were only a few feet away from the car when he lost consciousness again, and I felt the full force of his whole weight.

Widening my stance and bracing my feet, I took the extra weight, then reached out for the handle on the rear door. As soon as I got it open wide enough, I dragged Orin inside. Getting him settled in the car took precious minutes away and left me soaked to the bone and shivering. Running around the hood, I got inside and started the engine.

The old man at the corner store had said the hospital was only eight miles away. That should only take me around fifteen minutes—maybe twenty on account of the weather. My gaze flickered to the back seat where I saw Orin was still slumped, his usually harsh face slack. A shiver wracked his body, his eyelids fluttering but not opening.

I should've taken him to the hospital as soon as he refused to take the antibiotics orally. I should've pushed him. I had no idea how far the infection had progressed or whether his chances of recovery were good. All I knew was I'd failed in my first task as a nurse. I'd failed to put my patient's well-being above all else.

The road was slippery, but I drove as fast as I dared down the N-road toward Carrick-on-Shannon. The wipers whipped back and forth across the glass, clearing the rain briefly before my vision became blurry once more.

When I finally saw the signs for St. Patrick's Community Hospital, I yanked on the wheel and drove straight to the emergency bay.

"Hey! You can't park here," someone was telling me as I rounded the car to open the rear door.

I pointed at Orin, who was seizing once more. "I need help. *Please*."

The guy took one look at Orin and then started yelling. More people rushed from the emergency room doors, and I stepped back, wrapping my arms around my torso and holding on tight. I watched everything like I wasn't a part of it. Someone had pulled a gurney alongside the car. Someone else had opened the other rear door and was inside with Orin.

Then—somehow—they were lifting him out and laying him onto the gurney. He looked terrible, and my guilt tightened its grip.

"…name? Miss?"

I blinked, the nurse in front of me coming into sharp focus. We were standing out of the rain now, but I didn't remember moving to cover. "What?"

"I asked what his name was? The man you brought?"

Something told me that I had to be careful with what I said. Wiping the water from my eyes, I said, "I don't know. I'm staying at a B&B a few miles away, and he's the other guest. I found him unconscious in the kitchen."

She looked a little frustrated by my story but pressed on. "You don't know anything about him?"

"I think he said his name was Jim?"

The nurse scribbled that down. "You did a good thing bringing him." She eyed my soaked clothes. "Come inside. I have a pair of scrubs you can change into while you wait."

"Thank you. I should move my car, though."

Her shrewd brown eyes gravitated toward the car and then back to me. "One of the orderlies can do it. I'm worried you're going into shock."

I nodded. "Okay."

She started ahead of me, and I was about to follow when the back of my neck prickled with awareness. I turned my head to find a black SUV … wait, it was a black *Rover*, parked to the side. I frowned, wondering what the chances were of seeing that kind of car around here.

"Are you coming?" the nurse called, drawing my attention.

After one final look at the car, I followed her inside, where she led me to a waiting room near the general admissions area.

She gave me a long look. "I'll be back in a minute."

Settling into a seat, I squeezed my hands between my knees and let my shoulders roll forward. Orin had better pull through this. If he didn't, I would have to tell Finnan what had happened, and I had no desire to be on the receiving end of his ire. I heaved out a sigh and shut my eyes, suddenly exhausted.

I WOKE TO SOMEONE SHAKING MY SHOULDER. MY eyes were slow to open, but when they did, I saw the same nurse as before. In her hands, she carried a bundle of pink fabric.

"What's your name?" she asked.

"Fallon."

"Fallon, I'm Marcy." She offered me what she was holding, then pointed over my shoulder. "There's a restroom over there. Why don't you get out of your wet clothes? It'll make you feel better."

I nodded and rose from my seat. She was probably right. Sitting in my wet clothes only served to remind me why I was there. After I got changed, I returned to my seat to find Marcy waiting.

"Your friend has a nasty infection caused by a wound on his ribs. If I didn't know any better, I'd say it was a gunshot wound."

Maintaining eye contact, I said, "I don't know. I only met him at the B&B the other day."

Her gaze swept over me carefully. "You saved his life, you know? If that infection and fever had been left any longer, he would've been in big trouble." She squeezed my knee. "I'll let you know when you can see him."

Continuing the charade, I said, "No need. Like I said, he's just some guy staying at the same place as me."

Her shoulders lifted in a slight shrug. "No problems, Fallon. I'll give you an update in any case." She left the waiting room, and I sucked in a deep breath. The scent of disinfectant made my stomach turn as I was shunted violently back in time to when my mother had to come in for chemo. Only this time, I didn't have Grayson here to hold my hand and tell me everything was going to be okay.

For a brief moment, I considered calling him, but I didn't want to worry him while he was on his honeymoon. He and Sloane had fought way too hard and given up way too much for their relationship to thrive, including Grayson giving up his position as Warlord for the clan. They needed the break, and I needed to handle this on my own. I had to prove to myself that I could.

Pulling my feet up onto the seat, I wrapped my arms around my legs and buried my head against my knees. I did my best to block it all out—the smells, the noise …

The memories.

I chose to focus on what we were going to do once we got out of there. I thought Orin would need a couple of days to let the antibiotics do their work. We were already laying low, but we couldn't stay here. There would eventually be more questions—questions I had no idea how to answer.

About three hours later, Marcy was back. She had a coat over her scrubs and a handbag slung across her shoulder.

"I'm heading home now, Fallon, but I came to tell you that Jim has been given intravenous antibiotics and something to help bring his fever down. His temperature has already dropped, and it looks like the antibiotics are working on the infection. I personally cleaned his wound, and he'll be just fine in a couple of days."

"Can I go and see him?" I asked.

She gave me a look—one that said she wasn't buying the whole acquaintance act, especially since I was so adamant that I hadn't wanted to see him before. "Sure. He's been moved onto a ward. I can take you if you like?"

I bobbed my head and stood. My legs felt stiff from disuse. Marcy led the way through the hospital halls, into an elevator, and then out onto another floor. The whole thing was a ward with beds set into sets of six, three on one side, and three on the other, then divided by a wall.

She walked to the end section and waved me forward. "He's in bed six." Squeezing my hand, she started to walk away when I called out a hasty "Thank you!"

Marcy kept walking.

Returning my attention to Orin, I took him in. He had a hospital gown on now, and the edges of his tattoos peeked out the neck and under the sleeves. The thin blanket was pulled up to his chest and folded over neatly. Beside the bed was an automated infusion pump regulating the administration of antibiotics. I took a seat beside the bed and stared at him.

For the first time in nearly forty-eight hours, the color was back in his cheeks. His eyes were softly closed, all the tension that had been there before gone away. He would be here for at least a few more days, but at least I knew he was in good hands. I glanced at the clock above his bed. The hands were positioned at twelve and eleven, and I frowned. That would mean that I'd been here for nearly ten hours.

"You should get some rest," someone said behind me.

I turned around to find a young woman—a doctor, I supposed, given the stethoscope around her neck—standing there. She had curly red hair held back from her face in a loose ponytail.

"Your friend is doing fine."

"He's not my friend," I replied automatically. "Just a guy who's staying at the same B&B as me."

She gave me the same look Marcy had—the *bullshit* look—but didn't try and correct me. She stepped a little closer and picked up the chart hanging on the end of his bed.

"He's been given a sedative to help him sleep. He seemed quite restless after we brought him into triage." She leafed through a page, then peered at me from under her lashes. "Do you know anything about the bullet wound on his side?"

I made my eyes widen in disbelief. "A bullet wound?"

The doctor nodded. "He's lucky to be alive. Someone put some stitches in, and those sutures saved his life. They helped pull the two parts of his chest together and prevent any further tears or damage to his lung. It was a very close thing."

I looked back at Orin. "Maybe he did it himself?"

She shook her head. "I don't believe that. I think he had help."

Was she fishing? I cleared my throat. "Well, I'm glad he's okay."

The doctor noted something, put the chart back, and slid her pen into her coat's breast pocket. "You should get some rest. Come back tomorrow if you want to."

I nibbled on my bottom lip, knowing that if I came back, they would know that the story I told didn't wash. "I probably should. I wouldn't want to be left alone when I don't have any family or friends around me."

She nodded once. "Good." With a smile, she added gently, "Now, go home."

I rose from the chair, asking one of the nursing staff for directions on how to get out. Once I was outside the emergency department again, I found that the rain had eased off to a drizzle. I located the car and found the keys still inside. I glanced around, wondering how in the hell nobody had thought to steal it. Once inside, I reversed from the spot, flicked my lights on, and started back to the cabin.

8

ORIN

THERE WAS A BEEPING IN THE ROOM THAT I hadn't heard before … no, that wasn't right. I'd drifted in and out of consciousness for the past who knew how long, and that beeping had always been there. I opened my eyes. Then opened them a little wider when I saw the false ceiling, florescent lights, and metal railings. Where the fuck was I?

There was a curtain wall on one side of the bed, then a window on the other. Jesus, fuck, I was in a hospital ward. I looked down, pulling at the paper-thin gown covering my body.

"What the fuck?" I muttered, noticing the cannula in my arm. I followed the transparent tube up to the side of my bed where a machine was regulating the fluids pumping into me. My stomach turned in revulsion. I had no idea what drugs they were putting through me right now, and

I felt out of control.

Frantically, I began peeling the tape from my arm when a voice stopped me.

Her voice.

The girl with the horse-head-shaped birthmark on her shoulder.

"You have to leave that in," Fallon said.

I found her standing on the edge of my 'room,' arms folded, her expression wary. I had no idea what that meant.

"I have to get out of here," I said, my voice betraying the terror running through me.

She shook her head. "No, you have to stay. Your fever has only just broken, and you need to stay on antibiotics for at least another twenty-four hours."

Tearing off the tape, I tried to pull the plastic tube-and-needle-combo from my arm, but Fallon slapped her palm over it, stopping me. My panic, which had been building, suddenly began to recede. It was like I could breathe again. I looked up at her from under my lashes.

Fuck, she was beautiful.

"Orin, you must stay. Promise me you'll stay for another twenty-four hours. After that you can check yourself out, but please …"

She didn't say it, but the words *do it for me* hovered between us. Fuck. I licked my lips, waiting to see what she would do next. She didn't move away. She didn't break eye contact. She was waiting me out, and I had to respect the shit out of her for that. Swallowing roughly, I nodded, and she let go of my hand.

Wrapping her arms around herself, she walked to the

window and stared out.

"How long?" I asked her. "How long have I been here?"

"Almost twenty hours. You have a bad viral infection from your … *wound*. That was why you had the fever."

"I would've been fine eventually," I replied.

"No, you wouldn't have. The fever could have killed you." She shot me a look from over her shoulder. "And I couldn't let that happen."

"Why not?"

With a ghost of a smile tilting the corner of her mouth, she turned back to look out the window. "Because you're the Reaper."

I ran a hand through my short hair. "What the hell happened?"

"You passed out when you started showing me the bedroom. I managed to get you onto the bed. You began running a high-grade fever, growing delirious. Eventually, you seized. That's when I knew I had to get you to the hospital."

I ran my eyes over her petite form, trying not to let my gaze linger too long on her ass. She couldn't have weighed much more than a hundred and twenty pounds, soaking wet. "How did you get me out of the bed and into the car?"

"When I noticed you were seizing, I dragged you onto the floor to make sure you didn't hurt yourself. Pulling the blanket from the bed, I managed to get most of your body onto it, then pulled it through the house like a sled. Once I got to the front door, I roused you. You were on your feet just long enough to get close to the car."

Jesus, the lengths she went to. Even though I wasn't happy

to be in a hospital, I knew she'd done the right thing. In fact, if she weren't there, I knew I would've been dead.

"Thank you."

She spun around to face me at my gruff words. "Did you just … *thank* me?"

I let out a small huff.

Fallon leaned back against the window and stared at me. "You're welcome."

A flame of *something* began to flicker in my chest, but I snuffed it out quickly. "What story did you tell them when you brought me in?"

One of her brows quirked up. "Why would you assume I told a story?"

"Because your brother has been a part of the clan for almost a decade. You know how things go."

Folding her arms across her chest, she replied, "I said you were another lodger at the B&B I was staying at. Said I found you collapsed in the kitchen, and you'd told me your name was Jim."

The relief I felt at that information nearly floored me. "Good. The less they know about who I am, the better." I scanned her face, noticing the dark circles under her eyes. "How have you been?"

"Okay." Something outside caught her eye, and she turned to look at it more closely. "Shit."

"What is it?"

"That black Rover is back."

"Black Rover?"

"It followed me back from the store during the storm. And then when I came here to drop you at emergency, it was there again."

It wasn't the Mac Tíre—they didn't know where we were—which meant the Bèar Clan had caught up with us. Dammit, it took less time than I thought it would. We were nothing but sitting ducks.

"The windows?"

"Blacked out."

I yanked at the tape on the crook of my arm. "Help me get this thing out."

She didn't ask any questions this time—just jumped into action. Her fingers were warm where they traced the inside of my bicep down to my elbow. Once the tape was gone, she slid the canula free. Glancing around, she found a metal cart with medical supplies on it and rummaged around until she found a Band-Aid, then helped me from bed.

"Where are my clothes?"

She dropped to her knees, and my heart began to race. This woman on her knees was a big fucking kink for me. When she got back onto her feet, she was holding a clear plastic bag containing my jeans.

I ripped open the bag while she drew the curtains. "That's all they took off me?"

"You were still shirtless, so yeah. I'll turn around so you can get changed." She spun toward the window once more. I stepped into my jeans and buttoned the fly. Fallon turned around almost immediately, her mouth pressing into a line.

"What?"

"I wish I'd brought a shirt back with me, that's all."

I held out my hand to her. "Come on. We have to go."

She blinked down at my offered palm, and I realized what

I'd done. Yes, when people touched me, it made my skin crawl, but when I instigated it, I was okay … although I couldn't remember the last time I'd instigated it.

"Fallon," I said in a dark and stormy voice.

Biting her plump bottom lip, she slid her hand into mine, and the wave of relief and rightness that filled me staggered me for a moment. I'd have to analyze that shit later because we had to get out of there.

I ignored the nurses who demanded to know where we were going. I also avoided the elevator since they could be stopped by security. Instead, I punched at the stairwell's door handle and began our descent.

"How are you feeling?"

"Okay." The truth was, I still felt a little light-headed, but the need to protect Fallon from the Bèar Clan had taken over. This woman who had saved my life. This woman who, for whatever reason, wasn't scared of me.

"You have to tell me if you don't, okay? That's my only request."

I almost laughed. Nobody made requests of me. Sometimes, they begged. Most times they screamed until I cut their tongues out and they couldn't do that anymore. But I'd never had someone make a fucking request.

"Orin, I'm serious. You're not out of the woods yet."

I grunted. If Fallon wanted to play Florence Nightingale with me, I'd be down.

At the bottom of the stairs, we stepped into the lobby. The nurses upstairs had alerted security already, but the single guard waiting for us was standing in front of the elevator bank instead of covering the stairs. We easily slipped through the lobby and out the door.

Twisting my head around, I saw the Rover in question. I had no idea who was behind the wheel, but in the end, it didn't matter. The gun that protruded from the passenger side was real enough. I let go of Fallon's hand and yelled hoarsely, "Run!"

It took her half a second to realize what was going on. She bolted to the car and got the engine started. I began walking as fast as I could toward her, in time to see the Rover lurch forward in our direction. The muzzle of the suppressed gun flashed with each shot, the bullets hitting the cars surrounding me. I took cover as we came up beside one another and I got a look at the shooter. It was some little gobshite I didn't recognize, but who was probably looking for his ticket into the clan. This was a fucking initiation.

When he no longer had a clear shot at me, he turned the gun's muzzle in Fallon's direction, and an inhuman bellow broke free of my throat. The bullet *thwacked* into the rear window, shattering the glass. The bastard in the car sped off out of the hospital parking lot with a squeal of tires. For one heart-rending second, time slowed. If Fallon had been hit …

Rage filled my blood, the monster of my revenge knocking at the door of the cage inside me.

Yanking open the passenger door, I stooped to look inside. The bullet had lodged in the dashboard, mere inches away. "Are you okay?" I barked.

Her wide eyes were fixed on the hole, her chest rising and falling with labored breaths. "I'm fine." Her blue eyes shifted to my face. "What about you? Are you fine? Did you get injured?"

"No." The look of concern on her face threatened to put a fissure in the wall I'd built around my heart, but I refused to let it. I got in the car. "Come on. We need to go."

"Where? Back to your cabin?"

As much as I wanted to return to my only sanctuary, I shook my head. "No. It's time we returned to the compound. I've tried losing the Bèar on my own, but they've found us every time. We need to be with the clan."

Fallon put the car in drive and eased out of the hospital parking lot. She started heading northeast while I kept an eye out for any dark Rovers with blacked-out windows. When it was clear the bastard hadn't doubled back to follow us, it confirmed what I'd suspected, and I finally let myself relax a little.

My gaze flickered back to Fallon like it always seemed to do when I allowed it, and I found her expression pinched, her shoulders tight, and her hands wrapped so tightly around the wheel that her knuckles were white. I wanted to erase the lines of stress bracketing her mouth, but she was in my world now—a world where getting shot at wasn't a foreign concept.

"What?" she asked. At my raised brows, she added, "You're staring."

I rubbed at my stubbled jaw. "I just wish I hadn't dragged you into this."

"You would've preferred to die on my front doorstep instead?"

"You know what I mean."

She looked over at me for a moment before returning her

attention to the road. "I thought I knew the kind of life my brother lived. I thought I understood there was danger, but he was generally safe in his day-to-day life in Galway."

"He is," I replied, wanting to soothe her fears. "In Galway, we're safe. It's when we leave Galway that the real danger becomes present."

"But you leave Galway all the time, right?"

I nodded. "I do."

She nibbled her bottom lip, and although it shouldn't have been possible, the sight of it made my dick hard. I shifted in my seat. "And this is the level of danger and stress you live with daily?"

"Most times, I have a job to do. I go somewhere, do it, then return to Galway if I'm needed. Sometimes when Finnan doesn't have so many enemies or thorns in his side, I go to my cabin to get away from the violence."

This time she looked at me, her ocean-blue eyes locking on my face.

"What?" I asked. "You thought I enjoyed the violence that follows me around?"

Again with that fucking bottom lip. Without thinking, I reached out and ran my thumb over it, pulling it free of the confines of her top teeth. Her breath shuddered out, ghosting across the pad of my thumb. Her throat worked in a hard swallow, and I let myself enjoy this suspended moment—this illicit touch. Her eyes darted to mine for a second before returning to the road. Even though I didn't want to, I released her and turned in my seat.

"I don't enjoy violence, Fallon. I was trained in it. It's my job, but I don't enjoy it like everyone seems to think."

After a moment of mulling that over, she asked, "Do you think we can return to the cabin quickly?"

"Why? What do you need from there?"

"All my clothes are there. Plus, the medicine I found in your bathroom vanity. There were enough antibiotics there for the better half of a course. You need something to keep the infection at bay."

I shook my head. "It's too dangerous. If I were Farrell, that's exactly where I would go if my target was still alive after an attempted murder."

She chewed on her bottom lip this time, and I let out a groan.

Her head whipped in my direction. "Are you okay? What hurts?"

Just my fucking aching cock, I thought darkly. "You keep chewing your bottom lip."

Her eyes widened. "Sorry, it's a nervous habit. I do it without thinking … but why did you groan?"

Jesus, fuck, I could hardly take it anymore. "Because sometimes you torture me, Fallon."

She looked genuinely surprised. "Me? How?"

I shook my head, refusing to have this conversation with her now. How was it possible that she didn't realize how fucking beautiful she was? It was a damn crying shame, but it wasn't going to be me who told her. I was fifteen years older than her. On top of that, she was a clan member's sister. That was more than enough of a deterrent.

"If you're worried about clothing, I can get you some more."

"You don't have to do that. I can buy my own."

I quirked a brow at her independent streak. "Fallon, I've already bought you clothes. Why can't I do it again?"

"Because we'll be back in Galway then, and I'll be able to get my bank cards and phone from the house. I don't need to rely on you for help."

She didn't understand yet that I wanted to look after her. I didn't want to swaddle her and stifle her independence, but I did want to provide for her. With her brother gone and me being the reason she'd been dragged into this life, I wanted to support her.

Again, that was fucking weird because aside from Blakely, there hadn't been one person on this earth I wanted to protect more than her.

"It's probably not safe to go back to your old house."

"Why not?"

"The Bèar Clan will be watching the place now. They'll expect someone to go back there soon. I don't want you getting hurt on account of me."

"What about when Grayson and Sloane return?"

"They'll be gone for another three weeks at least. All this shite would've blown over by then. Just … trust me on this, okay?"

She began to pull her lip into her mouth, but then thought better of it. "Okay. I'll play by your rules for now."

Thank fuck for that.

9

FALLON

"PULL OVER."

It had been quiet in the car for so long that Orin's rough voice startled me.

I peered at him. "What?"

He had craned his neck to look at an SUV parked up on the shoulder. I was so busy thinking about the fact that I'd been shot at three times in less than a week that I didn't even notice the Rover.

The Rover with blacked-out windows.

He was already reaching into the center console, pulling out the gun I'd taken with us and checking it was loaded. "Fallon, *pull over*," Orin said, his other hand already on the handle.

Before I could bring the car to a complete stop, he was out of the door. I put it into park, turning around in my seat to see what he was doing. With the gun raised, he approached the other car slowly, moving around the back and to the far side where I lost sight of him.

When he reappeared, he walked back to the car and stopped beside my window.

"What the hell happened?"

"The gobshite who shot at us in the hospital car park has had his brains splattered all over the interior of that car."

"He's dead?"

A grim nod. "Very."

"Who shot him?"

"If it was an initiation into the clan, the clan member's shot him after he didn't succeed in killing me. I was the real target of the attack. The little fuck must've panicked when he took aim at you instead." He turned his face back to the car, his expression darkening. When he finally looked at me, his black eyes were murderous. "I was going to hunt the fucker down in any case. The Bèar Clan just did me a fucking favor."

I tried to not let his words warm my belly.

"Let's get moving."

Orin got back into the car, and I shifted it back into drive. We didn't stop again until we made it to a town called Roscommon, where Orin began directing me.

"Is this where the safe house is?" I asked, taking the left he'd told me to.

"No. That's closer to Galway. I wanted to stop here for the night."

"Why?"

"Because you look like you're going to be sick."

"I already told you I'm fine." The lie rolled out without a

hint of hesitation.

But I was *not* okay.

I could already feel the panic building inside me.

"Fallon." He said my name like he was ready for this battle—like he knew I would fight against this. "You were shot at."

"I'm aware," I snipped back. "And if you'll recall, it wasn't the first time, either."

He ground his molars together. "We're stopping, and I'm not having an argument with you about it. Turn right at the next street."

I flicked on my indicator and glared at him. "Is this town even safe for us to stay in?" Apparently, there was a whole other set of rules for the clans in Ireland.

"It's a neutral town," he replied.

"Neutral? So, it's not one hundred percent safe?"

"I'm with you. It'll be safe."

I shook my head. That wasn't good enough—not that I was going to say that to his face. "How much farther to get to the clan's safe house?"

A muscle ticked in his jaw. "We're stopping here. End of story. You look like you're going to pass out any moment. You need to eat properly, and rest."

"And I can do that at the safe house." I tried to insist, but Orin steamrolled right over me.

"When was the last time you slept?"

I frowned because I couldn't remember. Before he'd ended up in hospital, and even while I was there with him, I hardly slept properly. I was in a constant state of dozing where no real rest could occur. The honest truth was I was afraid to close my eyes. I was worried that I would relive the shooting, that the stain on my brain would grow larger and burrow deeper just like it had after the attack.

"I thought so," he rumbled. "Food. Sleep. Tomorrow, we leave for the safe house."

"Are you always this disagreeable?" I shot back.

"I wouldn't know. Nobody's ever said that to my face and stayed alive long enough."

And just like that, I was reminded that he was the clan's Reaper. He was their killer. He was the man who dealt in death. I pressed my mouth into a thin line, suppressing all the things I wanted to say to him. He had gone alpha male on me, and while a small part of me was enjoying that, another part of me was bucking against every single one of his shackles.

He may have thought he'd won this round, but I was accustomed to men like him—like my brother. They blustered and bullied their way into your life, then sought to control it in the only way they knew how: intimidation.

"Take that road," he said, pointing to the left. I pulled down a paved boreen that, after five minutes of driving, led to a sandstone cottage.

"Don't tell me. This one belongs to you, too?" I deadpanned as I stared out at the building.

"Don't be daft," he replied. "I picked this one because it was off the main road and private."

We drew to a stop in front of the building and got out. "And when did you have time to book a room?" I asked over the top of the car.

"Welcome to Briar Cottage," an elderly man greeted us

at the door. "Name's Jimmy. Do you need a room?" His watery blue eyes latched onto the shirtless Orin, and once more, I cursed not having brought him any clothes.

"Did you lose your shirt, young man?" Jimmy asked.

Orin stared at him in the same way he did everyone—like he was thinking about what they looked like with their skin flayed from their bodies. "Something like that," he finally said darkly.

Jimmy wasn't deterred. He simply heaved a sigh and turned around. "Park the car around the side. I think I have something of my son's you can wear." He disappeared through the front door, but not before adding, "Come through the back door when you're done."

Getting back into the car, we moved it down to the side of the house, parking beside a motorcycle. Orin looked at it for a long moment.

"Must be his son's," he muttered, more to himself than to me, I was sure. We walked around the back of the house, using the stepping stones set into the earth to stay out of the mud.

I followed him inside, staying close to his back but not touching him. I could feel the heat from his body though, and knew it was just him—not the fever anymore.

We found ourselves in a kitchen where warm pies were resting on the windowsill. I had no idea people still did that.

"This should fit you," Jimmy announced as he walked into the kitchen. He threw a t-shirt at Orin, who caught it one-handed before the fabric could touch his body.

"Thank you," he mumbled before sliding the navy-blue shirt over his head and pulling it down his torso. The fit was a little too snug for his musculature, but it would do.

"We only have one room left," the old man said. "The other one was rented out earlier today. Haven't heard much from him since he got here, and if you ask me, that's just the way it ought to be."

"Great," I said.

He looked between Orin and me. "You two will have to share a room. Is that okay?"

"It's fine," Orin replied, although his jaw was clenched tight as he said it.

"There's a pull-out couch in there if you want to sleep separately. Dinner is at six. *Sharp*," the man continued. "My wife, Betty, cooks the best Irish stew you'll ever taste. Keep the noise down, and we'll get along just fine."

Before we could respond, he was herding us down a hallway and toward the stairs. Jimmy went up first, and Orin maneuvered me to go next while he brought up the rear. At the top of the stairs, there were four doors. Two on the left. Two on the right. Jimmy shuffled his slippered feet over to the second door on the left and opened it.

"Bathroom. Shared with the other guest."

He pointed at the first door on this side of the hall. "Mine and Betty's room." Next, he pointed to the second door on the right. "That's your room."

Jimmy opened the door wide and stood aside. Orin went in first, nodding to me when he'd checked it all out. Jimmy only watched with barely disguised interest.

The room was nice. The bed was pushed kitty-corner up against the wall. A small chest of drawers was on the other side, while a sofa bed was opposite the bed.

From the doorway, Jimmy pointed out, "There's a WC in there, but if you want to shower, you have to use the main bathroom." And with that declaration, he left, shutting the door behind him.

I let out a breath and sat down on the sofa bed. "Well, he seems nice."

"He seems like a busybody," Orin mumbled, flipping the lock on the door, then going to the window to make sure that was locked too. Next, he was in the WC, checking things out. From my vantage point, I saw that it was just a toilet and small sink—barely room to turn around without bumping into anything. It must've originally been a closet.

Orin stepped from the WC, his eyes scanning me. "I'm going to go out and get some more supplies. Lock the door behind me." He stared at me for a beat longer, then retreated from the room, pulling the door shut firmly behind him. After a minute, he called out in a seductively low voice, "Lock the door, Filly."

Sliding from the sofa, I twisted the lock and rested my hand against the wood. I could feel him on the other side, waiting there like a specter. My awareness of him had only grown, and I suspected I would always know where he was.

Flopping backward on the bed, I stared up at the wallpapered ceiling and then turned my head in the direction of the window. The sun was beginning to set, casting the room in a kaleidoscope of colors. Rolling onto my side fully, I watched as the room went from orange to gold, pink, then, finally—against my will—my eyes slid shut.

TERROR GRIPS ME AS I RUN UP THE STAIRS AND INTO Grayson's bedroom. Someone is trying to break into the house, and I have to find the gun.

I have to find …

With clumsy hands, I pull open the closet door and step inside. Shoving aside some suit bags, I expose the false wall in the back of the closet and then press against the top right corner. The door opens on soundless hinges, revealing the matte black face of the gun safe.

Punching in the code, it opens not with a beep but with flashing green lights.

My head jerks around when there's a loud bang! and my heart slams against my ribs in a violent attempt to leave my body. I fumble the gun, forcing myself to tighten my grip and pull myself together. Orin needs me. He's still downstairs.

For a moment, I hear nothing until there's a loud crash and then someone walking through the debris of splintered wood and broken glass. I'm clutching the gun so hard my knuckles turn white.

There's a murmured voice, but I can't make out the words. Then my world tips on its axis when I hear a creak. The same step at the bottom of the stairs that I avoid stepping on when I'm trying to slip out without Grayson knowing where I'm going.

A sudden scuffle.

Pounding footsteps.

And I know I can't stand here any longer. I leave the safety of Grayson's bedroom and start down the stairs. I can still hear scuffling feet. Grunts and groans of pain. I'm halfway down when I hear their voices …

"Where's the bitch who lives here?"

"I don't know anything about any woman," Orin replies steadily.

"Bullshit. We know she lives here … Did you put a bullet in her *head? Get her out of the way? I heard you were ruthless like that."*

"There is no woman. She left a couple of hours ago."

The first man growls in frustration. "Will, go and check upstairs."

The other man appears, his head down as he gingerly touches the side of his head. There's blood on his fingers, a red smear left behind when he grips the banister railing at the bottom of the stairs.

The step creaks.

I bring up the gun …

Widen my stance …

Take aim …

Breathe …

And pull the trigg—

I woke with a gasp, my heart pounding like thunder in my ears. Covered in sweat, I slid from the bed and perched on the edge of the mattress, disoriented in the dark room.

Where am I?

I caught a whiff of cedar.

The Bed and Breakfast, I reminded myself. *Orin. I'm here with Orin.*

Orin.

He wasn't back yet, but I didn't want him to see me like this …

Broken.

Emotionally fractured.

On the verge of falling apart.

Walking quickly into the small bathroom, I turned on the light and looked at the woman staring back at me. My skin was white, a sheen of sweat still dotting my brow. My eyes were wild, though, the memory of the dream—of that *nightmare*—still had its claws in me.

I had shot a man.

I had shot a man *in the head.*

And now I was a fugitive with the Reaper of the Mac Tíre Clan.

On the run with a man who I was growing more and more attracted to by the day.

Closing the lid of the toilet seat, my head dropped into my hands, and I started to sob. My dreams had been plagued with reliving that moment on the stairs ever since it happened. It was getting to the point where I was terrified to close my eyes anymore.

It was just like after the attack. I hadn't slept properly for months afterward.

"Fallon?" Orin called.

Blindly, I reached out and tried to close the bathroom door, but then he was there, shoving it back open.

"What the hell happened?" he demanded, his voice hard like he was ready to tear down the world for me.

"I just need a minute," I told him, sniffling and keeping my face turned away from him.

A beat, then a harsh, "Are you *crying?*"

"No."

Then he was crouching down in front of me. Filling the small bathroom so completely that he took up all my field of vision. With his index finger under my chin, he forced me to look at his face. His dark eyes skated between my eyes, then dipped to my trembling mouth.

"Don't lie to me," he ground out, his jaw tight. "What's wrong?"

I pulled away from his intense stare, wiping the tears from my face with the back of my hand. "Nothing."

"It's not nothing. Is it something I did?" For some reason, he sounded mortified.

"No."

"Then what's wrong?" he bit out gruffly.

I took in two deep breaths. "I've not been able to sleep since … since …" Fresh tears leaked from the corners of my eyes, and I gasped when Orin thumbed them away. The gesture was so tender—so out of character—that the words fell unbidden from my mouth. "I fell asleep when you left. Then I had a dream." I fixed my gaze on his face. "I killed a man, Orin. I murdered him. In my house. And my mind shoves the event down my throat every time I shut my eyes."

"That was self-defense."

I gaped. "It doesn't change anything. I killed *him*. I can't get that image out of my head."

He rose to his full height, his lips pressing into a firm, stubborn line. "This is your life now, Fallon." His tone was hard. So different from the softness of before. "You should get used to it."

Anger licked through my blood at his dismissive tone. At the way he glared at me. At the way he spoke to me like I was a silly little girl who had stumbled into the lion's den with a steak wrapped around my neck.

My hands clenched into fists. "You might be able to live like this, Orin, but I can't. Now, if you can't stand the thought of watching me cry, shut the door and leave me alone."

He glared at me. I glared back, knowing that I couldn't back down first, otherwise he would see it for the weakness it was.

I huffed out a breath. "Just … leave me alone, okay? You don't have to try and comfort me when it's clear you're emotionally stunted."

Anger sparked in his eyes, and the next thing I knew, I was being hoisted into the air and cradled against Orin's broad chest. Carried in his strong arms. I struggled against him, but he only tightened his grip.

"Stop." His tone was firm and unyielding, and I immediately stopped trying to wriggle free of his grasp. He laid down on the bed, arranging me on top of his body so I was draped across him—engulfed by his warmth. His cedar scent invaded my nose.

"What are you doing?" I whispered.

In a gruff voice, he said, "Comforting you. Isn't that what you wanted?"

"Yes. But—"

"Shush," he barked, and I could've sworn I felt the ghost of his fingers brushing against my lower back.

I bit my lip. Despite his intense dislike of being touched, he was holding me to him. Tightly. His heart pounded steadily beneath my ear—a metronomic *thump, thump, thump* that I found myself setting my breaths to.

I was just letting myself melt into his touch when my breath caught in my throat. I'd felt his dick twitch where it was pressed to my stomach.

Orin's fingers drifted down to my hip. "I'm sorry," he said softly against my hair.

Ignoring the elephant in the room, I replied, "For being a stubborn bastard and manhandling me?"

"No. For the … against your stomach. Purely biological. Out of my control."

Oh. My cheeks flushed. I was mortified. I thought he was genuinely attracted to me, but he was right. It was only a biological response to stimuli. I cleared my throat and began to pull away from him, but his fingers tightened on my hip—holding me in place.

"You can let me go," I whispered. "I'm okay. I know you don't like touching people."

"Unsolicited touch is what I don't like." His voice vibrated against my ear.

"Oh." *He touched me first. Because he wanted to touch me. And he still wants to touch me because he hasn't released me, yet.*

Reaching out, he clicked the lamp off beside the bed, and the room descended into darkness.

"Relax, Fallon. I can feel how tense you are."

I couldn't relax though. I felt like I'd stepped on a rattlesnake, and as soon as I let my foot off, he would strike. I eased my fingers out of his shirt until I was inactively lying in his embrace. His huge chest expanded with an inhale before he let out the breath and dragged me a little closer.

"What are you—"

"Shh." There was pressure on the side of my head. A kiss? "Rest. I'll be here to keep you safe."

My eyes had adjusted to the darkness, and I briefly peered up into his face, feeling the heat and weight of his stare. "Is that your line? The one that gets women to fall at your feet?"

His rough reply rumbled through my cheek. "Go to sleep, Fallon."

Eventually, my hands found their way back to his shoulders, where I stroked him with a featherlight touch. He made a strange, sort of strangled noise, and I thought I'd gone too far. Curling my hand into a fist, I tucked it under my chin.

"Don't stop," he said.

"What?"

He cleared his throat. "I asked you not to stop."

I began stroking him again. "You confuse me," I whispered into the dark.

A hand brushed against my shoulder. "Go to sleep, Filly."

But I couldn't go to sleep. I was wide awake, my ovaries throwing ideas at me like dragging his mouth to mine and kissing him. Was it inappropriate? Yes. Did it stop me from having those thoughts? No. And if I was being honest with myself, I'd had them since the first time I realized who had passed out on my doorstep.

I'd never met Orin before that night, but that didn't mean I didn't know who he was. He was the Reaper—known only by reputation. I'd seen him from afar when Grayson had been picked up for jobs. He was an enigma. Elusive. Cold, I'd thought. But now I saw him for what he really was.

A man.

A man who craved the comfort of another warm body beside his even though he couldn't articulate that.

When you dealt in death, the living must be the mystery.

Lifting my head, I tilted my face up toward him to find his dark eyes already on me. There couldn't have been more than an inch between us—so close that his exhale fed my inhale. So close that even in this dark room, I could see every single dark lash that adorned his eyes. I bit my bottom lip, and his hawk-like gaze darted to my mouth.

His lips parted, and I saw the hesitancy in the stiffness of his jaw.

He wanted to kiss me, but at the same time, didn't want to. He was playing a game of tug–of-war and was the only participant. He must've been exhausted running between both ends of the rope.

Before the incident, I didn't think twice about kissing someone. A kiss was meaningless until you took the freedom of choice away. Then it became an act of torture. I had no intention of torturing Orin. I wanted him to want this.

To want me.

His chin tipped toward me in invitation, and I accepted. Licking my lips, I brought my mouth to his and kissed him. His lips were warm, but he wasn't actively participating. It felt as if an assault victim had retreated inside their heads where they could stay mentally safe while the unimaginable happened to their bodies.

This was not what I wanted our first kiss to be like.

I wanted him to want it, too.

I wanted passion.

Pulling back, I buried my face into his neck and did my best to keep the tears in check. If he ever suspected I was crying, he didn't mention it. If he felt regret for letting me kiss him, he didn't show it. I fell asleep with Orin Lynch wrapped around me, but his heart wasn't there with him.

10
FALLON

THE TASTE OF FALLON'S LIPS LINGERED ON MINE ...

Distracting me.

Torturing me.

Driving me insane.

I'd frozen when her soft mouth had pressed to mine. It wasn't because I wasn't attracted to her. I was so fucking attracted to her that my cock had decided to let its presence be known, and I'd had to brush off my reaction like it was a perfectly natural, involuntary biological reaction.

The fuck it had been though.

Nothing about that had been involuntary. Feeling her soft, warm body pressed to mine had made my brain short-circuit. I wanted to tear all her clothes off and sink inside her warm cunt, and the ball-grabbing need had confused me. Sex was about my domination and control over my partner. Sex was about restraint and never letting a woman be in control again.

I wouldn't expose her to that part of me—the dark monster that lived inside my head.

Besides, Fallon didn't need to be associated with someone with a past like mine. I was tainted. Dirty. My body only good for one thing.

Ava had taught me that.

Her cruel words and treatment broke me, but like everything in my life, I remolded myself into another version—one where I controlled every situation and refused to give another person that kind of power over me again.

I looked up at the uncovered window on the opposite side of the room as rain streaked down the other side. While I was out, I'd called Finnan to check in and receive an update on what he wanted us to do. Apparently, there had been several strikes on businesses in Galway that Finnan thought were messages for the clan. And now, he wanted me back in the fold. We were to return to Oranmore tomorrow— me and Fallon. The thought of bringing her even further into this violent life made me sick to my stomach. Her past actions couldn't be undone though, and I would rather have her close where I could keep an eye on her than far away and fending for herself. Not that I would ever let that happen. She was my responsibility now, and when it came down to it, I may not have had any qualms about pulling the trigger and killing mine and the clan's enemies, but I did care about her.

I shut my eyes and let the sound of her breaths, the heat of her body, and the scent of ylang-ylang wash over my beaten and battered soul.

WHEN I WOKE, IT WAS ABRUPTLY AND WITH A DEEP inhale. I was instantly awake. Alert. As was my dick, which had registered Fallon's presence before my consciousness had. She was still in my arms, pressed against me from chest to hip. No, it was more than that. One of her bare feet had snaked between my ankles, hooked there like she was afraid I was going somewhere in her sleep.

Frowning, I tried to figure out what had woken me. Outside, the gentle rain was gone, a storm raging in its place. The room lit up every few seconds, forks of white lightning arcing across the night sky beyond the window. Rain pelted at the pane, and thunder boomed.

I turned my head toward the door when I heard a weak shout, my senses alert in the same way they were when I was on a mission. Disentangling myself from Fallon, I shoved my feet into my boots, picked up the gun from the nightstand, and crept closer to the door.

"Come on, old man," said a voice—this one horribly familiar.

When the sound of footsteps receded, I glanced one last time over my shoulder at Fallon then opened the door. Lightning made the dark hallway illuminate with strobes, the roll of thunder dampening my steps. The door to the bedroom of the old couple who owned this place was slightly ajar. Easing forward, I nudged it open with my foot and swept the room with my gun raised.

"Fucking hell."

The old woman—Betty—had been shot in the head.

She was still lying down like she'd been shot in her sleep. If there was any way to go, though, that would be it. Her pillow and the upper half of the mattress beneath her body were soaked with blood, and the spill of bowels that death heralded was getting thicker by the second.

Across the hall, the door to the other guest room was ajar too, and I peeked inside. The bed was still made, but the blanket was askew as if it had been laid on. Peering around the door, I saw there was no luggage on the floor. Whoever had been staying here had obviously left.

Downstairs, I heard another *thud* and then two loud gunshots that I heard over the tempest. That should've been my first clue that shit was about to go down. The second was the smell of gasoline growing stronger and stronger.

Hauling ass back up the stairs, I exploded into our room, waking Fallon with a start.

She sat up, her hair wild around her face. "What are you doing?"

Fuck, there wasn't any time to explain. I could smell the first wisps of smoke.

"Is that smoke?" she asked, her eyes widening. Scrambling from the bed, she stared up at me with large, blue eyes. "Why can I smell smoke?"

I clenched my jaw so tightly I swore I could hear enamel grinding on enamel. "Farrell found us."

"Found us? How?"

My gaze shifted to the door behind us, the smell of smoke growing stronger. "I don't know how he found us, but we have to get out of here."

"How?"

We couldn't go out the front door. Farrell was smoking us out like you would a fox from a hole. I turned my attention to the window. Throwing open the sash, I peered out. The storm was still raging, lighting up the sky with licking forks of lightning. About six feet below our window was a tree. I could lower Fallon down there, make sure she was safe, then go and take care of Farrell.

Fallon followed my gaze and began shaking her head. "Nope. No way."

"Would you rather go downstairs and have bullets shot through you?"

She nibbled her bottom lip. "Okay." Sliding from the bed, she threw her legs over the side and approached me. "How do I do this?"

"Sit on the sill, then lower your body down. You should be able to feel the tallest branch with your toes … that's right. Don't worry, I have you."

I talked her through the whole thing while rain pelted me from one side and the heat of a fire warmed me from the other. Once I felt that Fallon had found her footing, I clutched the edge of the sill, my knuckles turning white. "Run to the car. Get in. Drive, Fallon. Go to Oranmore. Ask one of the locals for help. Tell them you're looking for sanctuary with the clan."

"What about you?" she asked with wide eyes. "What are you going to do?"

My jaw tightened. "I'm going to take care of this fucker once and for all."

The expression of horror on her face made me want to shield her from this life, but I shook off any grand thoughts of keeping a woman safe as easily as they'd come. I was the goddamn Mac Tíre Reaper. I never backed down from a fight. And when the enemy had Fallon in their sights, I would move hell and fucking earth to protect her.

I waited until she was on the ground and running before turning away. Giving my back to her was one of the hardest fucking things I'd ever had to do, but I did it and then moved to the door. In the hallway, thick smoke filled the space. I turned around and went into the bathroom, yanking a towel from the railing and soaking it in cold water. Once it was saturated, I drew it over my head and shoulders and made the dash down the stairs.

Embers landed on my exposed hands, but I shook them off quickly. When I reached the bottom landing, I found that fire had consumed all of the kitchen and most of the living room. The only thing that wasn't ablaze yet was the short hallway leading to the front door.

There was no more time.

I had to get out of there now.

I opened the door and then slammed it shut again when a bullet hit the wood frame beside my head.

"Orin, I don't want you anymore," Farrell called through the wood. "I want that little *bitch* who shot my brother."

Panic washed over me in a tsunami-sized wave.

I was in the house …

Fallon was out there.

With Farrell.

Fallon was the one he wanted.

Indecision tore at me. If I opened that door again, there was a very good chance I would be shot. Normally, that wouldn't fucking faze me. When your time was up, it was up, but the thought of leaving Fallon alone to defend herself against this motherfucker? It made me see red.

Hauling ass back up the stairs, I stayed low to avoid the billowing mass of writhing black smoke crowding against the ceiling looking for a way to get out. Covering my mouth and nose with the wet towel, I inched my way to the bedroom. Peering out the window, I was both relieved and terrified that I couldn't see Fallon. I had to trust that she had done as I'd asked and escaped. Then she wouldn't have to see me kill this bastard in the most violent ways my creative mind could come up with for wanting to harm the woman who was now under my protection.

I sat on the sill, then lowered myself down onto the tallest branch. Once I felt steady on my feet, I climbed down, my feet hitting the ground with a muted *thud* on the soaked grass and mud. Imprints of Fallon's bare feet were moving away from the tree and around to the side of the house where we'd parked the car.

She was safe.

She was s—

A high, keening scream sliced through the night.

The adrenaline that had been pumping through my body doubled savagely in my blood. Without any regard for my own safety, I bolted around to the front of the house, flinching when the front windows smashed, and glass exploded outwards. I protected my head from the shards, shielding my eyes when the flames licked and danced through their new openings. All the while, the rain tried to quell the fierceness of the inferno.

"Took you long enough," Farrell drawled, and through the flames, I saw him with his thick arm around Fallon's neck, holding her immobile.

My mind shifted into that dark place where rage and murderous intent reigned like a dictator with an iron fist. The monster snarled, baring its teeth.

I brought up my gun, training it at his head.

I could end all this right now.

I could take a shot, kill Farrell, and then get Fallon to safety, but …

What if the shot went a little to the right, and I hit Fallon instead? The thought almost buckled my knees. I stopped a dozen feet from him, feeling the fire at my back.

"Let her go."

Farrell's mouth tipped into a dangerous smile. "No, I don't think I will. She killed my brother."

My gaze ratcheted to Fallon. She looked like a caged animal. She was trembling. Her hands were wrapped around his forearm where it tightened around her neck.

"Let her go, and you can take me," I reasoned.

The other man sneered. "If I take you, all I can do is kill you. If I take her, at least I'll be able to fuck her before and after I kill her."

His words set off something inside me like I'd never felt before. The monster reared its dark head and roared. Without conscious thought, I lifted my gun and fired. Fallon screamed right before I pulled the trigger, and my eyes shifted to her for that split second to see that Farrell had pressed his gun to her side.

My bullet ceased all brain function before he'd even put

his finger on the trigger—his body knocked backward. She fell with him, scrambling to free herself from his lifeless arm. She shoved herself away from his motionless body, staying on her hands and knees as she began to hyperventilate.

I fell to the ground beside her and took her in my arms. Burying her face in my chest, she wrapped her arms around my back and held on just as tightly as she had before. A dormant part of me woke with a snarl—the protective part I had thought long dead. I'd tried to hide it away completely after Ava, but it seemed that this woman could make me feel it wholly—completely.

Even though it felt strange at first, the more I held Fallon, the better she felt in my arms. She was sobbing now, her tears mixing with the rain as it fell on us. I stared at Farrell's body, knowing that this changed everything. His vendetta against Fallon was a personal one, but I had killed another clan's Reaper, and there would be hell to pay.

"Let's get you in the car," I told Fallon, gently lifting her from the ground. She weighed nothing at all, and I relished the fact that I could hold her close to my body—my body that wasn't revolting at the thought of someone touching it. But Fallon wasn't just someone.

Fuck, these thoughts were dangerous.

I couldn't have her like I wanted to. I couldn't take what was left of this woman's innocence to satisfy some dark hunger in me.

What I *could* do was protect her, though, like she had protected me.

I owed her my life.

After settling her in the car, I got in and turned over the

engine. Positioning the vents so they were blowing on her, I said, "I have to take care of the body. I'll be back in a minute."

She'd gone into shock—staring blankly ahead. I didn't even know whether she heard me or not. Shutting the door, I returned to the front of the house and dragged Farrell toward the front door. The bastard must've been the one to set the fire in the first place because his clothes caught alight as soon as he was within reach of the flames.

If the fire burned hot enough, his body would be unidentifiable in a few hours, and judging by how highly flammable he was, he'd used more than enough accelerant to get the job done. This far out of town, I doubted the authorities had been alerted yet. With one final look at the house, I jogged back to the car and got in.

"Where are we going to go?" Fallon asked in a hoarse whisper, not meeting my gaze.

I would've given anything to wipe the desolation from her voice. Shifting the car into gear, I said, "Oranmore."

II
FALLON

SHOCK. I WAS GOING INTO SHOCK FOR THE second time in as many days. My body felt like it was being pulled through the wringer, my emotions bubbling too close to the surface. Orin was driving us back toward Galway, toward the safe house. His hands were relaxed on the wheel and his eyes focused on the road. Water still dripped from his hair onto his face, but he looked cool and calm like he hadn't just shot a man in the head.

My mind kept throwing out not completely irrational thoughts of what if he'd missed?

What if he missed his shot and shot *me* instead?

I could've been dead.

"You're staring," Orin said, eyes still on the road. "What is it?"

I licked my lips. "I was just wondering if I'll ever be as okay as you are with …"

Killing someone. The words I couldn't say lingered between us.

Orin knew though. His head whipped toward me—his black gaze narrowing on my face. "You think I enjoy taking life? That I'm heartless? Cold?"

"I never said that."

"You didn't have to," he sneered. "I can hear it in your voice."

"Orin—" I reached out without thinking …

His feral gaze slid down to where I clutched his forearm before darting away. At least he didn't shake me off. His jaw clenched tight before he finally said, "I am a killer, Fallon. I told you that before." He ran his eyes over me—*raked* over me. "Now I hope you can believe it."

He was trying to intimidate me, to scare me off, but I saw the flicker of shame.

"If you're a killer," I announced bravely, "then I am, too."

"You didn't have a choice," he muttered dismissively.

I didn't know why, but that got my hackles up. Why did his choice to kill diminish mine? What right did he have to shoulder this burden—this guilt—alone?

When I spoke again, my voice was strong—my indignant anger leaking through. "I had a choice. Live or die. Kill or be killed. I chose to live because my brother taught me that this world isn't fair, and it sure as shit wouldn't be fair back to me. Life is hard. We make decisions. We act on them. Good or bad, we have to live with it afterward. You are simply choosing to live, Orin."

Shadows lurked in his cold dead eyes. "And what if I told you I enjoyed taking someone's life?"

I let go of his arm and sat back against the door, but my body was still turned toward him. "Do you?"

He was quiet for a long while, then said, "I never want to lie to you, Fallon."

"Then don't."

His eyes cut to me, then away. "What if I said yes? That I enjoyed the rush it brought me."

I swallowed because the idea that someone enjoyed the kill was inherently wrong to me. I was studying to be a nurse—to help *save* lives.

I was about to answer him when he barked a humorless laugh. "You know what? Don't answer that. Your silence is more than enough of a response."

I didn't want him to feel like I didn't accept him. I may not have been able to trust him at the start, but he had proved himself to be someone I could rely on. We'd been through hell together, and the fight wasn't over yet.

Wrapping my arms around myself, I shivered despite the heat blasting from the vents. "I don't judge you for enjoying it. Sometimes, things happen in life that twist us around. Alter us completely. I know that this experience will harden me."

He didn't say anything to that for the longest time, and I thought the conversation was over.

"Don't let that happen," he said so softly I thought I misheard him.

"What?"

"Don't let that happen. Don't let this experience harden you. I let my life change me. Granted, some pretty fucked-up shit happened to me ..." He huffed out a breath and ran a hand through his damp hair.

"Like what?"

"What?" he asked like he was stuck inside his head with other thoughts.

"Like what? What happened to you?"

He shook his head, refusing to say more.

I sat there, staring out the window, letting his words turn over in my head. It was clear he had a past—we all did— but what was clearer was that he wasn't going to be talking about it anytime soon.

I WOKE UP WHEN I HEARD SOFT VOICES. PEELING open one eye, I found the rain had stopped, and we were parked in front of an imposing stone building that bore a striking resemblance to a castle. The façade was austere and gray, the stones weathered by time.

Orin was standing at the front of the car, his arms folded across his broad chest. Beside him were Finnan Quinn— the Clan Boss—and another man I didn't recognize. Orin's dark gaze kept flicking back to me, and when he realized I was awake, he walked away while Finnan was still speaking and opened the door.

I blinked at him.

"We're here," he said, holding out his hand to help me from the car.

"Well, fuck me," the other man said, his attention now on us, too.

"Shut it, Caolan," Orin barked. To me, he said gently,

"Come on, Filly. You need to rest properly."

Taking hold of his hand, I let him help me from the car. The stones beneath my bare, muddy feet dug into my heels, and I winced. Orin saw and swept me up into his arms, cradling me against his chest like a child.

"I'm going to take her to her room," he announced in a tone that didn't invite any further discussion. He walked past Finnan and Caolan. Both men stared, and as Orin passed, Finnan's hand darted out and grabbed him by the upper arm.

His green eyes were focused on me, but he spoke into Orin's ear. "Are you sure this is wise?"

Orin shrugged from his grip. "She's safer with me. Nobody in the clan speaks to her without my presence."

"Orin—" Caolan started, but Orin cut him off.

"Nobody," he seethed. "The girl is scared enough."

Both men stared at me in open disbelief. Once we were a few steps away, Finnan said something into Caolan's ear, to which he nodded.

Inside, large, ancient-looking flagstone floors stretched out in all directions. A large oak staircase was ahead, and Orin's long legs ate up the distance over the rugs and runners.

"You can put me down now," I told him, my arm still wrapped around his broad shoulders. Honestly, I didn't want to go anywhere, but I must've looked ridiculous being toted around like this.

Orin grunted but didn't relinquish his hold on me.

On the first floor, portraits hung on the dark paneled walls. Many of the paintings were surrounded by bulky aged-gilt frames, and I wondered how old some of the pieces were.

Orin finally drew to a stop in front of an oak door and opened it. Gesturing for me to go in first, I surveyed the room. There was a large bed against the wall to my right. An armoire on the left beside a door, which I assumed led to a bathroom.

"Is this your room?"

He shook his head. "Just a room. I want you to stay here while I go speak to Finnan. We need to start making plans."

Suddenly, the thought of being left alone didn't sit well with me. "Can't I come with you?"

Orin's expression softened, and he reached for me. I braced for his touch, but he seemed to think better of it, clenched his hand into a fist at the last second, and dropped it to his side. "Rest. I'll be back with food as soon as I'm able."

Before I could protest, he left the room, shutting the door behind him. Crossing the space, I went to investigate the bathroom, finding one can of deodorant on the counter, a toothbrush, toothpaste, and a bar of cheap soap in the shower stall. In the armoire, I found men's clothes hanging— all of them an iteration of something I'd seen Orin wear. Dark jeans. Black t-shirts. Leather jackets. I lifted a jacket out and slid my arms into the holes. The dark leather was cold against my skin but soon warmed. Dipping my nose to the collar, I inhaled deeply, smelling cedar, soap, and man.

This was Orin's room. He'd brought me to the place where he let his guard down, and once again I was confused by the man. Shrugging out of the jacket, I hung it back up, making sure to put it into the same spot again, then closed the armoire doors. There was nothing else for me to do here—no TV or books, games, or puzzles. It was as impersonal as a hotel room, and that made me want to weep.

Did Orin think there was no point in decorating his space with things that appealed to him because he thought he might be wiped off the face of the planet any second? If he did, that made me sad for him. Nobody should live like their last day was right around the corner. After the incident, and my recovery, I learned that life is a precious gift. I was lucky to come out the other end with my sobriety, and now I tackled each day like it was going to up and leave me.

Walking over to the bed, I traced my fingers over the thick quilt, then the pillows. My eyes drifted up the wooden frame, getting snagged on what looked like a thick metal eyebolt. My gaze drifted to the other three corners of the frame and found matching ones. Then, I looked up. There were more anchor points higher up.

Congruently, a thrill of lust and fear went through me, making my stomach drop and flutter at the same time. There would only be one reason to have anchor points like that on a bed, and it involved a hell of a lot of kink. Was that what Orin was into? Did he like to tie up his lovers? I hadn't noticed any metal brackets or chains at his cabin. Maybe that wasn't what he used them for here?

Despite my heated blood, the exhaustion I thought had been kept at bay by my small nap suddenly came back with a roar, and I laid down on the bed. I told myself not to fall asleep, but as the warmth of the quilt covered me and the scent of cedar washed over my senses, I was lulled into dreamless sleep.

12
ORIN

THANK FUCK I'D ESCAPED. I DIDN'T KNOW WHY I'D lied and told Fallon it was just a room and not *my* room. No doubt by now, she'd snuck a look inside the bathroom and at my clothes hanging in the armoire and now knew that she was in my personal space. It made me wonder how she felt about that. Did she hate the cold metal hardware affixed to the bedframe, or was she … curious?

I'd excused myself with a lie—a lie to get her some food—but the humiliating truth was I needed to remove myself from her presence before I took from her what I so desperately wanted to take. That was how I ended up sitting outside in the hall—my back to the hard wood paneling—while I talked myself out of going right back in there so I could breathe the same air as her.

If I could just see her with my own two eyes, I would know that this insane drive to protect her was unfounded.

She was safe here—safer than I'd been able to keep her when we were on the run—so why did I feel like I was missing something?

"I hope you know what you're doing."

My head jerked around, while my hand reached for my gun. I hadn't even heard Finnan approach, and I was a fucking idiot to have been distracted by thoughts of Fallon.

Releasing my grip on the gun's handle, I settled my arms back onto my knees and gave him a cool stare. "She's part of this now."

Finnan's shrewd eyes skittered toward the door before returning to me. "She's innocent in all this."

"She shot Farrell's brother."

Finnan's brows rose infinitesimally, then he walked in the direction of his office. Hauling my body off the floor, I followed, knowing I had to lay it all out. Bringing outsiders to the compound was not acceptable. I had to make sure Finnan knew all the whys. I shut the door behind me, finding Keir Flanagan—the Clan's Chief and second-in-command—already there. Finnan walked behind his desk and sat down.

"Start talking."

"I was driving back to Galway after a run-in with Farrell. He was waiting for me after I took out the cop Mannix had in his pocket. We shot at each other, and he got me." I touched the bandage on my ribs. "I got to Galway, but I'd lost a lot of blood. I saw Kent's house, thinking he would be able to help me, except I forgot he was … gone. I knocked on the door, then passed out."

"Jesus," Keir said from his seat.

"What happened then? How in the hell did Kent's sister get involved?"

"She opened the door. Farrell must've been waiting for that though because she told me her house was sprayed with bullets as he drove by." I left out the part about Fallon throwing herself over my body to protect me and pushed on. "She dragged me inside. Triaged me as best she could, then left me to rest."

"How bad is the wound?" Finnan asked, gesturing with his chin to my side.

"A few millimeters to the left and I wouldn't have made it."

"I swear, you have a lucky fucking rabbit's foot up your arse," Keir told me. "The number of times you've nearly died and somehow didn't?" He shook his head. "Fucking lucky bastard."

"You were being nursed back to health," Finnan cut in impatiently, his voice betraying how ridiculous he found the statement. "What happened then?"

"Farrell came back with his brother. I'd told Fallon to go and get any guns stored in the house, and while she was upstairs, they broke in. I got into it with one guy, which turned out to be Farrell's little brother. Farrell appeared and pressed a gun to my head just as Fallon started back down the stairs. They creaked, and Farrell sent his brother to check it out. Fallon blew the bastard away and then hid. While Farrell was crying over his brother's dead body, we slipped out the garage and got into her car."

I told him the rest of what happened—the near miss with the lorry, then the second stay at a B&B, where I'd had to shoot Farrell after he'd threatened to kill Fallon.

"There's a gap in your story," Finnan said. "You're missing at least four or five days."

I gave him my best blank stare, telling him that I wouldn't be discussing anything further.

He smirked. "All right. Keep your damn mystery."

"What are we going to do about Fallon?" Keir asked the question I'd been wondering about since we fled her house all those days ago.

Finnan got up, poured himself a glass of whisky, and took a long sip. "She killed a Bèar Clan member. Farrell might've been the only one to know, or he might've told Mannix King, and now all the Bears are after her." His gaze locked on mine. "What would you want to do with her?"

Claim her. "She can't go back to that house. She'd be dead within the week."

"Besides Mary, we don't have any active female clan members."

Finnan's eyes sparkled with something cruel. "She had a nice body from what I saw. Maybe we can get her working at Velvet. She can pay the clan back for the inconvenience that way."

My blood boiled at the thought of making her a clan whore. My hands fisted tightly, drawing Finnan's hawk-like stare. "You can't keep her, Reaper," he drawled. "She's a sister to one of our members. Granted, that member is a fucking arsehole, he's still a member."

"You can't tell me what to do in my personal life," I hissed, mentally holding myself immobile. "Fallon has to stay here."

"She's no good to me as anything but a cum dumpster."

I stepped forward, and Keir rose from his seat, angling his body in such a way that Finnan was partially obstructed. Finnan knew he'd pushed all my buttons and was fucking enjoying himself.

"I know what kind of sex you enjoy. Would you inflict that on that *girl?*"

I winced, knowing he was throwing that back in my face. Licking my lips, I wondered how to play this. It wasn't unusual for men to sit around and degrade women with comments, but it was quite another to discuss a man's preferences.

"Maybe she's got some skills that would be useful to the clan?" Keir suggested, trying to diffuse the situation. "Grayson mentioned she was studying."

"Nursing," I croaked. "She's studying to be a nurse."

Finnan's grin grew like he'd just won a game I hadn't known we were playing. "Nursing? Now, that could prove useful."

I didn't know why but knowing that Finnan already had a plan for Fallon made me want to put a bullet in his skull and walk away from the clan forever. I didn't want her to be used as a whore, but I also wasn't sure I wanted her to be used for her skills. What I wanted her for, I …

Stopped myself.

What I wanted with Fallon wasn't ever going to happen. Besides the age difference, which I knew would be a big fucking hurdle, there was my particular taste in fucking. I couldn't imagine a woman like that wanting to submit to someone like me—someone who enjoyed bringing another pain. Someone who enjoyed humiliating his partner.

Fingers snapped in front of my face, and I blinked Finnan, Keir, and the office back into focus.

"What?" I snarled.

Finnan's mouth twitched. "Fallon can stay. If she proves useless as a nurse, she becomes Velvet's new whore."

My blood pressure ticked up. "And what if whoring isn't how she pictured her life?"

My boss shrugged. "We could always drop her off to Mannix King."

As much as it sounded like a bastard of a thing to say, seeing Fallon as a whore was far better than seeing her as a corpse. My jaw felt wired shut as I asked, "Anything else?"

"Yeah." He clapped me on the shoulder, and my whole body shuddered from the contact. "You can go tell her the good news."

Taking in a deep breath through my nose, I stared at Finnan briefly before turning and yanking open the door. The force of my pull sent it slamming into the wall, and I smirked as I thought about leaving a dent behind. I hoped I fucking did because right now, I wanted to tear Finnan's tongue from his mouth and fucking feed it to him.

My anger rippled from me. Midway down the hall, some fucking Sentinel I didn't know took one look at me and scurried off. Good thing, too, because I was looking for a fucking fight.

"Orin," someone called behind me.

"What?" I didn't bother to turn. All I could keep my eyes on was Fallon's door ... which also happened to be my door.

Keir's large hand landed on my shoulder. "Stop. Please."

It took everything in me to do as he asked, but I did. Finnan was the kind of leader who pushed me to my limit. Keir was the kind to ease me into changes, making sure I was really okay with them. The pair couldn't be any different, and that was what made the clan work.

"What?" I repeated, less angrily this time.

We'd stopped no less than ten feet from my room. His black eyes slanted in the direction of the door and his brows rose. The bar through his right eyebrow winked in the light. "Are you sure you know what you're doing?"

"What the fuck, man? She's Grayson's sister. You think I'd go there with her?"

He shrugged. "Honestly? I don't know what you'd do. You've always been a mystery to me."

A small part of me was glad he didn't know me. I didn't want anyone to really know me … to find out my secrets … to pity me. I was not the kind of man others should pity, but there was something about him *wanting* to know. The wanting meant he cared on some level, and that was something I'd been chasing all my fucking life. The army had given me a taste of what a family could be, but instead of a mother nurturing me, it was a sergeant handing me a long-range rifle and teaching me how to snipe.

The clan had provided me with a little more stability, but I knew something was missing.

"She's safe with me," I rumbled, then opened the door and stepped inside.

I found Fallon on my bed, her unbound hair spilling all over my pillow. *My* fucking pillow. Something like hope flared to life in my chest at the sight of it. Did she know she was sleeping on my side of the bed? Did she realize that where she was resting her head would probably smell like me? That flicker of hope began to grow into a fully-fledged flame.

Unwilling to wake her, I went into the bathroom and shut the door quietly behind me. Hitting the switch on the wall, light flooded the space, and I quickly shut it off again. There were warm, muted LED lights under the cabinets and around the dropped ceiling that provided me with more than enough light to get showered and brush my teeth.

Stripping out of my clothes, I peeled off the bandage around my ribs before turning on the cold water and stepping inside the stall. The temperature always stole the breath from my lungs, but I gritted my teeth and stayed under the spray. The bar of soap I always used was sitting on the soap dish as usual, and as I grabbed it and started to lather it up, I thought about Fallon using the same stuff. I didn't want her to. The soap I used was fucking harsh—the kind of stuff that was used for disinfecting the skin.

Fallon was perfect in every way and didn't need this shit touching her body.

Rinsing off quickly, I toweled dry, then walked back into the bedroom. Fallon was still asleep, so I dropped the towel and started to get dressed. I glanced over my shoulder, however, when I heard the bedsheets rustle. She was still—thankfully—asleep, and for that I was grateful.

I let myself stare at her a moment, knowing that under the sheets, her soft body and curves would fit my hands so perfectly. That when I took her mouth, she would yield to me. I would want to take more, but I wouldn't let that happen. For me, fucking usually involved a fuck of a lot of power play. Most times, I would stay completely clothed while my sub would be completely naked. I liked the unbalance of it. It reminded me that I never had to be a sub—willing or unwilling—ever again.

After pulling on a pair of sweats and a black t-shirt, I walked past the bed, slowing down to get a look at Fallon's face. Her lips were slightly parted as she slept. My body ached to stretch out beside her, but the concept was so foreign to my fucked-up brain that I practically ran from the room.

I was so spooked that I ran straight into Keir. The other guy held his hands out in front of him so we didn't accidentally touch. "Woah, what's going on? Where's the fucking fire?"

Fuck. "Do you have another kind of soap for Fallon to use?"

I braced for the question of what was wrong with mine, but for whatever reason, he didn't ask. All he said was, "sure," then started down to his room. Stepping in after him, I looked around. It looked nothing like mine. Keir had decorated it with paintings and prints of the ocean and of Galway. A blue quilt was on the bed, an area rug on the ground, and a couple of comfortable-looking armchairs huddled around a small bookshelf.

Compared to this, my room looked like a prison cell—especially with the eye bolts positioned on the bedframe. This was where I brought some of the girls from Velvet since their rooms weren't properly equipped. It was also something the other clan members didn't know. They would've been bitching and moaning if they did, saying it was a security risk, but it wasn't when I blindfolded them before we even got in the car, and it didn't come off again until I dropped them back at the club afterward.

"Here," Keir said, reappearing with his hands full. "I've got soap or bodywash. Take whatever you want."

I took the bottle of bodywash and smelled it. It reminded me of her, and when I looked at the label, it said it was ylang-ylang and cedar. "Thanks," I said, then hauled ass out of there. I didn't want anyone else to see me gathering supplies for my woman.

Hustling back to my room, I deposited the bottle in the shower, took one final look at Fallon then went into the gym to work off some of my pent-up sexual aggression.

13
FALLON

THERE WAS A TAPPING IN MY DREAM. A RHYTHMIC *tap, tap, tap.* I was standing in the living room of my house, and the tapping kept coming, getting louder and louder until the glass in the front windows shattered and bullets rained down on me. I jolted up with a start, and I swallowed hard to ease the sensation of my heart in my throat. With my breath barreling out of me, I looked around the room.

This was Orin's room. I was safe. There were no bullets.

Tap, tap, tap.

My eyes locked on the door. Sliding from the bed, I padded closer. "Is someone there?" I asked.

"Aye, Fallon. It's Keir."

"Who?"

"Keir. Finnan's right hand."

My immediate thought was that Finnan wasn't going to allow me to stay, so I was reluctant to open the door at all.

Licking my suddenly dry lips, I asked, "Where's Orin?"

"He's hitting the gym."

"What do you want?"

"I have some food for you."

My stomach rumbled, and I pulled open the door a crack. Light from the hallway slanted in. A man with dark hair and eyes stood there. He had a bar through his eyebrow and had to have been well over six feet tall. He smiled at me then—a genuine, friendly smile—and I wondered how a guy like him had ended up in the clan.

"Can I come in?" he asked, glancing down at the tray he was carrying.

I stepped back. "Sure."

He stepped into the room, then stopped. I flicked on the light, revealing the sparse decoration and complete lack of furniture. His dark gaze landed on me briefly, and I could see the shock in them. He wiped it away a moment later with a smile. "Looks like Orin could use some decorating help."

"I think this suits his personality," I replied, dropping down on the edge of the bed.

"If you mean impersonal and stark, then aye, this fits his personality to a tee." He walked toward me with the tray and offered it to me. There was a plate of roasted chicken with some steamed vegetables and gravy. Mashed potatoes. A heel of bread. "I didn't know what you liked, so I got you a bit of everything."

I looked up at him. "That's very kind of you."

He nodded, and I thought that might be the end of the conversation, but he stayed. "Listen, Fallon ..." he began.

Then stopped. "I'm …"

I began to eat my chicken. "You're?" I prompted.

Keir ran a hand through his thick dark hair, and I had to admit that he was attractive in a wholesome kind of way. Dark eyes fixed on my face. "Do you feel safe with Orin?"

I physically recoiled at the question. "Why wouldn't I feel safe with him?"

He shook his head. "Orin isn't known for his … softness. He's our clan's Reaper. He kills men for a living, and from what I've seen, when he kills, it doesn't faze him in the slightest."

"And you're worried about him?" I asked, tearing off another strip of chicken with my fingers.

"No. No, I'm not worried about him. I'm worried about you *with* him."

It was my turn to shake my head. "I don't understand. Why would you be worried?"

Keir stared at me for a beat, then began to pace. "Orin can be a bit of a loose cannon. He goes rogue a lot, and Finnan tolerates it because he knows he can get the job done efficiently and effectively."

"Okay."

"Finnan also knows that Orin has a particular … taste when it comes to women."

My brows rose. "Taste?"

"He likes to dominate them. Do you understand what I mean when I say that?"

I snorted. "Of course, I do. Are you saying he's into bondage and submission?"

"He thinks we don't know he brings women here

sometimes." He approached the bed, brushing his fingers against one of the anchor points. "He thinks we don't know what he does in here with them, but we do. We've never stopped him because he's never lost control, but also because all those women *want* to be submissive to him. They know exactly what they're signing up for."

"And you're afraid for me because?"

He heaved a sigh and ran his hand through his hair again, making it stick up. "You haven't signed up to be his sub."

"What makes you think he's even interested in me like that?" I tried my best to ignore the stupid flutter in my chest. I knew I shouldn't be attracted to a man like him, but instead of feeling scared of him like I did most strange men, he put me at ease. Like he was my own personal stash of Xanax.

"I've seen the way he looks at you. Just be careful, okay? I'd hate to see you get hurt."

"Because I'm a delicate woman?" I shot back, anger bubbling to the surface.

"No. Because you're Grayson's sister. That means something more."

He turned to leave but stalled when someone bellowed, "What the fuck do you think you're doing?"

I turned to find Orin moving like a raging storm toward the door. He was in a black t-shirt that clung to every ridge, peak, and trough of his honed body. Sweat turned the fabric a darker shade of black—the same shade his eyes were currently flashing. Gray sweatpants hung low on his hips, and his feet were bare.

His anger flowed over the room, and I saw Keir visibly

stiffen. "I was just talking to her," he said, placing his hands up in front of him.

Orin got up in the other man's face, jabbing a finger at him. "No," he hissed. "Not while I'm not here. You can talk to her only when I'm here."

Keir tilted his head to the side to look at me standing behind Orin and raised his brows as if to say *See?*

I saw, and I wasn't afraid to admit that I liked this possessive streak Orin seemed to have when it came to me.

"Tell all the other motherfuckers here the same thing," he added, his voice a low growl. "Or you can deal with me."

Keir looked him dead in the eye. "Sorry, man. My mistake."

After one more fleeting look, he turned to leave with Orin following closely on his heels. He slammed the door shut behind Keir, then turned his ire on me.

Jesus. He was a stunning man.

A feral, dangerous, heartbreakingly stunning man.

"What did he say to you?"

Rising to my feet, I lifted my chin and met his gaze. "Nothing I didn't already know."

He stepped forward, invading my personal space until we were standing toe-to-toe. The scent of fresh sweat and cedar rose between us. I licked my lips, his dark eyes spearing me.

"Tell me what he said."

"Or what? You'll tie me up and make me submit to you?"

It was a taunt I shouldn't have made, but I wanted to see whether it was true. If it was possible, Orin's pupils dilated further, and I knew in that moment that I was standing with a man who barely had control of himself and his urges.

We breathed in each other's air for a long minute, his eyes

moving between mine as he searched for the answer. Then, his mouth curled up into a snarl. "Don't talk to anyone else."

A humorless laugh escaped my lips, and I stared at him incredulously. "How do you suppose you're going to enforce that? Keep me locked up in here the whole time?"

He grunted, then stalked over to the plate of food I discarded on the bed. He picked it up and sniffed the contents before walking to the door and throwing it into the hall. After he slammed the door shut, he turned to me once more.

"I was eating that," I spluttered.

"I'll be the one to feed you from now on."

I couldn't believe he'd said that. "I'm not your property, Orin. You can't keep me caged and expect me to be a meek little woman about it."

He grinned, his mouth stretched out to bare all his teeth. "I can keep you caged, Filly. You're mine to protect now. From everything. Even myself if I have to."

My breath left me on a shudder. Protect me from him? "What do you mean protect me from you? You wouldn't hurt me."

"How would you know? I could be a sadist."

I shook my head. "You're not. I know you want people to see you in one light, but you forget I've already seen you in another." Even though there was a chance he would bolt, I edged closer. "I know you won't hurt me."

This time when he smiled, his grin was malevolent. "That's where you're wrong. I've hurt women before. If the clan demands it. If *I* demand it. Retribution isn't something I play around with. Man. Woman. Fucking child. If someone needs to die, they die. End. Of. Story."

As he spoke, he leaned further and further forward until our noses were practically touching. Our mouths an inch from each other's. Even though it was stupid and reckless, I wanted to tilt my chin up and slant my mouth over his. I wanted to taste him, feel his reckless abandon wash over me. Everything he was saying was probably true, but there was one thing he was lying to both me and himself about. He would never hurt me.

Ever.

I knew it in my bones.

I tilted my chin up, inviting his mouth to touch mine. His eyes widened as he stared at me, at what I was offering him. I could practically taste his desire to kiss me, but then he started shaking his head and backed away. Turning, he opened the door and fled.

14

ORIN

FUCK! WHAT THE FUCK WAS I THINKING? I STOOD on the other side of my bedroom door, lust and fucking *desire* waging a war inside me. I wanted to take her mouth. I wanted to take more, but I couldn't. Fifteen years were too goddamn many between us. Not to mention she was Grayson's sister.

Grayson's sister who I wanted to see bound and naked before me.

Fuck!

My hand trembled as I ran it through my hair. I had to get away from her. I'd assumed that going to the gym and doing some kickboxing would ease the ravenous hunger I had inside of me, but it had done nothing to subdue the ferocity of my feelings. Then seeing Keir alone with her? My mental monster had flipped the goddamned table of rational thought and started to rampage.

Keir—my brother—didn't even know how close he'd come to eating a fucking bullet for being alone with her. I probably should've fed him the damn thing when I realized what he'd told Fallon about me. She'd specifically mentioned the word *submit*, which meant Keir had told her all about my kink.

The bastard probably thought it was just something I was into, but the truth was much more painful. Stalking down the stairs and into the kitchen, I began yanking open cupboards, looking for everything I needed to cook her a better meal than day-old chicken and steamed vegetables. I was going to make her a fucking pasta dish that would ruin all other pasta dishes for her. Plus, the routine and rules of cooking would help ease that monster back into his cage.

I got lost in the motion of chopping vegetables and opening tins of tomatoes. Adding herbs and just a sprinkle of brown sugar to cut through the tartness of the tomatoes. I cooked until my rage was under control, and I could go and speak to Fallon like a rational fucking human being.

I drained the pasta, then dumped it into the sauce on the stovetop. Shay and Quillen came sniffing around when I started placing large spoonsful of pasta into a deep bowl.

"I didn't know you could cook," Shay said, trying to snatch a piece of penne from the pan.

I glowered at him.

"Can we have some?" Quillen asked.

"You can have some when Fallon is done eating. Not before." Annnnd just to drive the point home, I pulled the gun from the small of my back and shoved it into Shay's chest when he tried to steal some more. "*Not* before."

He backed away with a half-smile on his face. "Got it."

I grabbed a fork from the drawer, and the bowl of parmesan cheese from the counter that I'd grated while waiting for the pasta to finish cooking. When I walked back into the bedroom with my peace offering, I found that Fallon was in the shower. And I knew this because the fucking bathroom door had been left cracked.

I set the bowls on top of the nightstand and looked around the room—trying to see it through her eyes. The furniture was sparse, but that was because aside from bringing women here to fuck, I didn't spend a lot of time at the compound. My job took me to different places, never staying too long. Then when I did have time off, all I wanted to do was stay at my cabin and be left alone.

Being at the cabin with Fallon would've been different though. I wanted to see her in my kitchen or curled up on the couch with her nose buried in one of my books. Waking up and knowing she was safe was turning into a new kink for me, and I could only blame the shift on the fact that she kept saving my life, and I kept saving hers. We were a mafia version of Mr. and Mrs. Smith, but Angelina had nothing on my Filly.

Fuck.

On Fallon.

Not *mine*.

Yet. The thought popped into my head without permission, and instead of pushing it back into the box that held every impossibility I thought I had for my life, I cupped the idea in my hands for a moment. What if she was mine? What if I could have her? Keep her safe? I shook my head. None of that could ever be. I needed sex in a specific way, and I could never degrade her like that.

So, for now, I would keep her packed away in the *Never Going to Happen so Stop Dreaming, Asshole* box in the back of my mind. Once this shit with the Bèar Clan was over, she could return to her safe life, and I could go back to knowing she and I would never become more than what we already were—two people who had to rely on each other for a short time.

The door to the bathroom opened, and I froze in place. I'd been so consumed by my thoughts that I hadn't even heard the shower stop.

Fallon's blonde hair was darker wet than it was dry. She'd towel-dried it a little, leaving the strands clumped together around her face. Her cheeks were pink, and the color spread as I dropped my gaze down to her body. The towel around her was cinched shut at the top of her breasts and barely hit her mid-thigh.

My mouth salivated.

"What are you doing back here?" she asked. "Come to rail at me again?"

"I brought you food. *Real* food." Jesus, fuck, my voice was raspy.

She followed to where I was pointing, seeing the steaming bowl of pasta. She inched closer, brushing past me as she did. The scent of the bodywash I'd left for her swept over me in a sensual caress, and I moved back a step.

She picked up the bowl and brought it closer to her face. With her eyes locked on mine, she inhaled deeply and smiled. "My favorite kind of pasta and sauce."

I tried to not let that statement impact me too much, but, fuck, it felt good.

Now that I knew she was happy with what I'd made for her, I walked over to the door and made sure it was locked. One of her brows rose in question.

"You're in a towel. I want to make sure none of those bastards come in here while you're like that."

"But you can see me like this?" she taunted gently.

Fuck. This woman. I swallowed. "I would never do anything to you."

She held my gaze for a long minute before dropping her eyes to her bowl. Under her breath, she asked, "Even if I wanted you to?"

My whole body froze. Muscles locked down on bone. I was pretty sure my blood stopped pumping except for one specific area of my body. I must've misheard her. She couldn't want …

I pulled the bowl from her hands and took the fork, spearing a piece of pasta. Holding it out to her, she only stared.

"You're going to feed me now?"

She was right. What the fuck was I doing? I started to lower the forkful, but she stopped with a shake of her head and opened her mouth.

I fed her the mouthful, taking an obscene amount of pleasure in watching her chew and swallow what I had cooked for her.

"I need you to stay away from Keir."

She raised an eyebrow. "That's funny. He said the same thing about you."

"I'm serious, Fallon. None of these men can be trusted."

"You trust them." She opened her mouth for another forkful of pasta, chewing thoughtfully while she awaited my answer.

"I really don't," I muttered. "I don't trust anyone."

She cocked her head to the side as if she wanted to know whether she was lumped into the category, too. "That's sad then."

And there.

She'd done it.

She'd tapped on my chest and found out one of my secrets without having to put a fucking gun to my head. What was it about this woman that made me spill everything to her? Whatever it was, I couldn't stand in the warmth of her truth serum any longer. Thrusting the bowl at her, I turned and marched into the bathroom. Before I shut the door, I told her over my shoulder, "Eat everything. If you want some more, I'll get you some after I have a shower, but *don't* leave this room."

Twisting on the cold water, I stripped off the sweaty clothes I'd done kickboxing in and stepped under the stream. As always, a hiss escaped me.

Then there was a knock on the door.

"Are you okay in there?" Fallon called. "I heard you hissing in pain."

"I'm fine!" I yelled back, letting her hear my frustration if only to keep her away.

When she said nothing more, I assumed that was the end of it … until the door opened wide, and Fallon walked into the bathroom. She still had the fucking towel wrapped around her breasts, and my dick stood at attention once more.

"What the fuck are you doing?" I roared.

She ignored me, pulling open the shower door and staring at me. Her eyes were on the wound on my side, but then they dropped lower, taking in all my body and my bobbing dick, vying for her attention.

Fallon licked her lips and returned her eyes to my face. "Is it your wound? Does it hurt?" She came closer, and I put my hand out to stop her. I didn't want her in this fucking freezing water with me. She pushed past my hand and stepped inside the cubicle with me, pulling the bandage away.

The stream of arctic water hit her in the back, and she yelped, colliding with my body as she rushed to get out of the way.

"Why is the water cold?" She cupped her mouth and spun to face me. "Please tell me I didn't use up all your hot water."

Reaching out, I turned off the faucet until there was only a trickle dribbling from the head. "No, you didn't."

Her eyes widened. "So, you *choose* to have cold showers?"

What could I tell her? That I felt like I didn't deserve hot ones? She would pry, probe, and question until she knew all my secrets and she already knew too much.

"And why do you have an erection right now?"

I blinked. *I can't believe she actually said that.*

"Men aren't supposed to be able to maintain an erection when exposed to temperatures below fifteen degrees Celsius."

"Surprise," I replied darkly. "I'm one of a kind. Now either get out of here or get on your fucking knees." I said it to be crude. To scare her away. I expected her to run from the cubicle, but when her eyes dropped to below my waist, and her tongue darted out to run along her plump bottom lip, I was ready to let her wrap them around my cock and suck me down.

She reached up to her towel and began to loosen it, but I stopped her with my hand wrapped around hers.

"No."

She blinked. "But you said—"

"Fuck, Fallon, I don't expect you to suck my dick just because I told you to."

She blinked up at me from under her wet lashes, and my cock bobbed. "What if I wanted to?"

"You want to suck my cock?" I had to ask because I had to know if she was being serious with this shit. At the bob of her head, I asked, "Why?"

She shrugged. "Maybe I find you attractive?"

She'd posed it as a question, and my sick fucking mind had to know whether she did want to do this—truly do this—and whether I would let her. If I were honest, I'd rather slip my tongue into her pussy and make her come on my tongue, which was … new for me. Normally, I didn't want my partners to find any pleasure, but with Fallon, I wanted her to experience it.

"Do you find me attractive?" Fuck, what was I? A teenage boy?

She nodded, then gestured down to my dick, which had only grown harder the more we spoke about sucking and blow jobs and my dirty thoughts of swallowing down all her honey. "And you're attracted to me."

I opened my mouth to deny it, to stop this shit before it was too late, but she placed a finger over my lips. "Don't try and lie to me. Your body doesn't lie."

Don't try and lie to me. Your body doesn't lie.

Don't ... lie to me ... body doesn't lie.

Body doesn't lie ...

Those words echoed in my head, pounding through my ears, and burrowing deep into my memories. And just like that, I was dragged back to when I was a thirteen-year-old kid who was powerless to stop a woman who was supposed to nurture and care for me. I was back in that room, being tied down and ... and ...

"Don't touch me." The words came out as a stifled moan, ripped from my throat almost violently.

Fallon stopped immediately, looking at me with a stunned expression on her face. "Orin?"

I shook my head and bolted from the bathroom. Not bothering to dry off, I shoved myself into another pair of sweats and a t-shirt, then ran from the room. I was suddenly spinning out of control, I didn't know where to go or what to do. I was a glass spinning top on a table, teetering closer and closer to the edge. I was going to fall off and shatter on the floor, and when I did, I feared I wouldn't be able to put myself back together again.

I ran outside the compound, getting into the first Rover I saw. The keys were still in the ignition. I turned on the engine and peeled out of the driveway. I felt as if I was sinking into the past, and the only way to regain my footing was to cement it in the present. To gain control. To have the power and never cede it again.

When I finally stopped the car, it was in the parking lot behind Velvet. I moved on autopilot, finding my way into the back rooms, and stumbling down the hall like I was fucking drunk until I found her in the main body of the club.

Raven.

The girl who was my preferred sub.

She caught a glimpse of the look in my eyes and approached, dropping her gaze to the floor and rolling her shoulders forward to make herself look smaller. With her head bowed, I could hardly hear her over the music when she said, "I'm ready, sir."

She slipped into the submissive version of herself so effortlessly.

"You know what I expect of you," I told her, my voice changing, becoming the Dominant she needed, and I craved.

"Yes, sir." She turned and started down the hall.

Wordlessly, I followed, only stopping when another man shouted, "She was my cunt!"

I stopped. Turned. Bored a hole in the man's head until he backed down, then continued down the hall to the final room. This looked like all the others, but anchor points were hidden behind the eggplant-purple curtains. I didn't like using the communal room. I didn't like the idea of any other man being in here in the same capacity as me, but after what happened in the shower with Fallon, I was desperate.

Desperate for control.

Desperate to feel grounded.

Desperate to feel powerful once more.

When I opened the door, Raven was folded on her knees, head bowed, naked, and waiting. I locked the door behind us and rolled out my neck. I was going to take my agitation out on her flesh, and she was going to thank me for it.

"Stand up."

She rose to her feet, keeping her head down. I walked around her, inspecting her naked body. She was trembling, but I knew it had nothing to do with fear. It had to do with anticipation, and I enjoyed the way that made me feel. Walking over to the small chest of drawers, I pulled out a thick leather collar. The buckle was heavy in my hands, and as I wrapped the leather around Raven's delicate throat, I wondered what Fallon would look like wearing a collar.

Raven let out a sigh as soon as the buckle was secured and the leather strap had been slid out of the way. She was looking forward to this as much as I was. Moving back to the drawers, I pulled out the telescopic spreader bar with leather loops on either end to secure it to her ankles. Most times, the inside of the loops were soft, but I chose the ones that were unfinished and raw. I wanted to see the red welts left behind when I was finally done with her.

Kneeling, I affixed one side before ordering her to widen her stance. She did until I had stretched her to her limits, leaving her pussy wide open and ready for the taking. She was already so turned on that her arousal was dripping down the inside of her thigh.

Raven craved this release as much as I did.

It was the perfect arrangement.

I rose to my feet to inspect my handiwork and rubbed my fingers along my mouth. She was unable to move and teetering on her heels as the spreader bar kept her legs apart. Wrapping one hand around her arm, I moved her into position—facing away from me—and against the back wall. Reaching behind the curtains, I found the three lengths of rope complete with the hooks I needed, and clipped one to her collar, and one to each side of the spreader bar.

Raven's hips undulated with barely contained excitement. She enjoyed the restraint part of our play, and I enjoyed her restraint. Next were her hands, which I wrapped in the same red rope and lifted above her head, securing her hands to the ceiling anchor. Stepping back, I admired the shape her body made and the angles I could fuck her at. Like this, she wouldn't be able to suck my dick, but I didn't need that. I just wanted to fuck her. Hard. Ruthlessly.

I needed to forget.

Lowering my sweats, I took out my erection and began to stroke. Raven tried to peer over her shoulder at me, but after a growled, "Eyes on the wall," she stopped trying. I rewarded her for her good behavior with a paddle on the ass. Her hips rolled forward as if she was taking a cock inside her—moving over and over again.

Stepping up to her back, I stared at her perfect, unmarred skin and resisted the urge to damage her more. I was already sending her home early today with the burns that will be around her wrists. I didn't need to mark her any more than that. Grabbing my cock, I slapped her on the ass with it, then slid it between her folds. She was so wet she was dripping, lubricating my dick with every stroke.

She moaned, finding her pleasure from one simple touch.

I groaned because all I could think of was Fallon.

Wondered if she would react this way for me.

What would she think of the way I fucked?

Would she judge me for needing to be in control?

My erection grew painfully hard, and I did something I'd never done before. I allowed myself to think of another woman while I phantom-fucked Raven. It was a first for me. Never had someone haunted me like Fallon did. As my dick slid through Raven's pussy lips, pushing against her clit, I let myself dream for a moment that it was Fallon beneath me, wordlessly begging for me to take her, to fuck her hard and rough, to make her come with a cry that the other patrons would hear. Fisting my cock at the base, I slapped it hard against her opening, and the smell of sex and anticipation in the air—everything about this scene I'd conjured up in my head—made me want her even more.

I was panting by the time I pulled back, and I forced myself to reach into my pocket for the condom I'd slipped in there while I collected all the other props I needed. Tearing the foil wrapper, I rolled the latex down the length of my cock, making sure it wouldn't accidentally break. I never wanted to have children—there was too much pain and misery in the world for them to endure.

Anchoring a hand on Raven's hip, I slid the crown of my cock past her wet lips and into her slick channel. Her whole body undulated at the invasion. Pulling out of her almost all the way, I slammed back inside. I needed to fuck Fallon out of my system. Having her was never going to be an option. Fucking whores, paying double for what I wanted to do to them, was the only way for me to find a release.

Fuck, it would be so much easier if I didn't want to fuck,

but fucking was the only way to keep the demons in my head at bay. Gliding back out of her again, I tightened my grip on her hip and ground my way to the hilt once more. My balls slapped the front of her pussy, the wet sounds of our union echoing around the room.

Raven pulled on the bonds of her arms and shifted from side to side on her feet.

"You're not allowed to come, Raven," I grunted out, slapping her on the ass as I pulled out once more. "You don't get to come. Ever."

"Yes, sir," she babbled. "I promise. I won't."

My hips pistoned into her, touching a deeper place each time, but I needed to go deeper. I needed to make her truly helpless. Pulling out, I undid her hand restraints and repositioned her body so she was bent over at a ninety-degree angle and facing me. Her hair was covering her face now, the ends so long they were dragging on the ground.

I gripped her jaw and tilted her head forward. "Open."

She did, even sticking out her tongue.

Tearing the condom from my cock, I slid it past her lips and into the warm recesses of her mouth. She created a suction immediately, sealing her lips around me and drawing down. Raven didn't have a gag reflex, so when I hit the back of her throat, she kept me there. Sucking. Moaning. Licking. Fluttering her tongue against the underside of my dick.

Fuck.

Securing both my hands around her jaw, I held her immobile and fucked her mouth until I was spilling all over her tongue and down her throat. She hummed as she took everything I had to give her, and when I was finally sated, I pulled free and zipped myself back up.

There would be no aftercare. No fucking moment of sweetness. I had come to take something from her, and she'd given it to me willingly.

I walked into the club to find Mary—the clan's Pull.

She took one look at me and her lips pressed into a tight line. "Raven need a ride home?"

I nodded.

"How bad is it this time?"

What she meant was did I whip her until she literally couldn't move from all the pleasure rolling through her body. Raven was a pain slut—a masochist in the purest form. When she and I came together, it was a battle to inflict the most pain, and to suffer the most pain. Tonight's session had been tame compared to what we normally did—downright vanilla—and I could only blame that on a certain blonde who had burrowed beneath my skin.

"A few rope burns."

Mary bobbed her head and picked up the phone, calling whoever the fuck she needed to call, while I left Velvet the same way I'd come in, slipping out the back door and into the night.

15

FALLON

THE BOWL OF PASTA THAT I'D FINISHED AN HOUR ago was still sitting on the nightstand where I'd left it. After Orin had gone, I didn't know what to do. I was confused by his reaction to me and wondered what the hell he'd meant when he said I shouldn't touch him. One minute, he seemed as if he was ready to let me suck his cock, then the next … it was like a switch had been flipped.

What had I said that had made him change his mind?

And where had he run off to?

After getting dressed in one of Orin's black t-shirts, which swallowed me down to my mid-thigh, and a pair of sleeping shorts, I'd tried to follow him. But as soon as I walked into the kitchen and living area, there were a bunch of men I didn't recognize. Just like I knew would happen, panic started to bubble up, and the knowledge that I was alone in a house with strange men tipped me over the edge. I'd run back to the room, locked the door, and then locked the bathroom door.

After an hour, when it was clear nobody was going to try and break in, I emerged, sat on the bed, and waited for Orin to return. My gaze shifted from the empty bowl to my feet, then back to the bowl.

When was he coming back, and where had he gone?

My head jerked around when the handle on the door depressed, then released.

"Fallon? You in there?" Orin called.

I scooted off the bed, unlocking the door and yanking it open. The happiness I felt drained away when I got a look at his face. He looked as if he'd been dragged through the wringer, and as he walked past me to the bathroom, he smelled of another woman's perfume.

Tears stung my eyes, but I refused to let them fall. "Where were you?" I demanded of his retreating back.

He didn't bother to answer. He just pushed the door closed behind him, but it didn't close all the way so there was a couple of inches gap that I could see through. He stripped out of his clothes, then turned on the shower. I knew better than to barge back in there again, so I curled up on the bed and waited for him.

When he emerged from the shower five minutes later in a towel, I sat up. His dark eyes traced the way my hair fell over my shoulder.

His jaw tightened. "I need to go."

"Go?" I swallowed. "Where are you going?"

"Limerick. I have a job to do."

A *job*. A murder. "How long will you be gone?"

He shrugged his broad shoulders, and I traced the slope of his traps down to his broad shoulders and chest. He may have been older than me, but his body was still in phenomenal shape, and the tattoos that covered every inch of his chest and torso only enhanced the sharp definition of his muscles.

Licking my lips, I asked hesitantly, "Can I come with you?"

His brows rose. "You know what I do, Fallon. You really want to be an accessory to fucking murder?" He said it so casually—so cruelly.

"I've already murdered someone."

He huffed a laugh. "You killed in self-defense. What I do is slightly different."

I glanced down at my hands, which were white-knuckling the comforter.

"You'll be safe here, if that's what you're worried about."

Looking up at him once more, I wondered how he always knew what I was thinking. "I don't want you to go, and if you do, then I want to return to my house."

He frowned. "You want to return to the house that's been shot at and where you also killed a man." He shook his head. "You can't go back there. That's not your house anymore."

"And this is?"

Again, with a shrug. "I've lived in worse places."

For some reason, that statement felt loaded with secrets— weighed down by mystery. I hugged my knees closer to my chest and wrapped my arms around them. I didn't want him to go. He was the only one I trusted.

"You don't have to be scared."

I blinked at him. "How do you know what I'm feeling?"

Even though it looked like it was the last thing he wanted to do, he approached the bed. "I'll make sure the Sentinels bring you three meals a day. Clean towels. Books to read. Anything else you might want."

"Fuck the Sentinels," I told him fiercely, then held his gaze as I asked, "Where did you go tonight?"

His expression soured. Getting up, he placed more distance between us, and I felt every single inch of it. "Out."

"You were with a woman."

He didn't even bother to look stunned. "What of it?"

"You ran to her after you rejected me," I said softly. "That does dent the ego."

He made a strangled sort of noise, then his warm hand wrapped around my wrist. I looked at him from under my lashes. "I … I don't know what you want me to say."

"The truth would be nice. I offered to suck your dick, then you freaked out, left me in the shower, and went to another woman. If you're already in a relationship, tell me. I'm a big girl. I can take it."

"It's not that."

"Then what is it? What made you run like that?"

The muscle in the side of his jaw flexed angrily. "I'm too old for you."

"I don't care."

"Yeah? Well, I do." He released his grip on me and ran a hand through his slightly wet hair. "You're fifteen years younger than me, and you're the sister of a clan member."

"I don't care."

"You should. I shouldn't still be alive. The number of times I've been shot at and stabbed. The number of men, women, and children I've killed would mean life in prison if the cops ever caught me and made the charges stick. I'm not a good choice of man for you."

All these things were true, but I hadn't even considered them. "And what if I just want to fuck you?"

His mouth twisted as if the crudeness of what I'd said offended him. What do you know, a murderer with sensibilities.

"You don't want to go there with me."

"Why not?" My voice was rising—with my frustration. With my rejection. Yes, that shit had stung. I was not ashamed to admit that.

Orin was getting angry, too, because he started to pace. He glared at me every few seconds like he couldn't believe we were having this conversation.

"Why not?" I demanded again.

"Because I like to inflict pain on my partners!" he shouted, drawing to a stop. "I like to dominate them, restrain them, take away their choices. I like to fuck like that to … to …"

"To what?"

He stared at me like he had no idea what he'd just said or why. "Jesus," he muttered, striding to the armoire and pulling out a leather jacket. "Stay here, or so help me, I will take you over my knee and teach you the meaning of obedience."

His words shouldn't have affected me so deeply, but the idea of being at his mercy was suddenly something I wanted to experience. He looked at me one last time before marching from the room.

16
ORIN

WHEN FINNAN HAD CALLED ME ABOUT A JOB down south on the way back from Velvet and told me to come and see him as soon as I got in, I was relieved to have a fucking reason to leave Fallon and remove the temptation she inspired. Now, after seeing the devastation on her face when she figured out that I'd been with another woman—that I had *rejected* her—I wanted to keep away from her so I wouldn't fall at her fucking feet and beg for forgiveness.

I knocked on Finnan's office door.

When he opened it, he gave me a once-over, then said, "You look like shit."

I grunted, unable to disagree with him, and stepped inside. "What do you want?"

Sitting behind his desk, he ground his molars, obviously unimpressed with my tone. He could suck my fucking dick if he didn't like the way I spoke to him.

"Sit down."

Reluctantly, I took the seat in front of his desk.

"There's been a change of plans."

"Don't leave me hanging in suspense," I drawled.

Finnan's glare was arctic. "Torin has disappeared."

I sat up a little straighter. "Run that by me again."

"Torin." He practically bit the word off. "He's gone, and I need you to find him."

Torin was the member turned rat for the Bèar Clan. He also happened to be Finnan's half brother. The punishment for turning on your clan was death, but Finnan had been dragging this shit out. It had been almost three months since Grayson's now-wife, Sloane, revealed it all. She'd been snatched by the Bèar Clan, only to be rescued by Torin. She found the money book that linked him to our rivals and ruthlessly bargained her life for his.

I frowned. "What about the job in Limerick?"

"Resecuring Torin is more important."

Leaning back in my chair, I studied the other man's face. "What the fuck happened, Finnan? I thought he was being held somewhere secure."

His jaw bulged with his growing irritation. "He was."

I shook my head. "This could've all been over months ago." I'd offered to put the bullet in his skull myself.

But Finnan wasn't having any of that. "No," he barked back, his hands curling into fists on the top of his desk. He seemed to breathe in deeply for a moment before adding, "I haven't decided what to do with him yet."

Hinging forward in my seat, I said, "And every hour you

let him remain breathing is fucking our clan up the arse!"

Finnan's eye twitched, but he had no response.

I blew out a frustrated breath. "Do you know where he could've gone?"

Steepling his fingers across his mouth, Finnan looked like he had the weight of the world on his shoulders. "He'll be heading north. Try Westport."

"What's in Westport?"

He heaved a sigh, rubbing at the back of his neck. "Just go up there and see if you can locate him."

"And what do you want me to do when I find him?"

My boss remained strangely—and uncharacteristically—quiet.

Motherfucker. He was still hesitating over this shit. This was exactly why I didn't get attached to people.

Liar, an insidious voice whispered.

I bit out my next words, wondering why in the fuck it was me who was pressing Finnan with this. This was fucking Keir's job. "The rules are there for a reason, Finnan." My voice was cold. Unyielding.

"I know."

"And *I* know he has to eat a bullet for what he did."

He slammed his fist onto the desktop. "I fucking *know*!" His nostrils flared as he stared me down. "I know, but he's ..."

"Your brother," I finished for him, saying the words he couldn't bring himself to say.

"Could you kill your brother?" Finnan demanded, his anger growing.

"Never had one, so I couldn't tell you."

A *mother* I could kill, though.

He heaved a sigh, his gaze fixed on the desk. When he finally brought his eyes back to my face, there was a ghost of regret hovering there. "Bring him in. Unharmed."

I thought Finnan was a fucking idiot for stringing this thing out, but I wasn't the goddamned boss. I just followed orders. Rising from my seat, I moved to the door. When I reached for the handle, Finnan's words stopped me. "Take Nightingale with you."

Nightingale. I clenched my jaw. "Why does she need to come?"

"You might need her."

I did need Fallon, just not in the way he was implying.

"Plus, Grayson told me some shit about her. She doesn't like being alone around strange men. She doesn't seem to mind you, though, so take her with you. It'll give me time to think about what I want to do with her after this shit with the Bèar Clan blows over."

Clenching my hands into tight fists at my side, I returned to my room where I found Fallon pacing the length of the floorboards. She turned to face me, wrapping her arms protectively around her upper body.

Finnan's words echoed in my head.

She doesn't seem to mind you, though.

"I thought you were leaving."

"I am. You're coming with me."

"What?" Her eyes darted around the room before landing back on my face. "You're taking me to Limerick with you?"

Dammit, I had to ignore that fucking flicker of relief in her voice. I also tried to ignore how amazing she looked wearing one of my shirts. "No. Get dressed. You've got five minutes to pack."

"Where are we going?" she called out as I turned to leave.

"Out." I shut the door and went downstairs, finding Keir nursing a glass of whisky in the kitchen.

"You're leaving?" he asked. "Taking Fallon with you?"

Narrowing my eyes at him, I replied, "Yeah, I am."

"Good."

"Why is that good?"

He shrugged and simply said, "She trusts you."

Ignoring the way my heart squeezed at that, I turned at the sound of quiet footfalls behind me. Fallon stepped into the room, placing a small bag at her feet. Keir—the bastard—smiled at her, and I wanted to punch him in the face. Nobody got to smile at my Filly but me.

"Keep it in your fucking pants," I grumbled to him, then turned to face the woman who was turning my ordered world upside down. "Are you ready?"

She bobbed her head.

"We'll be back in a couple of days," I told Keir, then walked toward Fallon. Her blue eyes skimmed down my body, then back to my face, her cheeks growing pink. I didn't know why, but I liked seeing that on her. Knowing that I could elicit that response.

"Did you pack a bag?" she asked quietly.

Fuck. "It'll only take me a moment. Do you want to come with me, or …" I peered over my shoulder at Keir. "Will you be okay?"

"She has nothing to fear from me," Keir said.

Ignoring the bastard, I repeated my question to Fallon.

"I'll be fine."

I stared at her a beat longer, then turned my eyes to Keir. "Don't fucking touch her. Don't fucking approach her," I warned, jabbing my finger in his direction. To Fallon I said, "Give me five."

I strode up the stairs and back to my bedroom. Pulling a duffel bag from under the bed, I filled it with enough clothes for a couple of days along with my toothbrush. Back in the kitchen, I found Keir trying to engage in conversation with Fallon, but she was only giving him one-word answers.

I shot Keir a warning look. "I thought I told you to leave her the fuck alone."

"Aye, you told me not to touch her or approach her. I was just trying to talk to the lass."

Fucking Keir with his *fucking* loopholes.

"Come on." I waited for Fallon to follow me outside. Once she was buckled into the Rover beside me, I peeled out of the driveway and started heading in the direction of Westport.

"Where are we going? Did your plans to go to Limerick change?"

I grunted. "Finnan wants me to look for someone."

Her eyes widened. "To kill?"

My head jerked around at her whispered question. "No. To bring back."

"Who is it?"

"Torin."

A frown marred her features. "Torin? What do you want with Torin?"

The fact that she knew who that was made my hackles

rise. "How do you know Torin?"

"He's Grayson's friend."

"He's also a traitor to the clan."

She shook her head. "What? No, he couldn't be. He's too nice to betray anyone."

I barked a humorless laugh. "Torin only showed you a side to himself that you wanted to see. The bastard is a snake. He sold out our clan to save his own skin."

After a long minute of silence, she asked, "Where are we going exactly?"

"Finnan doesn't know. He only has a hunch. But he went missing, and Finnan wants him back."

She worried her bottom lip with her teeth. "What are you going to do with him once you get him back?"

"Nothing I want to do," I muttered darkly.

"What's that supposed to mean? You don't want to hurt him?"

"Quite the opposite."

She gaped at me. "You want to kill him?"

"I want to prove to all the other clans that the Mac Tíre are not fucking pussies when it comes to punishing insurrection. Every day, every *hour*, Finnan sits on this fucking issue, tears away our credibility, and buckles our reputation."

Fallon blinked at me. "Everything is black and white for you, isn't it?"

My hand tightened around the steering wheel. "The world is black and white, sweetheart. If someone hurts me, I hurt them back. It's simple."

"I used to think that way too, until …"

As if on a string, my head jerked toward her. "Until?"

"Nothing. Don't worry about it."

She wanted to keep her secrets? Fine. I would let her.

"Where is Torin right now?"

"Don't know exactly. We just have to look for him, I guess."

"Fantastic plan."

"Don't be a smart-arse," I whipped back at her.

"Or what? Going to put me over your knee?"

I was hard in an instant. Actually, that wasn't true. I'd been semihard since she came into the kitchen, but now, hearing her ask if I wanted to take her over my knee, my cock had gone from semi-firm to a fucking steel pipe.

I peered over at her to see whether she was interested in goading me more. "Is that what you want?"

Her cheeks flushed a lovely shade of pink, and then I could see it all. Fallon's body draped over my fucking knee, her ass bare and ready for my hand. She would whimper with the first stroke because she'd be embarrassed that she actually enjoyed impact play, but soon she would be mewling for my touch, begging me to spank her harder and harder until she came spectacularly in my lap.

"Yes."

Licking my lips, I pushed a little deeper. "I don't fuck like most men."

"I know. You told me. You like to inflict pain." Once more, she nibbled her bottom lip. "Would you hurt me?"

The word *never* hovered on my tongue, but that was something I couldn't promise because pain was the only thing I was capable of delivering on. Pain and a rough fuck.

"I might in the heat of the moment." I took my eyes off

the road to look at her. "Does that scare you?"

She nodded.

Fuck. "Do I scare you?"

This time, she shook her head. "No. You *terrify* me."

Fucking finally.

"But not in the way you think," she added quickly. "I'm terrified by how much I want you."

My eyes closed briefly before I peeled them back open and concentrated on the road. "All I have to offer you is pain."

"I don't believe you."

"You should." The words came out on a harsh bark, and I immediately regretted raising my voice. "Look, I'm sorry, Fallon, but you drive me insane sometimes."

"Why?"

"Because I wanted you on your knees for me in that shower. I wanted to take what you were offering."

She shifted her body around so she was facing me. "Why didn't you? I wanted you to."

Jesus, fuck, her words were like heaven on my ears. I contemplated telling her the truth—all the dirty details of my past, but I wasn't sure she was ready to hear it all. What kind of woman would want a man who had had that done to him?

For the next few miles, we were silent. Until …

"I was gang raped when I was sixteen."

My gaze flew to her, but she wasn't looking at me. She was staring at her hands in her lap.

"I was dating an older guy at the time, and we'd gone out. Partying. Dancing. Drinking. I'd gone to the bathroom, and when I returned, he'd bought a drink for me."

"What was his name?" I asked, and my voice didn't sound like my own.

"His name doesn't matter."

My hand slapped at the steering wheel. She jumped in her seat, and I felt like an absolute asshole. "Tell me his goddamned name, Fallon!" As soon as the words were out, I regretted them. Not because of what I was demanding but because of the tone I'd used. "I'm sorry," I managed to get out from between my gritted teeth. "I just …" I dragged a hand through my hair. "I want to peel the skin from his body and drape it at your feet."

I sounded like a fucking unhinged psycho, but it wasn't far from the truth. There wasn't anything I wouldn't do to keep Fallon safe, even if that meant keeping her safe from me.

"Owen Ward."

My jaw unclenched, and I stored that name away for later. "What did that bastard do to you?"

"He'd spiked my drink, then once the drug had taken effect, he, along with his four buddies, took me back to his place. I was conscious and aware the whole time, but I couldn't move. I couldn't … couldn't fight them off. Owen stood over me while it happened, watching it all with a spark of anticipation in his eyes. He always wore a Saint Patrick pendant, and he rubbed it with his thumb as he watched them take their turn with me."

I swallowed down my burning rage, muting the darkness inside me.

"Sometimes, when I close my eyes, that's all I can see. Instead of goodness, a saint represents horror and pain for me." She shook her head. "After they were done, I had to lay there feeling their cum dripping out of me. I had to lay there and wonder whether they were coming back for more. I had to lay there, alone, while tears dripped down my face and wonder whether I had encouraged it or would get pregnant from the attack."

Unable to stop myself, I reached out and gripped the back of her neck. "You didn't deserve a fucking thing, you hear me?" I tightened my fingers until she looked at me. "You didn't ask to be gang raped. No one ever asks for that shit."

She nodded, the movement dislodging a tear that had been clinging to her cheek. She wiped the back of her hand over her face.

She continued with a broken voice, "After the drugs had left my system, I ran home to Grayson. I didn't want him to see me like that, but there was nowhere else I wanted to be. He made me go to the hospital, where they performed a rape kit. I went to the police with that information, and the four men who raped me were charged and sent to prison."

I will kill those bastards as soon as they get out. The dark thought stunned me—not because of the violence it promised, but because of how territorial and protective I felt of Fallon. Not that I should've been surprised. The woman was so deep under my skin that she was never coming out.

"They're already dead," she replied softly, and I realized I'd spoken that last thought out loud. "Grayson hunted down each and every one of them when they were released from prison. He made sure their deaths were just as violent as the violation of my body was on me."

I squeezed her shoulder a little. "You're so fucking brave, Filly." I shook my head. "What I don't understand is how you're okay with another man touching you."

A ghost of a smile played on her lips, and I wanted to lean over and take them. "I'm not okay with it." She blinked at me, willing me to read what was between the lines.

Except you was what her stare was saying.

Except me. She wanted my touch, but did she crave it as much as I craved her?

She blew out a deep breath. "I wasn't okay after the attack—"

"Please, you don't have to tell me if you don't want to."

"I want to. I think it'll make you understand me a little better."

Did I want to know more? If I did, there was a good chance I would put a bullet into the skull of anyone who wronged her. If I didn't, I wouldn't become more attached to her than I already was.

I chose the former.

"Tell me anything you want to tell me."

Her jaw tightened with determination. "Okay. After the attack, I couldn't sleep. Every time I closed my eyes, I relived the assault. Guilt and shame nipped at the heels of my exhaustion, and I dealt with it all by drinking and taking drugs. I figured if I could quiet my mind somehow, I could rest.

"I started with alcohol. It helped numb the pain and made me forget, but when it stopped helping I turned to drugs. Coke was my initial choice, but it was a slippery slope, and I was soon addicted to meth as well. I spiraled so much that when I looked in the mirror, I hardly recognized the woman I'd become. Grayson stood by me the whole time, supporting me, but not supporting my choice of coping mechanism ..." She trailed off, and if I didn't know any better, she was back there in that dark place again.

I squeezed to let her know I was there.

"I OD'd, but that wasn't what made me change my ways. It wasn't until the second time, after I witnessed a girl I knew, another addict, whore herself out for her next hit. She gave away her body so she could do more drugs. That was my wake-up call, I guess you could say."

"You guess?" I asked.

"After witnessing her desperation, I took so much in a short amount of time that I OD'd again. This time, when I woke up, I was in hospital, and Grayson was there. He didn't know I was awake, so I got to watch him sit beside my bed with his head bowed. It looked as if he was praying, but I knew he stopped believing in God a long time ago. Grayson looked how I felt on the inside. Gutted. Hollowed out. A shell of what he was. When he realized I was awake, the relief that washed over his face was like a dagger through my heart.

"It was then that I recognized who I was really hurting by doing what I was doing. I was trying to escape my demons, and find the help I needed, when all the help I could ever need was sitting right beside me. As soon as I was released, he helped me get into a rehab center, where I stayed four times longer than I needed to in order to get clean and stay clean. I went to therapy twice a day the whole time, talking about all the feelings I still had attached to the attack. I eventually learned that what had happened hadn't been my fault, that I was the victim, that the men who chose to do this were the ones in the wrong.

"Once I was out, I had to choose what I wanted to do with my life. I knew drugs weren't the right choice. I wanted to help people though, and nursing seemed to be a good way to do that."

Fuck, she had been through so much. Like me, she was a survivor. She had bared her soul to me, but I wasn't ready to bare mine in return. Not yet, at least. She'd had the benefit of intensive therapy, facing all her inner demons and exorcising them, whereas I had nurtured the monster that lived inside me—the monster that had been born out of dark revenge and violent thoughts.

The only thing that made us similar is that we were both victims of rape. I knew it was fucking sexist to draw the comparison, but a man who's been raped feels like less of a man because of it—at least that's how I felt. I felt like I should've been stronger, better prepared, and able to fight off my abuser. But I'd only been a kid and was completely alone in this world.

I cleared my throat, surprised to find we were in Westport already. Pulling into the parking lot of a pub that had accommodation upstairs, I shut off the engine, and we sat in silence for a moment.

Fallon peered up at the building. "We always seem to be staying at quaint little places."

"Let's hope this one doesn't burn down while we're here." I'd meant it as a joke, but Fallon's eyes widened in surprise.

"Do you think that's going to happen?"

"No," I replied gruffly. I got out of the car and walked around to her door to open it. "Come on."

After she was out of the Rover, I walked her into the pub with my hand on the small of her back. The place was packed, and everyone stopped and stared at us. Ignoring them all, I strode to the bartender.

"We need a room."

The middle-aged man's eyes darted from me to Fallon. "Are you all right there, lass?" he asked.

There was the sound of a stool sliding backward on the flagstone floor, and I peered over my shoulder to see that one man was getting to his feet while another had stepped forward. I smiled at them, letting them see the monster that lurked behind my eyes. One man swallowed. The other retook his step.

"I'm fine," Fallon said, wrapping her arm around my waist. On instinct, I tensed, but when the warmth of her body and the scent of her skin got caught in my nose, I relaxed. "My fiancé and I were just traveling to see family, but I hate driving at night." She beamed at me. "Right, honey?"

"Right," I bit out. I met the bartender's eyes. "So, how about that room?"

Seemingly placated by Fallon's explanation, he reached under the bar, making me tense. I reached one hand behind my back, then let it drop away when the guy produced a key.

"Second door on the left," he said.

I took the key and then turned around to face the pub's patrons. They were all staring at me—at the woman I had wrapped a possessive arm around. Walking toward the stairs on the other side of the room, I motioned for Fallon to go up first, then I followed her. The noise of conversations resumed the minute we were out of sight.

"They seem friendly," she commented absently.

"Yeah, right."

She watched as I slid the key into the lock and opened the door. "They seemed genuinely concerned that you were kidnapping me or something." She went to step into the room, but I stopped her.

"Wait. I need to check it."

"Check it for what?"

"Make sure it's secure."

She stepped aside and let me enter first. Once I was sure the only way in or out of the room was by the door, I gestured for her to come inside.

"You act like your life is under the threat of danger every single minute."

"It is," I told her. "Do you want to get washed up before we eat? I can get us some food and bring it up here."

"I'd rather eat downstairs if that's okay?"

My brows rose. "Are you sure?"

"Positive."

"What about being surrounded by strangers?"

"As long as I'm not in an enclosed space with no way out, I'll be fine."

I studied her for a long minute before nodding. "Okay, we'll do it your way. Do you want to wash up? I can go and get our bags."

"Sure."

I left Fallon in the bathroom and returned to the pub, where the speculative and outright hostile looks continued. As I strode to the door, someone yelled, "What are you doing with that girl, Reaper?"

I stopped. Turned. Scanned the crowd looking for who had spoken. A nervous-looking man was shifting on his feet.

I directed my question at him. "What did you say?"

"I asked what you're doing with her. She looks too young."

I stepped closer to him, and the people standing around him scattered until it was just me and him. "I don't see how she's any of your business."

Sweat beaded on his upper lip, and although he was trying to be brave, I saw through the bravado. "You need to let her go."

I stared at him, making him squirm. I should've pulled out my knife and stabbed him in the fucking neck for questioning me, but I didn't because I didn't want Fallon to see that sort of violence. Instead, I turned around, throwing over my shoulder, "You need to mind your fucking business. Nobody talks to her. Am I understood?"

A murmur of *aye* went up, and I stepped free of the smell of beer and too many people and walked to the Rover. After retrieving our bags, I returned to our room. Fallon was sitting on the bed, flicking through the TV channels but not settling on one.

"Took you long enough."

I raised a brow at her as I passed the bag over. "The locals were telling me to leave you alone."

"Really? Did you dispense some of that legendary hospitality when you gave them your answer?"

I tried to keep the smile from my face, but she drew it from me anyway. "No, but that's not for wanting to."

Her mouth flexed into a grin. "I'll get washed up then we can eat."

17

FALLON

WHEN WE ENTERED THE DINING ROOM ONCE more, I felt all eyes turn on us. I wasn't sure why these locals were being so protective, but I could tell that Orin was getting pissed off by it all. He chose a table at the back of the room, then sat facing the door. Grayson did the same thing when we were out in a public place.

He handed me a menu, then watched the room as I looked it over. After a moment of pretending to look at the dishes and their descriptions, I put the menu facedown on the table and met his eyes.

"Why is everyone acting so weird right now?"

"I don't know what you mean by weird." He stretched his long legs out under the table.

I peered around the room. There was open hostility there but also fear. "Like everyone wants to save me from you."

"They do."

"They do?"

He nodded. "They think you're here against your will. They think I've captured you and am refusing to let you go."

A smile pulled at my lips. "Is that right?"

"I'm the monster they're all afraid of, and you're the princess they're all trying to save."

I didn't like being referred to as the princess. I'd much rather be the knight. "Little do they know," I murmured in reply.

"You hate the reference." He said the words with such conviction that there was no way I could confuse it for a question.

"Yes, I hate it. I never want to be the victim or even thought of as the victim ever again."

Something passed over his eyes—there one minute and gone the next. "I can understand that." His words were a crawl, a dark promise. "You need to eat. Order something."

The waitress appeared just as he spoke, and I noticed she was throwing furtive glances at Orin the whole time. It was as if he were a lion, and she wasn't sure what he would do next—*who* he would eat next.

"The stew, please," I told her.

"Something to drink?"

"Water is fine," Orin said before I could reply.

The waitress looked to me, waiting for confirmation that what he'd said was, in fact, true.

"Water," I said.

With a heaved breath, she turned to Orin. When she spoke, her voice was a few octaves lower than when she'd spoken to me. "And for you, sir?"

"I'll have the same as the lady." Then to prove that he wasn't the big bad wolf they all thought he was, he smiled, except Orin's smiles were utterly terrifying to behold. Instead of putting someone at ease like most smiles would, the way he bared his teeth made it seem like a very likely threat.

Once she was gone, he returned his expression to neutral impassivity.

"You enjoy the role of monster," I told him.

"You think so?"

"I know so. You want to scare people away. That way they can never get close to you."

He huffed a dark chuckle. "Believe me, I don't have to work very hard to keep people away. They seem to avoid me all on their own."

"And that makes you happy?"

"Nothing makes me happy anymore," he replied, but a look in his eyes said maybe there was *something* that brought him joy.

Only a few minutes had passed before our waitress was back with a pitcher of water and two glasses. She deposited them on the table, then darted away just as quickly. Orin leaned forward in his seat, and I watched as the muscles and tendons in his arms shifted under his tattooed skin. There were veins in the meatier parts of his forearm, and the overwhelming desire to reach forward and lick them gripped me.

Shaking myself, I inched back further in my chair to stop myself from doing just that. Orin watched my face as he poured water into both glasses, then nudged one my way. Keeping my eyes locked on him, I took a swallow of water, then set it back on the table.

"Where will we go tomorrow?"

"We'll continue north. There are a few towns I've been told to ask around in."

"And if we can't find him?"

"Then we return to the compound, where you can be safe, and I can do my job without worrying about you getting hurt."

I nibbled on my bottom lip, until Orin's croaked "Stop" gave me pause. His dark eyes were locked on my mouth. I made a slow show of licking where my teeth had just been, and he shifted under the table. It gave me such a rush to know that I was affecting him this way—me, who had zero confidence when it came to the opposite sex and had no interest in eliciting that reaction from another man.

But Orin wasn't just another man.

"Do you think the Bèar Clan have given up on trying to find us?"

"If I were them, I wouldn't have. I would simply be biding my time until there was an opportunity."

My heart lurched a little in my chest. "Do you think I'm in danger?"

"You're with me, Filly. Of course you're in danger."

At the use of my nickname, I frowned. "Did Grayson tell you about my nickname?"

"No."

"Why do you call me Filly, then?"

Instead of answering, he stared at me like he always did,

and I fought the urge to squirm. He was silent for so long that I thought he wasn't going to answer me at all, until he said, "You have a birthmark on your left shoulder. It looks like a horse's head to me."

"I know, but why Filly specifically?"

"You're a young woman. A young horse is called a filly. Is that not the reason you were called it by Grayson?"

I shook my head. "My ma had started calling me Filly when I was five because I was horse mad. I wanted to have one so badly, but she'd said that horses were expensive, and they didn't have the kind of money that was needed to own and really look after a horse."

"Do you ride?"

"I did up until ma died. Then I stopped because I couldn't handle the thought of knowing she wasn't there to watch me anymore."

"I can stop calling you that if you like?" He said the words carefully—seriously—like the thought of offending me or making me sad were abhorrent to him. "If it causes you too much pain."

"No. I like it when you call me that. It doesn't ... hurt anymore."

"I'm glad."

We were still looking at each other when the waitress arrived with our meals. She placed mine down first, then Orin's before rushing away from the table. I watched her go.

"You certainly have a way with the ladies."

"I have a reputation with the ladies, although how they've found out about it, especially up this far north, I have no idea."

I picked up my fork, trying to act nonchalant. "What's your reputation with the ladies?"

"That I tie them up. Beat them. Bleed them."

A gasp escaped me. "And is it true?"

He leaned forward in his seat, holding me captive with his dark eyes. "Every. Single. Time."

I couldn't move for a whole thirty seconds as he stared at me, willing me to say something in reply. But I was mute. He huffed out a breath and picked up his fork, starting in on his stew.

I began, too, because what the hell else was I going to do? Letting the sound of the bar fill my ears, I focused on eating, feeling Orin's dark eyes on me every few seconds.

"Where do you find these women?" My voice was a broken whisper.

"They find me. They know I can give them what they need."

I paused with my fork halfway to my mouth. "And they … enjoy being bound and bled?"

"Yes."

I knew that Keir had told me as much about him, but to hear it from Orin's mouth in such detail, sent a tremble through me.

"Do you think you'll ever not … do those things to your partner?" I asked in a soft voice.

"No."

"What if she doesn't like it?"

"I would never pursue a woman who didn't." When I didn't say anything in reply, he added. "But sometimes, a woman doesn't know she likes being a sub. Sometimes, she needs to be taught the rules, to know the limitations, to allow her Dom to show her all the benefits."

"What if a woman was interested in trying, but wasn't quite sure how to approach the subject?"

His brows rose in question.

"Hypothetically, that is," I added on hastily.

He looked down at his bowl again. "She would have to find someone she trusted who could ease her into it."

"What is it about the dynamic that appeals to you?"

His eyes cut to mine. "Why are you asking me these questions?"

"Because I want to get to know you, Orin." I glanced down at my bowl, feeling as if the tables were unbalanced. I'd told him all about my experience in the hopes that he would open up to me too.

"You mean you want to experience the way I fuck?"

There was no use in denying it. I bobbed my head.

"Even when you've been scarred by past experiences. I'm not a gentle lover, Fallon. I like it rough. I like to have control. I like to make my partner feel pain because I get off on it."

The more he spoke, the more my body responded to the growling purr that had worked its way out with his words. Yes, I may have been broken in the past, but I trusted Orin. He had saved my life. I had saved his. We were irrevocably bonded in our own fucked-up pasts, and I wanted to experience this part of his life too.

"I want to try." I peered into his face to gauge his reaction. "I want to try it your way. With you."

He looked horrified. All the color drained from his

face, and he dropped his spoon onto the table. It clattered loudly, competing with the sound of his chair scraping back against the flagstone floors. Rising to his impressive height, he stared at me for a moment, a muscle in his jaw ticking. "You don't know what you're asking for, Fallon," he snarled before whirling around and marching up the stairs.

People stared at him as he left, and then they turned their gazes to me. Clearing my throat, I drew a breath in through my nose, then let it out. I wasn't going to let his tantrum deter me. Picking up my spoon once more, I started on my stew again.

I glanced up when I sensed someone hovering beside the table. It was our waitress.

"Are you sure you're all right?" she asked, her brown eyes darting to the stairs before coming to rest on my face again.

"I'm fine."

"Do you know who that is?"

"Yes."

Her eyes widened. "And you're aware of what he does?"

"More than aware."

She shifted on her feet nervously. "Are you being held against your will?"

"Look …" I started to scan her shirt, looking for a name tag but finding none. "What is your name?"

"Lottie."

"Lottie, I know who he is. I know what he does. I'm here willingly." If only she knew just how willingly. "You have nothing to worry about."

Lottie glanced over her shoulder. "There's someone here who would like to talk to you."

My shoulders stiffened. "Who is it?"

"Me," a deep voice said.

My eyes fell onto the shadow that consumed the table in front of me, and I looked up at the man who had approached. He didn't look familiar, but there was something about his energy that was off.

"W-who are you?" I asked, cursing that I'd stammered my way through the question.

"The name's Lorcan Kane," he said. When I showed no sign of recognition of the name, he turned to Lottie. "Get everyone out. Lock the door behind you."

Shit.

He turned green eyes to me—green eyes that at any other time would be gorgeous to look at, but right now, on this man, they filled me with dread. "Now, I need you to listen and listen well. You're going to leave. The Mac Tíre Reaper and I have some business. If you alert him to my presence, I will kill you. If you try to tip him off, I will kill you. If you refuse—"

"I get it," I interrupted. "You'll kill me."

He nodded.

"Who the hell are you?"

One dark brow winged up. "You've not heard of me?"

"Should I?"

He shook his head. "I belong to the Fiach Clan. I'm their Reaper."

I almost jumped out of my seat, but Lorcan's hand on my shoulder stopped me.

"You don't need to be afraid of me. You're an innocent in all this and I will let you go *if* you leave quietly."

"W-why are you doing this?"

"You probably don't know of Orin's sins, but I do. Both my clan and the Bèar Clan are aware of what he's been doing, and he can't get away with it."

Fuck, fuck, *fuck*. I dropped my gaze to the table before bringing it back to his face. "Are you going to kill him?"

"Yes," Lorcan replied simply. "So, go. Now. And don't ever come back to this town."

With my hands on the edge of the table, I pushed my chair back and rose to my full height. If I stayed and called for Orin, Lorcan would kill me before I got the words out. If I walked out the door like he was trying to convince me to do, I would condemn his life. I wasn't in the business of selling out family, so I needed a plan C. Something that would ensure Orin's safety, as well as mine. But what?

"Can I leave out the back door?" I asked. "I don't want everyone out there to see me."

He seemed to think about it a moment before nodding. "Fine. But go now."

Taking in a deep breath through my nose, I willed my legs to move toward the bar's back door. I found what I was looking for as soon as I turned the corner—a closed door that I knew concealed another set of stairs. This building had once been a grand house, and the servants' stairs would've been hidden away back here. Squeezing my eyes shut, I prayed that the door wasn't locked and grabbed the handle. I turned it, letting out a breath when the knob twisted to the left and the door opened. I slipped inside, then ran as quietly as I could up the stairs. At the top of the landing, there was another door where a strip of light shone out from underneath it. I prayed that my good luck continued and twisted the handle on this door too. It opened soundlessly, and as I peered out, I saw Orin already standing in the hallway.

I called his name, making his head whip around.

Striding over to where I stood, he demanded, "What are you doing there?"

"Trying to save your arse." I glanced behind me to make sure the Fiach Reaper hadn't followed me. "There's a man named Lorcan Kane downstairs. He says he's …"

"The Reaper for the Fiach Clan," Orin finished for me, his mood darkening. "Fuck." He stared off into the middle distance for a moment before he asked in an angry rumble, "Did he threaten you?"

I swallowed, knowing it was hopeless to try and lie to him. Somehow, he always knew. "Yes, but—"

"I'll fucking tear him apart." His eyes had clouded over with intense rage like a storm threatening to break on the horizon. I didn't want him to charge downstairs and get himself shot, so, without thinking, I reached up and placed my hand on his chest. He was warm and firm beneath my palm, and I couldn't ignore the way his breathing hitched.

"Orin, please. He told me he'd let me live if I left you here."

His chest was rising and falling with shallow breaths, and I curled my hand into a fist and withdrew it. His raven eyes remained on my face.

"You came to warn me instead?"

"We've been through too much for shit to end this way," I told him. "There's another way out though. Come on."

He stepped into the servants' stairs, and I followed him in. The tiny space was immediately sunk into darkness when I shut the door behind us. I felt my way along the wall until my fingers brushed up against something hard and warm. I'd reached Orin at the bottom of the stairs, and his hand curled around mine for the briefest second before the pressure disappeared.

He opened the door a sliver, peered out, then eased his big body from the cramped stairway. The pub beyond was quiet, except for some pacing footfalls in the dining room. I took a step closer to the entry into the dining room when Orin grabbed my hand and yanked me closer to his body. He held his finger up to his mouth in the universal sign for *shhh*, then began moving toward the kitchen.

The waitress who had served us was crouched down behind the stainless-steel workbench. Her eyes widened when we stepped into the room.

"Please," she whispered. "It was my boss who called them. He's second cousin to Gannon Sweeney. His loyalties lie with them. The next few towns are also loyal to the Fiach Clan."

I could see the irritation written on Orin's face. He glanced around. "Tell me there's a goddamned way out of here."

Lottie pointed at something behind her. "Beside the walk-in freezer, there's a back door." When she dug into the front of her apron, I saw Orin's shoulders tense, then relax when Lottie pulled out a set of car keys. "Mine is the red Focus. Take it. Get out of here."

"What if they find out you helped us?" I asked as Orin accepted the keys.

"The Mac Tíre Clan has helped my da for years. I owe them this."

I nodded to Lottie as we rushed past her and out the back door. The night air was biting against my cheeks, but we found the car we had been gifted. Orin unlocked the door remotely, and I started opening the passenger door.

"No," Orin said. "You're driving. You have to look like you're leaving alone."

Hustling over to the other side, I got in while Orin squeezed himself into the back seat and hunkered down. There was a blanket over the rear seat, so I grabbed it and settled it over him.

"Where are we going?" I turned on the car and checked the rearview mirror.

Orin's voice was muffled as he spoke. "If what the girl said is true, the northern part of county Galway have defected. Finnan couldn't have known that. We need to return to Oranmore."

"Okay. Oranmore. I can do that."

I stalled the car coming out of the car park, and Orin whispered, "Easy," to me.

"Sorry. I haven't driven a manual car in a while." I tried again, this time getting the balance between the clutch and the accelerator timed perfectly. The car moved forward, and as I glanced to the right, I saw the bartender and most of the patrons waiting outside. Apparently, murder did nothing to dissuade people from finishing their drinks.

I turned to the left, driving carefully down the road until the pub was out of sight. Gearing up, I started back the way we'd come.

ABOUT AN HOUR AND A HALF LATER, WE WERE BACK inside the safety of the compound, and I pulled the car to a stop in the turning circle. I got out to find Keir already standing there.

His brows rose in question. "Did Orin lose the Rover?" he asked.

"The Fiach Reaper came looking for us," I replied. "It was either this or walking back."

Keir's eyes roved over the small hatchback. "Where's Orin?" Movement in the back seat caught his eye. "Ah, there he is."

Orin extricated himself from the blanket and back seat, then pulled himself from the car. He looked pissed off for having been crammed into the back, but it had been his idea. He walked straight past Keir, barking the question, "Where the fuck is Finnan?"

"Office," the other man called, then to me, he said, "You want some hot cocoa?"

Of all the things he could've said to me, that wasn't what I was expecting. I glanced at Orin's retreating figure, then back to Keir. Now that I'd met him a few times, my anxiety about being alone with him had gone from an eight down to a three. "Okay."

I followed his broad back into the house and through to the kitchen. Because it was open plan—despite the outside looking like a stately home—I could see that the TV had been turned on to a football game. There was also a sweating bottle of beer on the table beside the couch.

Keir got started on the cocoa, pouring milk into a small saucepan and setting it on the stove. The blue flame licked the bottom of the copper pot.

"Do you like your cocoa with whipped cream?"

"Do you have any?"

He moved toward the fridge and opened it. His eyes scanned the contents before he reached in and grabbed something. He turned back to me with a triumphant smile that seemed to soften his face. "I knew we still had some."

For some reason, I found it funny to think of someone from the clan going shopping and filling their fridge.

"What's that smile for?" he asked, putting the can of whipped cream down on the counter between us.

"It's nothing."

He folded his arms and leaned his hip against the granite counter. "Come on. It'll be a few more minutes before the milk is heated enough. What's so funny?"

"I was just thinking about who does all the shopping for this house. I can't imagine Finnan wandering the aisles of Tesco, picking up fresh fruit and bread."

That comment earned me a chuckle. "No, it's definitely not Finnan who shops."

"Who is it then?"

"One of the sentinels goes usually, but the whipped cream? I bought that last time I was in town." Keir winked at me, a smile on his face. Then his eyes shifted up over my shoulder, and the smile wilted.

I turned to find Orin there, his energy volatile, as he stared at Keir. "What the fuck are you doing?"

Keir actually stepped back a pace. "Man, chill, I was just making her a hot cocoa."

He turned those black-as-sin eyes on me, and a thrill went through me. "Fallon."

It was only my name, but he didn't have to say anything more. I rose from my stool and walked toward him. His eyes never left me, and as I walked past him, my arm brushed his, sending a shock wave through my body. Orin was at my back, a heat-seeking missile following its target.

Once I was inside his room, he shut the door and leaned against it. Still staring. Still stripping me bare.

"Are you okay?" he asked—no *demanded.*

"Fine. We were only talking."

He growled, his top lip peeling off his teeth. "I don't want you talking to him."

"Why not?"

Instead of answering me, he said, "I'm going out. You need to stay in this room the whole time I'm gone."

I grabbed his arm as he strode past me, making him freeze. His muscles were practically vibrating beneath my fingers. I knew I was pushing past his boundaries here, but if he didn't want me to touch him, he could so easily brush me off. The fact that he was allowing it spoke volumes.

I swallowed over the lump in my throat and asked, "Where are you going?"

He turned his head, his dark eyes dropping to my mouth, then back again. "Out."

Suddenly wild with jealousy, the words seethed out of me. "You're going to see her? The same woman as before?"

"None of your business." He tried to pull away, but I

didn't let him. I dug my fingers in, drawing a hiss from his perfect mouth.

"If you're leaving to find sex, let me … let me be the one to give you what you need."

His eyes nearly bulged out of his head. "What?"

"Do to me what you were going to do to her."

"You wouldn't like it," he reasoned oh-so-calmly.

"I've never tried it."

"I like my sex rough. Are you ready for that?"

There was something in his voice—a hesitancy that said more than his words ever could.

Lifting my chin, I met his eyes. "I'm ready. Show me what it's like. Show me how you need to fuck."

He dropped his head, shaking it. "Jesus, Fallon, you don't know what you're asking of me."

I eased the pressure of my fingers. "I do know, Orin. I know I want to be with you in whatever capacity you'll have me. If that means I must be submissive to you, then I will. If that means being bound, then that's what I'll do. If it means being unable to touch you, then that's what I'll do, too."

His pupils blew out to consume his whole iris. "You don't know what you're saying."

We stayed there for a long while, caught between my offer and his desire to take it. My gaze dropped to his hips, where an impressive erection was pushing against his jeans.

"I do," I said with a finality he couldn't deny. I released him, giving him the opportunity to move away or stay.

We stayed suspended there in time, staring at each other, breathing each other's breaths, tasting each other's hunger.

My willingness to bend to his will.

His reluctance to show me this side of himself.

Eventually, he said, "No, you don't." He stalked away from me and into the bathroom, shutting the door behind him loudly. I stood there for a minute, thinking about how I could get him to see I was ready to try it his way. Walking closer to the bathroom, I placed my hand on the wood separating us and decided he was worth it.

I dropped to my knees, sat back on my heels, and bowed my head. Then, with my pulse trying to crawl out of my throat …

I waited.

18

ORIN

JESUS FUCKING CHRIST.

I sucked a deep breath in through my nose and stared at Fallon kneeling outside the bathroom door. My dick, which had been hard before, was now uncomfortably straining against the zipper of my jeans. I should've turned around and left the goddamned room, but I couldn't seem to move away.

"Fallon, what are you doing?" I asked, my voice nothing but a deep rumble filled with lust and reservation.

She didn't answer.

"Answer me."

A shiver ran through her, and I didn't think it was from fear. "W-waiting for you."

Waiting for me.

I'd been waiting for her too.

Spending time with her had been the greatest pleasure

and pain of my life.

Knowing I could never have her was my greatest torture.

I couldn't have sex any other way, and she was willing to try it. I had to decide. Stay and try to keep control of my lust, or leave her and find Raven, knowing that the other woman liked the pain I wanted to dish out.

I stood there for so long that Fallon started to lift her head, but it dropped quickly when I asked, "Waiting for me, *what?*"

A sharp inhale. "Waiting for you, sir?" she asked in a soft voice.

"Good girl." Reaching out, I ran my fingers lightly through her hair, feeling how soft the strands were, knowing that this might be the only chance I had to touch her so freely. Because after this, I was sure she would run for the fucking hills. "You call me *sir* when we're in a scene."

"Is that what this is?" she asked, tacking on "sir" at the end.

I found my lips tugging up into a smile. "Yes, it is. But this is going to be the only time we're together."

"Why, sir?"

"Because I'm too fucking old for you, and you should be with someone who doesn't need to tie up their partners to find sexual gratification." Before she could protest, I ordered, "Stand up."

She did without question but kept her head bowed. Circling her, my eyes raked down her body, and I wanted to see her curves without any barriers between us.

"Strip."

Her hands went to her jeans, and she only hesitated for a

moment before fumbling with the top button and drawing down the zipper. Wriggling free of the fabric, she kicked the jeans off, then lifted her shirt up and over her head. All the air in my lungs left me in a rush as I stared at the midnight-blue bra and panties she was wearing.

I swallowed. "Everything, Fallon. If we're doing this, take off every-fucking-thing. Do as I say."

Reaching behind her, she unhooked her bra, drawing the straps down off her shoulders. I couldn't see her breasts yet given I was standing behind her, but my imagination was running fucking wild. When she hooked her thumbs into her panties, I bit back the moan. The sheer fabric skimmed over the perfect globes of her ass as she drew them down and kicked them away.

Fallon was curvy—a fucking goddess if ever I saw one. I was used to women who whored for a living, and who had a certain body type. But not Fallon. I liked her curves, her slightly softer, more rounded parts.

"Turn around." Fuck, that didn't even sound like my voice. It was deeper somehow, filled with more goddamned lust than I ever thought was possible. Fallon moved slowly, turning around to face me. Her eyes were still on the ground, and I sucked in a hiss as her submissive behavior hit me square in the chest. It was like being struck with a heat-seeking missile, only this one had a singular target in mind: my fucking need to possess her. I wanted her. More than any other woman I'd ever engaged with in this dangerous game.

The revelation knocked me back a metaphoric step, but I recovered a moment later. Yes, I wanted her, but she didn't need more. She only thought she did.

I needed to show her that this wasn't what she wanted in her life. That *I* wasn't what she wanted. I couldn't infect her with this darkness in me. If this was my only chance with her, I was going to take my time and savor every last second … before I made sure she never sought this out again.

"Look at me."

Her blue gaze met mine, holding steady against the onslaught of nervous energy I was sure she was feeling.

"Are you sure this is what you want?"

"Yes."

I ground my molars. "Then we do it my way. Understood."

She nodded, then drew her bottom lip in between her teeth.

With my thumb, I dragged the flesh free, gently stroking her mouth. "I won't be fucking you tonight, Fallon."

Disappointment shimmered in her eyes. "But—"

With a firm shake of my head, I silenced her. "No. I can give you a taste of what it would be like to be with me, but I won't … *ruin* you like that." I fixed my eyes on her mouth again, running my thumb over her plump bottom lip. "I should punish you for tempting me the way you do, though. For making me feel so out of control and territorial."

Her lips parted and she panted, "I want to experience it all. I want you to do to me what you do to that other woman."

Hearing the mention of Raven filled me with fucking shame—also a new sensation.

"I won't hurt you like I hurt her, Fallon. She's a pain slut. She craves it like I crave the domination of a woman's body." I stepped closer, finally letting some of the leash I was keeping myself on slide through my fingers. "I won't give you everything, but you still need to be punished for pushing me to this. For wanting this."

Her gaze grew heavy. "How will I be punished if you refuse to hurt me?"

My smile was dark. "Have you heard of orgasm denial?"

"No."

"What about a forced orgasm?"

She shook her head. "No."

She was a blank canvas. My own personal playground for tonight. And as many things as I wanted to do with her, I knew all I had was this moment. This time. I couldn't push her too hard and too fast, so I had to decide where I was going to draw the line. Fucking was out, but there was one thing I'd wanted to do with her that I'd never done with another woman.

Unbuckling my belt, I slid it through the loops of my jeans, the *shhht* sound seeming too loud in the confines of the bedroom. Fallon watched my movements like a nervous mouse.

Turning, I walked to the bed, feeling her eyes on me the entire time. I sat down, spreading my legs wide, then crooked my finger at her.

"Crawl to me like the good little whore you are."

I braced for her refusal, and when she stared at me for a few seconds, I was sure it was coming. But then she lowered herself onto her hands and knees and started to crawl toward her pleasure.

When she was kneeling between my legs, I slid my fingers along her jaw and around the back of her head. If it were anyone else, I would make them suck my cock until they were choking on it, but I shook those thoughts from my head. Fallon's pleasure had to come first.

Releasing her, I rasped, "I need you bound for this."

She nodded and thrust her hands out in front of her. She was so willing it made something in my chest crack open. Some barricade that had calcified in place cracked right along with it. Wrapping the belt around her wrists, I made sure the knot was tight, but not so tight that it would leave a mark.

"Is this okay?"

She nodded.

"I have two rules. Number one is no touching. The second is I want you to use a safe word if you feel like something I'm doing isn't for you. You say the safe word, and I stop. Simple. Do you understand?"

Another nod, this one followed up by a swipe of her tongue over her lips.

I bit back the growl trying to work its way up my throat. "Your safe word is bullet. Repeat it."

"Bullet."

"Bullet will stop me instantly from whatever it is I'm doing."

"Okay."

"Okay, *what?*"

"Okay, sir."

"Good girl."

I sat back a little and stared at her. Her chest was rising and falling quickly, and her cheeks were high with color. "I'm going to do something to you that I've been thinking about since we met."

"What's that?"

I cocked a brow at her, wanting her to forget again. She must've seen the thoughts in my head because she quickly tacked on a "sir."

"I'm going to put you over my knee and spank your pretty arse." I patted my left thigh. She hesitated. "I promise I won't hurt you. I'll only make you feel pleasure."

Fallon did as I bid, standing up and positioning herself so she was draped over my knees. She rested her elbows on the mattress beside me and peered over her shoulder. Savoring this moment, I rubbed one ass cheek, then the other. My hands were greedy to begin, but I knew I had to take it slowly. Applying a little more pressure, I rubbed her other ass cheek until I felt her physically relax into my touch.

I was in strange, unchartered territory here. I hadn't ever done low-impact play. All my previous partners demanded I cause them pain, but that was not what this was about.

When I was sure Fallon was ready, I raised my palm and slapped her lightly on the ass. She drew in a small gasp, the sound of which made my dick so fucking hard in my jeans.

"Okay?" I asked, my voice rasping over the words.

"Yes, sir," she whispered. "More, sir."

"Good girl," I told her, rubbing the pink mark from her ass. Lifting my hand, I paddled the other side, her gasp turning into a moan. Fuck, yes, she was loving this. Lifting her ass a little higher, she wordlessly begged for more, and I gave it to her. The sound of my hand meeting her pinking skin was fucking music to my ears.

My heart was racing as I worked her into a frenzy of lust. Her hips rolled against me, trying to find the friction she was after in order to come.

"Don't come until I tell you to," I told her, deciding to deny her orgasm this time. Next time would be a different story, though.

She whimpered and stopped undulating her hips. Her head was touching her bound hands, and I could see how labored her breath had become. "Yes, sir."

Running my hand down between the valley of her ass, I slipped a finger in between her legs. I teased at her entrance, feeling how wet she already was. I would've bet that even she was surprised by how much she had enjoyed that. Sliding my finger over her drenched opening, I pushed inside by half an inch, watching to see how she would react. At first, she was tense, but she soon relaxed into my touch. I slid in a little farther until my second knuckle was inside her. She moaned, her inner muscles working hard around the digit and in that moment, I knew she would've felt amazing coming on my cock.

Which will never happen, I told myself. This wasn't about fucking her. This was giving her a taste of my world and praying to God that she wouldn't ask me for more.

"Shall I keep going, Fallon?" I rasped.

"Yes, sir. Please, sir."

Taking in a deep breath through my nose, I released it and slid my finger all the way inside. Her slick inner walls grabbed on tight, and I warned, "Remember what I said."

She nodded frantically, stifling a moan with her hand. "I'll try, sir."

Withdrawing my finger, she whimpered and writhed the whole time until I returned it to its starting position. She mewled that time, and my dick jumped. That sound. Fuck, that sound would be the fucking death of me.

I waited until she had relaxed enough before I slid another finger inside her slick channel. Raising her ass, she pushed back against me, begging me for more. I could feel her inner walls start to pulsate with need, and as soon as I did, I withdrew my fingers.

I slapped her on the ass cheek one last time, then helped her stand. She stared at me—dazed and confused—as I went into the closet and retrieved a chest. Fallon watched me open it and pull out a pair of soft Velcro cuffs and a spreader bar. The bar was telescopic, so as I extended it out, her eyes widened.

"What's that for?"

I dropped to my knees and wrapped a hand around her ankle. Her skin was warm—soft—and I took a moment to enjoy that softness on my palm. Undoing the Velcro on the cuff, I wrapped it around her right ankle and secured it in place. I did the same on the other side, making sure they were snug against her skin. Grabbing the spreader bar, I clipped the hooks into the D links on the cuffs around one ankle, then nudged her legs wider. She made a small noise of protest and I stopped.

"Do you need to say the safe word?"

She shook her head, some hair that had come loose from her ponytail brushing against her shoulders. "No. I was just surprised."

"Surprised by what?"

"How exposed I feel."

"If you're worried that I don't enjoy the way you look right now, let me assure you that I do." I gave her a solemn look. "Do you want to continue?"

"Yes, sir."

"Good girl."

Positioning her at the foot of the bed, I helped ease her into a seated position. With her legs wide, I could see how pink and perfect her cunt was. Her bound hands were still in her lap, her fingers tightening and relaxing the longer I looked at her.

Normally, I wouldn't touch my partners other than to reposition them or attach equipment, but with Fallon, my fingers ached to touch her. Giving in to the sensation, I ran my hand along her jaw, my long fingers reaching around to the back of her head. "Are you nervous?"

"A little."

"That's okay. You can be nervous. All I need to know is if you want to stop."

She shook her head, and her hair brushed up against my skin. Ylang-ylang filled my senses, forcing my eyes to close in euphoria. "I don't want to stop, sir. I want more."

If she wanted more, I was going to give it to her. As I dropped to my knees, I said, "Remember what I said. You can't come until you have my permission. Understood?"

"Yes, sir," she whispered, eyes wide as she traced my movement closer to her center.

With her bound and restrained, I felt the monster inside my head stretch out a little further. Normally, it was only sated once I had taken my partner's pain, but it was as if it sensed the need to move a little more slowly, be a little more careful.

"I'm going to eat your delicious cunt now, Fallon." Before she could reply, I swiped my tongue through her folds and elicited the most delicious gasp from her plump lips. Again, I was in unchartered waters here with her. Giving a woman pleasure was never my intention when it came to fucking. I had certainly never put myself into this position of vulnerability either, but the knowledge that this was a one-time thing helped me overcome any hesitations and just fucking enjoy the taste of her on my lips.

Fallon's gasp was in my ears.

Her ylang-ylang taste was on my tongue.

My eyes ate up everything about her.

She tried to widen her legs, and when she wasn't able, she widened her knees and hips, trying to give me more room. I shoved my shoulders between her thighs and feasted on her pussy, running my tongue through it, sucking her clit into my mouth, spearing her center with my tongue. Her honey was dripping all over me, and I fucking loved it.

When her inner thighs began to shake, I reared back from her. She was glassy-eyed and breathing heavily.

"Why …"

I made a show of licking my lips—of tasting her. "You were going to come, and I haven't given you permission yet."

She moaned as if she was in pain, then blinked up at me with those blue eyes. "When will you give me permission?"

"When I'm good and ready." I dived back into her cunt, savoring everything about the experience. The way she squirmed and writhed, how her hips flexed toward me, chasing my mouth and tongue and teeth. I brought her to the edge once more, then sat back on my heels to look at her.

Her face was flushed, her chest heaving with labored breath. A fine sheen of sweat coated her skin, but it was her blue, unfocused eyes that did me in. She looked as if she was standing at the gates of heaven, except it wasn't an angel who had gotten her there.

It was the devil.

"When are you allowed to come?" I asked, sliding a finger into her pussy.

She threw her head back and rolled her hips. "When you tell me I can."

"When I tell you you can, *what?*" I demanded darkly.

"Sir. When you tell me I can, *sir.*"

I withdrew my finger and slid it into her parted mouth. She latched onto the digit, sucking it hard. "Do you like the way you taste? Because I do."

Fallon nodded her head. "I want to taste you, too."

My cock twitched, and as much as I wanted her lips wrapped around me, I shook my head. "This isn't about me. This is about you and your pleasure."

I could tell she wanted to protest, so I leaned forward and sucked one of her nipples into my mouth while I pumped two—then three—fingers into her drenched cunt. Her inner walls began to tremble again, and I rolled my eyes up to see a line of concentration on her face as she tried to stop the inevitable. I knew that when she finally did come, the force of it would be exponentially better than it normally would be, and that was all because I had taken control of her pleasure.

"Orin, please," she pleaded. "Please let me come."

"I'll let you come in a minute, Filly. I just want to watch you fight it a little longer."

She bit her lip, her eyes locked on my face as I pushed her closer and closer to breaking point. When I was sure she wouldn't be able to last another second, I gave the command.

"Come. Now."

Her eyes squeezed shut, and she let herself go. Her breath was a rush against my neck as she collapsed forward, and I had no choice but to let her rest her head between my jaw and collarbone. Her inner walls clamped down hard onto my fingers, but I didn't stop thrusting inside her, milking her orgasm and making it mine.

Mine.

I had earned it.

Her whole body shook with her release, and I would've given anything to see the rapture on her face, to see how she looked when she came undone under my fingers. More air chased down my chest as she breathed through her orgasm until I finally nudged her back upright again.

Fallon's cheeks were flushed, and the drowsy look in her eyes made me want to do it all over again.

"How was that?" I asked her, pushing some stray strands of hair off her cheek and neck.

"I didn't realize it could be that powerful."

I motioned for her to hold out her wrists. Unwinding the belt, I rubbed her wrists where the leather had bitten a little too hard.

"Does this hurt?" I asked, refusing to let go.

"It's okay," she replied.

Once I was done with her other wrist and massaged it out, I turned my attention to the spreader bar. The Velcro sounded too loud in the room after the silence had fallen. I took one cuff off, rubbing her skin to soothe away the sting, before releasing her other foot.

When I sat back on my heels, she was looking at me.

"If you don't mind, I'll take a quick shower," I told her. "Then you can get in after me."

She bit her bottom lip. "Or, we could take one together?" she asked.

My dick was on board with that, but I wasn't. Not yet.

I began shaking my head, but she stopped me. "I promise I won't touch you. I just want to be close to you for a little longer."

I knew it was a bad fucking idea, but I couldn't bring myself to deny her. I turned and walked toward the bathroom, knowing she was trailing after me.

19

FALLON

MY KNEES FELT WEAK. HELL, EVERYTHING ABOUT me felt weak. Orin stepped over the threshold and into the bathroom, peering at me over his shoulder. The look in his eyes was cold and distant, and I wanted the passionate man who had just taken me to heaven back again. Leaning into the stall, he turned on the cold tap, and for a moment, I thought that was how he was going to leave it.

But then he added the hot, and steam was soon billowing out and fogging up the glass screen. He turned back to me, his gaze hungrily eating mine as he stripped out of his clothing. He undid the buttons on his shirt with deliberate slowness that spoke of his incredible control, then shucked the fabric from his shoulders. I let myself drink him in—his hard shoulders and rounded chest. Everything about his torso was perfection—a well-oiled machine, honed and perfectly crafted.

The tattoos on his chest looked brighter under the bathroom light, and I wanted to run my hands all over them. Squeezing my hands into fists, I knew I couldn't though. Orin had let me into his world. I had to play by his rules for just a little longer.

Undoing the button on his jeans, he hooked his thumbs into the waistband and then drew them down his strong legs.

Breathless.

I was breathless for a moment when my eyes landed on his rigid cock. It stood out proudly from his hips, long and hard. The tip glistened with a drop of pre-cum, that I was fascinated with. What would he do if I fell to my knees right now and took him into my mouth?

When my attention finally returned to his face, the corner of his mouth curled in a knowing smile. "You want this?" he asked, wrapping his hand around his cock and running his palm up its length. All the muscles in his forearm and bicep flexed and relaxed with the movement. He chuckled. "Of course, you want this. You're already licking your lips."

"Please," I whimpered.

He stopped, pinning me with a hard glare. "Who do you belong to, Fallon?"

I answered without hesitation. "You."

His answering smile was fierce. "Who made you feel good just now, legs forced open, wrists bound?"

A tremor ran through me. "You."

He stepped toward me. "Who else gets to fuck your perfect pussy?"

"Nobody. Just you."

His eyes were so dark, lust and something else lurking in their depths. "That's right. Only me. And when I finally take your cunt, I'll ruin you for every other man who comes after me."

Hope flared like an ember in my chest. He'd said *when* he finally took me.

I shook my head. "I don't want any other man."

"My style of fucking might scare you off."

"It won't."

His eyes zeroed in on my mouth, and I licked my lips to see what would happen. An inferno broke out in his gaze, a blast so strong that I swore I felt the heat of it from where I stood. Raising his hand, he looked as if he wanted to run his fingers over my mouth like he had before but stopped himself.

"It might make you hate me."

My whole body trembled. I was so desperate for his touch that I almost reached for him myself. I stopped myself at the last minute though. I had to play by his rules. If I wanted him to give me more, I had to do as he said.

As if he saw that whole decision-making process flash across my face, he stepped away, and into the shower stall. "Come."

On wobbling legs, I followed him in, stepping inside and closing the door behind me. Orin was standing in front of the spray, his eyes still burning.

"On your knees."

I dropped. God help me, I dropped to my knees at the harsh command, and my body rejoiced. Heat flooded my skin, and moisture started to pool between my legs. My eyeline was level with his bobbing cock, which he fisted in a tight grip.

"Open your mouth and stick out your tongue."

I complied, practically salivating over what was to come. Closing the small distance between us, he slapped his cock against my tongue, then rimmed my lips with the engorged crown. When I tried to close my mouth around it, he withdrew.

"My rules, Fallon." His tone was dark.

"Yes, sir," I replied, opening my mouth so wide that my jaw cracked.

He slid his cock into my mouth before withdrawing it. Once more, then he gave the command.

"Now, suck."

Sealing my lips around his shaft, I sucked him in, swirling my tongue over the thick veins that ran along the underside.

"Eyes on me."

I lifted my gaze to his face, finding his eyes were flaming with desire. Humming, I started bobbing up and down on his thick cock in earnest, taking him as deep as I dared.

"Further," he grunted, thrusting into my throat as I swallowed him down. He breached that part of my throat where comfort stopped and reflexes kicked in, holding me there until the muscles in my throat relaxed and accepted his invasion.

"Do you trust me?" he asked.

My eyes shone with my answer. *Yes, I trust you.*

For just a moment, awe slid across his features, the emotion buried quickly after. "I want to fuck this part of your throat, but I need to have the control. Do you understand?"

I blinked up at him.

For the briefest second, his fingers dusted over my bottom lip. "Tap my hip if it gets too much for you."

Another blink to show him I understood the rules of this filthy, erotic game.

He withdrew a couple of inches, then slammed back inside me. My throat constricted around him—making a wet gagging sound—and he groaned. Saliva flooded my mouth and started to drip down his cock, which only seemed to get him off. Orin's pace picked up, each flex into my mouth feeling like it was going deeper and deeper until I couldn't find the air I needed.

My fingers hovered over his hip.

I trusted Orin—of course I did—but this was too much. Too far.

Too extreme …

But then something happened.

My body relaxed completely, and my mind became blissfully empty. My body started to fully accept the invasion, and there was something liberating in that. In the knowledge that all he wanted to do was bring me pleasure, that he would wring every last drop from me. My fear had stopped me from enjoying sex, but with Orin, things were different. I knew he would never hurt me.

"Touch yourself," he gritted out between his clenched teeth.

I snaked a hand between my thighs. My body was so in tune with his that at the first brush of my fingertips against my clit, I knew it wouldn't take me long.

"Is my little whore close?" he asked, his voice sounding

more strained than before.

I blinked, getting off on the power display, on the way he seemed to be having trouble holding himself back. Because *I* was the one driving him crazy. I was the one pushing him past his feral limits. I came with a long, drawn-out moan, his cock still thrusting deeply into my throat.

"Fuck!" he barked, pulling out of my mouth and coming on my face as my orgasm crested and took over my senses. My pleasure and his layered until we were stuck in an erotic loop. Warm spurts of his cum hit my cheeks and lips, dripping down onto my chest. His eyes were slits as he stared at me, at how he covered my face. When he'd squeezed the last drop from his cock, he released it and stepped backward.

I rose from my position on the tiles while he watched with unbridled lust. Shifting to the side, he let the spray hit me. Closing my eyes, I slid my face fully under the water, letting it clean me off. I shivered, however, when cold air swirled around me.

Rubbing the water from my eyes, I saw Orin was outside the shower, wrapping a towel around his waist.

"Orin?" I called.

He glanced over his shoulder, his eyes darting down my wet body, then back again. A muscle in his jaw ticked. "What?"

"Where are you going?"

He frowned like he couldn't quite understand the question. "Leaving you to shower."

Before I could ask him to stay, he strode off, shutting the door behind him.

20
ORIN

TOO FAR.

I'd gone too fucking far.

What the actual fuck was I thinking?

Running a hand through my hair, my fingers clawed, and I blew out a breath to force myself to keep moving. The desire to turn around, walk straight back into that bathroom and take more from Fallon was nearly irresistible.

Because, *fuck,* she had looked beautiful taking my cock. Even thinking about it now made my body twitch and dick harden. My downtime between fucks was short, but this was ridiculous. My body craved more of her, but it wasn't going to happen again. Yes, seeing her bound and at my mercy lit a fucking fire inside my heart. Yes, seeing her take my cock without complaint made me want to burn down the world for her on the off chance that I could keep her, but …

I knew she didn't belong to me. And she never would.

One time. It was only supposed to be one time that we fucked.

You didn't actually fuck her, a not so helpful voice echoed in my head.

I hadn't penetrated her cunt, but I had penetrated her mouth. I'd fucked it and taken my pleasure, but only after giving her hers. I shook my head. It didn't matter anyway. This was the last time I would be with her. She was too innocent for my world, and despite her telling me this was what she wanted, I knew it wasn't sustainable. I didn't make love. I fucked, and I fucked hard. A woman like Fallon deserved sweet and gentle.

She wouldn't ever find that with me.

Dropping the towel, I was searching through my drawers for a fresh pair of jeans when there was a sudden pounding on the bedroom door. Sliding on the jeans, I pulled them up and did the zipper but left the top button undone. I opened the door. It was Keir.

He took in my state of undress, then tried to peer over my shoulder and into my room. I blocked him.

"What do you want?"

"There's been a—"

It was then that the perimeter alarm went off, and any post-sex haze slid right off me.

"Breach," Keir replied.

"Where?"

"Finnan wants you on the roof and covering the eastern forest."

"I'm coming now."

I left Keir at the door, striding to my closet, where I kept my cache of weapons. I opened the gun safe and pulled out three handguns and my sniper rifle and stand. As I emerged, Fallon was standing in the entrance to the bathroom with a towel wrapped around her. Her eyes were wide, and they got wider still when she saw the rifle slung across my bare chest.

"What's going on?"

"Perimeter breach." Checking over one of my Glocks, I handed it to her. "Stay in the room and shoot any motherfucker you don't recognize."

"Where are you going?"

"To defend the goddamned compound."

I took one step away from her, then hesitated. What the fuck was I doing? I needed to go, but the desire to tell her to stay safe and I'd be back was overwhelming. With one final glance over my shoulder, I hustled out of the room and ran down the hall where the stairs to the roof were.

The floodlights were on, but there were still dead spots in the landscape where the light didn't reach. Shots rang out in the darkness, the shooters giving away their positions with the flash from their muzzles. Laying down my rifle, I crouched to set up the stand, then mounted the gun. When everything was ready, I looked down the scope.

"Come on, you bastards," I muttered as I settled in and waited.

The sound of shouts and grunts carried from the other side of the building. Some of my brothers must've engaged in hand-to-hand. I didn't have to fucking worry about them though. They would look after themselves. All I had to focus on was keeping more people out.

A shot rang out in the direction of the fighting. Directly ahead, I caught the shooter in my sight—a flash of white from his hair—and pulled the trigger. The rifle recoiled, slamming into my shoulder and bringing back the familiar ache I had grown accustomed to while serving in the army.

Another shot was fired, and I shifted the rifle to where it had come from. I picked off that guy easily, too.

And another.

And another.

Seven more shots rang out, all of them hitting their intended targets.

Bringing down the rifle, I scanned the tree line, looking for any further movement.

That was when I heard it. A shot from inside the house, and as far as I knew, only one person was left behind. Leaping up, I left my rifle where it was and ran back down the stairs. The house was silent once more except for a muffled scream for help. I sprinted down the hall, sliding to a stop in my bedroom.

What I saw would fucking haunt me.

Fallon was on the ground with a man on top of her. He had her sleep shorts down, and he was struggling to undo his own pants. A cool calmness crept over me as I walked into the room, pulled out one of my Glocks from the thigh holster and put the muzzle to the back of his head.

"She's mine." I jammed the metal in a little harder.

The man grunted but still hadn't looked at me. "You can have her after me."

"I don't think you understand what I'm saying. The girl

is mine. Sticking your dick in her will only sign your death warrant."

He growled this time. "Who the f—" His question died in his throat as he came face-to-face with my Glock. I shoved it into his mouth, breaking a few teeth while I was at it. Fallon was whimpering beneath him, holding her shaking arms out in front of her. Her limbs were shaking and seeing her so upset set the monster free in my head.

"Stand up. Slowly."

He flinched as he looked at the cold look in my eyes. I wondered if he could see the darkness lurking there, slinking from shadow to shadow as he waited for the bloodbath to begin. The guy stood, his now flaccid dick hanging out of his pants.

Fallon scrambled to her feet, drawing her shorts back onto her hips, and pressed herself against the wall.

After patting down the motherfucker one-handed and removing a gun and a knife, I shifted my gaze to Fallon.

"Are you okay?"

She didn't meet my eyes, but she was trembling.

"Fallon!"

Her blue eyes finally moved to my face. "I'm okay," she whispered. "I'm okay."

I shifted my attention back to the man who thought he could take what was mine—what I had claimed. "Start walking."

I marched the guy out of the room with Fallon following behind me.

"Are you going to hurt him?"

"Yes."

"Are you going to kill him?"

"Yes."

I waited for her to beg me to spare his life, but she said nothing. Instead, she hung back at the doorway and watched.

Over my shoulder, I said, "Lock the door. I'll come find you after I've taken care of this shit."

She nodded and disappeared into the room. I waited until I heard the door lock, then proceeded down the hall and stairs. I was still leading the bastard by a gun in the mouth, and I smiled when I entered the living room to find six bodies laid out on the rug.

Finnan was pouring himself a drink while Caolan, Keir, and the twins hauled another man into the room.

My boss looked at me, then at the man getting real intimate with my Glock. He took a sip of his whisky. "Where did you find him?" he asked casually.

"Doesn't matter. I found him." My gaze shifted to the bodies lined up. "My kills or yours?"

"These are the motherfuckers who stormed the house," Caolan replied. "I saw your handiwork when I went to check the perimeter. You got eleven. Perfect hits."

I nodded, acknowledging the compliment he was paying me. Nobody else had the skills to be that accurate in low light. Nobody except for me.

"What are you going to do with that one?" Keir indicated to the man with me with the jerk of his chin.

"Don't fuck around, Orin. Put a bullet in his fucking head and be done with it," Finnan snarled, slamming back the rest of his drink.

Turning to face the man, I saw he was sweating. Good. He

was fucked ten ways from Sunday right now. Keeping the gun in place with one hand, I tore the shirt from his body with the other, looking for the tattoo of his clan. Every single bastard had one—somewhere. And there his was— on the right side of his ribs.

"Fuck," I hissed. "Fiach."

Finnan's brows rose in question. "What the fuck are clan Fiach up to now?"

"Maybe Sweeney's finally decided to make a move against you?" Keir said, crouching down to check the bodies at his feet for tattoos, too.

"It's been almost three months. What the fuck took him so long?" Finnan asked in a bored drawl. He approached the man giving my Glock a blow job. "What the fuck is your boss up to?"

Given he had a gun in his mouth, he was reluctant to talk.

"Put him out of his goddamned misery," Finnan spat, returning to the bar once more.

The Fiach member started to scream around the metal in his mouth, and I knew his tongue was going to be the first thing to go tonight.

"Where are you going?" Keir called after me as I headed to the basement door.

"To take care of business."

I shut out his words of concern and pulled open the door. Shoving the man in front of me, I pushed him in the back and sent him sprawling down the stairs. He landed in a heap, moving slowly to get back onto his feet. I stalked forward, letting him see more fully the monster he'd just set loose.

"I'm sorry," he said, hands up in front of him. "I'm sorry I touched her. I'm sorry I even looked at her. I'm—"

"It's too late for that." My voice was a violent rumble like thunder threatening on the horizon. "You touched what belonged to me. And for that, you'll pay with your blood, your pain and, eventually, your life."

Grabbing him by the arm, I shoved him farther into the room. His foot got caught, and he fell backward, his arms pinwheeling as he tried to find his equilibrium again. Before he could, I shoved him back into the lone chair in the center of the room. Taking the first set of cuffs dangling from the back, I restrained his legs first, then his arms.

There was a workbench on the adjacent wall, and I found what I wanted in the first drawer. I drew the knife out slowly, heightening his fear until it saturated the walls. I wondered how much more this room could witness before it spilled its secrets. It had seen every single bloody deed I had ever committed. It was my priest and confessional. It was my damnation.

Walking back to the guy, I hacked away at his pants until he was naked from the waist down. If he wanted to use his dick as a weapon, I was going to make sure I took it off him.

"Please," he whimpered. "Please."

"Fallon said the same thing to you. Were you going to stop?"

Pressing his lips together, he shook his head. "Is this about her? I'll do whatever you want to make it up to her. I didn't know she was yours."

"Liar. I told you she was mine, but you didn't stop."

His eyes widened as he replayed what had gone down

between us, and I saw the moment it dawned with crystal clear clarity when he realized I was right. He had told me I could have her after, but I didn't share.

"I'm sorry."

I shook my head. "It's too late for that. We all make choices. Good. Bad. Neutral. You just made the wrong one today when you went into that room and found that girl." I stepped forward menacingly. "And now, you'll pay the ultimate price for that decision."

Grabbing him by the jaw, I forced his mouth open and then dragged out his tongue. The blade sank into his flesh, the tissue and sinew giving up its fight with the sharpened metal. He screamed, or tried to scream, but there was too much blood filling his mouth. It dribbled down his chin, and I watched him choke as it rushed down the back of his throat, too.

Discarding his tongue, I turned my attention to his limp dick, slicing it off in one quick motion. More blood flowed, dripping down onto the floor as he began to bleed out. Taking the tip of the blade, I set my sights on the clan tattoo on his ribcage and began to carve it out of his skin. Some killers kept hair. Others, an item of clothing or a photograph of their work. For me, it was a tattoo.

Once the inked skin had been cut out, I laid it out on the workbench so I could preserve it later. The guy's muffled screams had turned into nothing but moans now, but I still hated the sound. It triggered something in me that I didn't want to necessarily forget, but I didn't want to relive every damn day either.

Which made me think about Fallon.

How she must be scared right now. How she must be reliving that shit again after tonight.

I needed to get back to her, and for the first time, I wanted to make my enemy's death a quick one rather than the long, drawn-out process it normally was. I fixed my artic gaze back to the Fiach Clan member.

Taking him by the jaw, I forced his eyes to me. "You touched the wrong woman tonight. She belongs to me. Anyone who touches something that belongs to me, dies."

I slid the blade in between his ribs, aiming for his heart. The steel hit the organ from the side, puncturing it and sending shit sideways for the motherfucker who thought he could have what didn't belong to him.

Watching the life drain from his eyes satisfied the monster. He had been sated for another day. Stepping back, I walked to the incinerator in the back corner of the basement and turned the dial, setting the temperature. The clan had upgraded from wood to gas, so the blue flames jumped and writhed as soon as I hit the start button.

I opened the door, shielding my face from the intense heat it was already throwing out. I slid out the metal slab, then hauled Mr. Touchy onto it. I shoved him inside and shut the door. As I watched him burn, I thought about justice. I'd brought justice to Fallon tonight. I had done the right thing, but something inside me also asked whether Fallon needed this kind of justice. Whether she'd asked for it or whether I'd simply taken it for her. What the hell was I thinking having her? I couldn't have her. My world was ugly shades of black, white, and gray, and hers streamed in color. Despite the shit that went down, she still looked at

the positive side of things …
    Except, I wasn't positive.
    I was darkness, and she was my light.
    I wouldn't snuff out that light with my life.
    I fucking refused to take something so pure.

21

FALLON

WHEN ORIN RETURNED TO THE ROOM, HE STRODE straight into the bathroom without giving me a second look. He was covered in blood. Scrambling from my perch on the edge of the bed, I tried to open the door, thinking it would be locked, but it swung open easily.

Orin had his hands planted on the counter, his head dropped low. When I entered, though, he turned to face me. My immediate thought was that I had to check him for injuries. I reached for him without thinking—without warning him—and he jacked up to a stand.

"Don't touch me," he snarled.

He looked like a cornered, wild animal. His eyes were huge, his posture stiff. He was ready to attack, but I didn't care. I needed to know he was okay. Ignoring his command, I tried one more time to run my hands along his back and chest, looking for any signs of bullet or stab wounds. This time, he backed up a physical step.

"I said don't *touch* me!" he barked.

I held back my wince. "You're bleeding."

He glanced down, then back at me. "It's not mine."

"Who does it belong to then?"

"The man I killed."

"The man …" My eyes widened. "The man who tried to …" I couldn't even finish the question.

He answered anyway, nodding his head. "Yes, that man."

I swallowed thickly. "Where is he now?"

"Burning."

Fuck, fuck, fuck. He had killed a man, then incinerated his body all because of me. I looked away, nibbling on my bottom lip, trying to make sense of this. I knew he was a killer. I had *seen* him kill when it was a matter of life or death, but this kill was purely for revenge. He had ended one man's life because he had touched me. At the time, that was just what I'd wanted, but now in the cold wastelands of introspection, I should've said no. I should've told him not to do it.

"Now do you see the monster I am?" he asked in a dark rasp.

I looked at him through the mirror. "You're not a monster."

"I *am* a monster, Fallon." He flung his arm out wide, pointing at something in another part of the house. "I tied him to a chair, cut out his tongue *then* his dick, peeled his clan tattoo off his body like I was filleting a fish, before finally sliding a knife into his heart—all while I was staring into his eyes. The kill was intimate because he had fucking *touched* you. He'd touched you and I told you, you were mine."

Removing his dick I could understand, but …

"You cut out his tongue?"

He flashed me a sardonic grin. "It helps stop them screaming."

I looked away, shaking my head. I shouldn't have been surprised by his answer. I shouldn't have been surprised by anything he did, but I was fucking blindsided by this.

"Are you going to leave me now, too?" He bit the words out. "Just like everyone else?"

I thought the unequivocal answer was no, but now …

"I don't know," I mumbled, turning and walking back into the bedroom. Orin slammed the door shut, and I stood there a moment wondering what I could do. Would I even be allowed to leave after witnessing what I had? Did I really want to? Jesus, I didn't know what to do.

My thoughts were interrupted when there was a knock on the door. Moving on autopilot, I opened it and saw Keir on the other side. He smiled at me—a nice smile—not one hinged with malice like Orin was so good at. Why couldn't I have been attracted to someone like him instead?

A frown formed between his brows when he caught sight of my face. "Jesus, are you okay?"

"I'm fine." I brushed off his concern and took a step back.

His eyes darted over my shoulder, and the relief that crossed his expression when he saw the bathroom door shut was visible.

"Were you looking for Orin?"

"No. I was looking for you. I wanted to see whether you

were okay after what happened."

My cheeks flushed with color. Of course, Orin had told them how he'd found me. With my eyes fixed on a spot on the floor, I nodded. "Fine. Orin …" My words stalled.

Keir heaved a sigh. "Yeah, Orin." He studied me for a moment. "Has he hurt you?"

My head jerked up, and I shook it. "He would never."

That earned me a frown. "I've never known him to be gentle with anyone."

I shrugged because there was no other way to answer that. I couldn't tell him that in Orin's own way, he was gentle. It was like saying that a lion could be nurturing. It wasn't something you witnessed very often or were lucky enough to witness at all, but that didn't mean it wasn't possible.

"Look, I want you to give him some space tonight. Whatever happened tonight messed with his head, and I think that some time apart might be wise."

As much as I hated to admit he was right, I felt like maybe he was. Orin had pushed me away when he was in the bathroom. He asked me not to touch him, so sleeping in the same bed would not help the issue.

"I think you're right."

Keir's brows rose. "You think I'm right?" he repeated.

"Yeah. I think he needs some space tonight."

He nodded, relief crossing his features. "Grab some things, and I'll take you to a guest room."

After snatching up some clothes, I followed Keir down the hall, stopping at a room only two doors away from Orin's bedroom. He opened the door and stepped inside. It was like a carbon copy of Orin's except it didn't smell the same as his did.

"You'll be comfortable here until morning," he told me, running a hand through his hair. He looked exhausted.

"Are you okay? Did anyone get hurt tonight?"

"We lost one of our Sentinels, but other than that, we were fine. Orin took out most of them from the roof before any reinforcements could get in." He smiled at me. "It's late. Get some rest. Good night, Fallon."

"Good night."

Keir stepped out of the room and closed the door behind him. I turned around and stared at the room, feeling lost inside. It was crazy to feel this way though. Orin was literally down the hall, and I had spent a lot of time on my own. Why should this be any different from those times?

I turned on the bathroom light before shutting the door until just a sliver of light pierced through the room. I hadn't had to sleep with the light on in a very long time, but my nerves were shot, and the way Orin had spoken to me had left me rattled. Climbing into bed, I curled up on my side and shut my eyes.

Sleep was elusive though. I lay there listening to the noises of the house, to the men who passed by on the runner outside. I listened to my own breathing and erratic pulse and wondered what I was going to do now.

I was close to drifting off when I heard Orin roar, "Where the hell is she?"

Heavy footsteps pounded toward the stairs, and I sat up in bed. Why was Orin so pissed that I wasn't in the room anymore? He said he didn't want me to touch him. This was the best way to achieve that. His footfalls thundered back down the hall, and then he was standing in the doorway to the room, his large, bare chest pumping restlessly so that his tattoos writhed and danced over his skin.

"What are you doing in here?" he demanded in a soft growl.

I sat up properly. "I could ask the same of you."

His jaw flexed. "You're supposed to be sleeping in my room."

I folded my arms across my chest and gave him a look. "You told me not to touch you."

He glared at me, that same muscle in his jaw jumping. "You sleep in my room. With me. End of story."

"You can't tell me not to touch you then demand I come and sleep beside you. That makes no sense."

Shaking his head, he marched forward muttering something about being a ridiculous woman and threw back the quilt in one swift movement. With one arm under my legs and the other around my back, he lifted me over his shoulder and returned to his room. I was too shocked to wriggle out, only remembering that I had this choice once we were back in his bedroom.

"Put me down!"

"Aye, I'll put you down," he grumbled, dumping me onto the bed.

I bounced off the mattress, then lay there, breathless for a moment, blinking up at him before scrambling into a sitting position.

Shoving the hair from my face, I seethed, "You think you can just manhandle me back in here? What if I don't *want* to be here anymore."

"You do." He pointed at my protruding nipples.

I folded my arms. "It's a biological response to stimuli." I hurled the words he'd once said to me back at him, and the muscle in his jaw ticked. "I want to go back to the other room."

"No, you don't."

Arrogant arse. "And why wouldn't I? Being alone is better than dealing with you."

There was a knock on the door. "Is everything all right in there?" Keir called.

"Fuck off!" Orin yelled while I called back, "Fine. Just dealing with this jackarse!"

Orin glowered at me. "Calling me names now?"

"It wouldn't be the first time," I replied sweetly.

"I should take you over my knee for that disobedience."

Whether it was his words or the way his voice deepened, I didn't know, but suddenly all bravado and bluster left me. My body flushed with heat. I wanted what he was threatening me with. I wanted it all, with him, but I couldn't let him use sex as a distraction. I needed to know what the hell was going on in his head.

I sucked in a shallow breath and pleaded with my body to let my heart stop hammering so hard. "Not until you tell me what's wrong. Why did you recoil when I was only trying to help you? Why did you push me away?"

If his glare before had been cold, it was downright arctic now. "Now isn't the time for this."

"Now is the perfect time for this," I volleyed back. "I left to give you some space, and you come back into the room like a fucking tornado and physically move me back to your room. That's messed up, Orin."

"I am messed up, Fallon," he replied in a mocking tone. "Haven't you learned that yet?"

I knew. I'd learned the lesson. But that didn't mean I was going to let him off without some sort of further explanation. "Not good enough. I want to know more than what you're willing to show the world."

"Why would you want that?"

"Are you fucking kidding me?" I yelled. "Haven't I made myself perfectly obvious?"

This made him frown. "What? That you have a thing for killers?"

"I have a thing for *you*, Orin. I want to know you, but you're keeping me at arm's length here. I don't know what else you want from me besides my submission."

He stared at me for a moment before rasping out words I never thought I'd hear. "I want you. All of you. In all the ways possible, but I can't let you have all of me."

"Why not?"

His eyes became unfocused as if he were lost in the past. "Because there's a monster inside me. There's a darkness that swirls around my heart and eats away at my soul. Because every person I've allowed to get close to me either goes away or fucks me over. I don't want that to be your fate, Fallon."

I blinked rapidly at his words—at his confession. Wetting my lips, I asked, "You think I would fuck you over?"

He threw me a caustic look. "Everyone eventually fucks me over."

"If that's true, then why the hell do you want me here, in

your bedroom, in your bed."

"Because."

He said it like that was all the explanation I needed. "Because?"

He ran a hand through his hair and glowered at me. "I need you beside me. I need to know you're safe, and the only way I can do that is by having you here in the room with me."

I didn't say anything in reply. There was nothing I could say. He had laid his fears out to me, and I had to accept them. Were they rational? Absolutely not, but if staying close to him helped ease his fears, I could do that.

I slid from the bed. "Okay."

He arched a brow as he watched me pull the thick quilt back and settle onto the mattress. I looked at him standing there.

"Are you getting in?"

Orin grunted, then came a little closer. He had on a pair of sweats that were hanging deliciously low on his hips, and as he came up beside the bed, I wanted to run my tongue down the deep V that was carved into his hip.

When he seemed to stall at that point, I patted the mattress beside me. When he still didn't move, I lay down and rolled over onto my side, giving him my back. The man was like a skittish animal that couldn't seem to trust that I wasn't going to hurt him.

Eventually, the bed dipped, and the scent of cedar wrapped around me. I sighed deeply, so content to be close to him again. The warmth of his body was an assault down my spine, covering me, and wrapping me up. I let my eyes drift shut, let my breathing even out, but they opened once more when I felt Orin's arm snake around my waist and pull me back against his chest.

We were touching from shoulder to thigh, my ass pulled in close to his pelvis, his chest pressing against my shoulder blades. I thought that might be the extent of his touching until he dropped his head into my hair and inhaled deeply.

The sound he made lit me on fire—part moan, part groan, part sigh of relief. His impressive length started to press against my ass. I wriggled, unable to help it. Orin's fingers tightened.

"Stop that. Things are already hard. You're making them harder by rubbing your gorgeous arse against me like that."

I bit my lip. "Sorry. Won't happen again."

But it did happen again, and I wasn't even ashamed of myself. The feel of his body wrapped around me made me light up inside. I yelped, suddenly, when he swatted my ass, sending fire and lust streaking through me.

His fingers dug into my hip. "Stop. Moving."

"I can't help it. There's something hard and insistent prodding me."

"I'll give you hard and insistent," he muttered under his breath.

He pulled me in even tighter to his hips, and I knew he wanted to take more from me, but he was too afraid to ask for it, so I had to be the instigator.

"If you want to fuck me, you can," I said.

He growled. "If I wanted to fuck you, I wouldn't be asking you first. Those little sleep shorts you insist on wearing would be on the ground already, and my dick would be so far inside you, you'd feel me there for weeks after."

A stupid needy whimper left me, earning me a husky chuckle.

"You like the sound of that, Filly?" he asked, his breath brushing over the bare skin on my neck. "You want me to impale your cunt? Fuck you so hard your pussy would be begging only for me from now on?"

I clutched at the arm around my waist, digging in my nails. "Yes. I want all of you, Orin."

His grip suddenly tightened, and he pulled away slightly. "You don't want all of me. My darkness will destroy you."

Frowning, I turned around and looked at him. "Why do you say things like that?"

"Like what?"

"Like I don't want you. I do want you, Orin. I want you so fucking bad that sometimes it hurts seeing you look at me like you want to touch me, but you always stop yourself."

"It would be better if I left you alone." His tone was serious, but the lust in his eyes was unmistakable. Running a hand along my jaw, he tightened his fingers. "It would be better if I didn't use you as the fuck doll I want to use you as … but I can't leave you alone. Fuck knows I've tried."

My mouth opened, but no words came out. I could hardly breathe as the meaning of his declaration hit me.

"You said you know how I fuck? How I cause pain to my partners?"

"Yes."

"And you still want that? You want to experience that with me?"

"Yes. I want all of you, whether it's good or bad, gentle or rough. I want to know what you like."

His hand wrapped around my hip in a bruising grip. "You shouldn't say that to me."

"Why not?"

"My self-control is holding on by a fucking tether, and one word from you will break it."

My breath was shaky as it left my lungs. Biting my bottom lip, I said, "Take me as you want to. Use me as a fuck doll. If you want to hurt me, hurt me. I'll take you whatever way I can have you, Orin, but please let us have a chance."

I didn't know where the words had come from, only that they were true. I wanted all of him. Every dark corner of his heart. Every insidious thought he had. I wanted him to use me like he needed to. It was fucked up, but then again, so was I.

His pupils dilated so wide that I could hardly see where his irises began. "Do you remember our safe word?"

"Yes."

"Say it."

"Bullet."

"If at any time you want to stop, say *bullet* to me, and I'll stop."

We were going to do this. Holy shit, my body was on fire with anticipation. "Okay."

"Afterwards, I'm going to walk away from you, Fallon. After I fuck you like I've wanted to since the first moment I saw you, I'm going to walk away."

The feeling of anticipation dissipated like smoke, and all I was left with was a feeling of dread. "W-what?"

"This will change everything between us. I couldn't handle

the thought of seeing you again after I've broken you. I may be a hard bastard, but I can't do that. Do you understand?"

"Yes, but—"

"Enough talking then," he said, cutting me off. His tone had deepened into that dominating one he'd used before, and God help me, my body responded to it. "Take off all your clothes."

I slid from the bed, stripping down to nothing, then stood there for his pleasure. He drank me in, and I noticed his cock getting longer and harder beneath his sweats.

"Touch yourself. Make yourself come while I watch."

Swallowing hard, I traced my hand down between my breasts, along my stomach, and between the juncture of my thighs. I was already wet, and my fingers slid through the slickness that had pooled there.

Rolling my fingers across my clit, I bit back a gasp, loving how this was making me feel. Orin's eyes on me were hot and ravenous. Despite the heat in his gaze, he watched me in a detached sort of way, and I knew it was because he was still fighting this thing between us. My eyes drew down to his hips, where his cock was twitching. The thought of him filling me added another erotic layer to my fantasy, and I picked up the pace against my clit.

I stared at Orin until the pleasure became too much, and my eyes slid shut.

"Open your eyes. Look at me when you come."

With a gasp, I refocused on his face. He was still watching me, his cock like a steel rod between his legs. He hadn't touched himself yet. Hadn't moved from his position at all. He was simply watching me.

My fingers were working overtime when his gaze moved from my face to my pussy, and a tiny whimper escaped me.

Before he could ask, I slid two fingers inside me, letting out a groan of pleasure. My hand had nothing of Orin's cock, but it was a start. I grew wetter, my arousal dripping down the inside of my thighs as I pushed and thrust myself closer to orgasm.

"Please, sir," I said, the words popping out unbidden. "Please, can I come?"

His mouth parted. He nodded, then watched as my hips began to flex and retreat, flex and retreat. I imagined they were his fingers buried deep inside me. I imagined his mouth on my breasts, taunting my stiff nipples into impossibly hard peaks. I wanted his touch. I came with a cry that left my knees weak, and I had to catch myself on the edge of the bed as I continued to come, continued to look at Orin with dark hunger in his eyes.

When my pleasure finally ebbed away, I was wrung out, leaning on my elbows against the mattress. The air felt cool against my heated skin.

"Stand up."

I did, wobbling on my feet.

He licked his lips. "Do it again."

"What?"

"Make yourself come again. While I watch. While you watch me stroke my cock. While you wish it was buried deep inside that greedy pussy of yours."

He wanted me to come. Again? My body was oversensitive from the pleasure that had just been unleashed on it.

"I can't."

He pulled down the front of his sweats, releasing the thick head of his cock. "You can't?"

I shook my head. "My body won't let me."

"It's not your body anymore, Fallon. It's *mine*, and I want you to come again. Now." He spat into his hand and ran his palm along the length of his erection. He kept his eyes on me the whole time, watching me, waiting for me to comply. When he reached the crown of his cock, he twisted his wrist, making his head kick back. I watched his Adam's apple bob and brought my hand between my legs once more.

I worked my fingers against my clit, feeling myself getting wetter and wetter. Orin was like my own personal porn channel, and I studied the way he moved, the noises he made, the way his eyes got darker and darker with lust the closer I came to finishing.

"Are you close?" he asked, unable to hide the strain in his voice.

"Yes."

"Yes, what?"

"Yes, sir. I'm close. I'm close."

He got onto his knees, still working his cock with his hand. A drop of pre-cum glistened on the end, and I wanted to taste it so badly.

"Don't stop, Filly," he murmured, seeing how badly my legs and arms were shaking. "Don't stop until I tell you to." A grunt left his lips as he increased his pace. The muscles in his neck and abdomen strained with the pleasure he was unleashing on his body, and by proxy, my body clenched down tight.

"Please, sir."

He got to his feet, balanced on the bed, and brought his cock close to my mouth. "I want you to suck on my cock until I come, then you can come."

I nodded obediently, opening my mouth and letting him slam it to the back of my throat. I gagged. Orin threaded his fingers through my hair, holding me close to his hips, forcing more and more down my throat.

"That's it, my little whore. Take it all for me."

His words, although depraved, set off an explosion in me. My orgasm was steaming toward me, but I had to wait. I had to let him come first.

Relief flooded me when his hips punched one last time and he emptied himself onto the back of my tongue and throat. The taste of him triggered my own orgasm, and I moaned my release around him.

Orin's hand in my hair tightened, tugging at the strands and heightening my release. "Don't swallow," he commanded. If it was possible, the pleasure from my orgasm doubled, and I came even harder, my moans dragging out Orin's pleasure and sheering off any semblance of civility from his face as he completely dominated me.

When the last drop had been wrung from his body, he tapped my jaw. "Open. I want to see my cum on your tongue."

I complied, showing him my prize for being such a good girl.

Shoving a finger inside my mouth, he touched what he'd left behind, then roughly commanded, "Swallow."

I did, knowing I would never belong to another man after this.

22
ORIN

FUCK, THIS WOMAN WAS GOING TO BE THE death of me. As I watched her swallow my cum, the feeling of possession that had staked a claim on my body began to infiltrate into my heart. I'd told Fallon that after tonight I would walk away from her. I would rather know she was alive and hating me than by my side and in fucking danger every minute of the day.

Stepping off the bed, I kicked off my sweats and then went into the closet to pull out a length of shibari rope. When I reemerged, she was still standing in the same place, her skin flushed with sweat, her eyes dark with lust. When she saw the rope, she cocked her head to the side.

"Are you going to tie me up?"

"Yes."

"Is this what you do with all your toys?"

"They're all bound in some way or another." I ran my

hand over the rope coiled in my hand. "But I want your beautiful body restrained by this." I pointed to a spot on the floor in front of me. "Come here."

She walked toward me, and I drank my fill of her beautiful body. I loved her curves and the way her waist looked tiny against the swell of her hips and breasts. She was my ideal woman, which was why I always chose women who were the complete opposite.

She looked up at me with such trust, and I never wanted to take that away from her.

"What's the safe word?" I asked again.

"Bullet."

"Use it if something doesn't feel good. I'll stop in an instant."

She dropped her gaze. "Yes, sir."

With my finger under her chin, I tilted her face back up to me. "I mean it, Fallon. If something doesn't feel good to you, then say so. The scene will end. You won't be punished for stopping things."

She nibbled on her bottom lip, then nodded. "Okay."

I started out slow, binding her chest with knots and ties, creating the diamond pattern across her collarbones and around her breasts. I had never allowed someone to tie me up, so I had no concept of how she was feeling right now, but all I knew was that she looked like fucking perfection.

Hooking my finger under the edge of the ropes, I tugged her closer, seeing how rapid her breathing had become. "How does that feel?"

"Restrictive, but … good."

Drawing my fingers along her skin, I dragged the tip

of my index finger over her taunt nipple protruding from between the diamond pattern, then squeezed it between my thumb and forefinger until she moaned and tried to squirm away.

I pinched a little harder. "Do you need to say the safe word?"

"No," she whispered, panting softly.

Satisfied that she was still willing for me to continue, I grabbed another length of rope and wrapped her upper arms, pinning them to her side so she couldn't move the whole top half of her body. The red shibari rope contrasted with the milky smoothness of her skin. Skimming my fingers across her restrained body, her breathing accelerated as she stared at the dark look in my eyes. She was trussed up and helpless, and a frisson of pure lust shot through my body.

Grabbing hold of the rope between her breasts, I nudged her backward toward the bed. She whimpered a little—accompanied by a soft mewling—as I urged her to sit down on the edge of the mattress. I got to my knees in front of her, my greedy gaze drinking up the sight of her glistening pussy.

"Is this drenched for me," I asked, sliding two fingers through her folds.

She gasped, pushing back against my thrusting digits. "Yes."

"Does this cunt want to be fucked? Will you be my good little whore and take everything I have to give you?"

She nodded, her eyes rolling back this time as I circled her clit with my thumb. I could feel her inner walls already clenching tight around me, and I withdrew them from her body. She moaned.

"You don't come until I tell you to. Understood?"

"Yes, sir."

In my head, I had a plan to put her over my knee, punish her for making me want her this badly, but as I stared at her breasts restrained by the red rope, I wanted to worship her instead. Reaching out, I pinched one jutting nipple, making her gasp.

"I love that fucking sound you make," I murmured, then pinched again. She mewled this time, the sound of it shooting down to my semihard dick. Rising to my feet, I stood in front of her, bringing her mouth close to my cock once more. I told Fallon to open her mouth.

"Suck me until I'm hard again, then I'll fuck your cunt like you've been wanting me to."

Opening her mouth, she took me in. I let her set the pace this time, letting her bob her head. Without the use of her hands, she couldn't lean too far forward, or she would lose her balance. Reaching down between us, I pinched her nipple again, her responding moan humming through my shaft.

It didn't take long before my cock was full and ready. Easing Fallon onto her back, I hooked my hands under her knees and dragged her to the edge of the bed. Stuffing a pillow beneath her back, it elevated her hips, putting her soaked opening at my hip height. Rubbing my thumb along her clit, I watched through hooded eyes as she writhed against me. Her cunt brushed up against my cock, and I dragged the head through her folds, knowing it would drive her insane.

"I'm going to fuck you bare, Filly," I told her.

She nodded. "Please, sir."

There wasn't even a hint of hesitation. "I'm going to fill your greedy pussy with my cum over and over again. I'm going to *own* it."

"It's yours, sir," she whimpered again, rolling her hips against me, trying to find the friction she so desperately craved.

Gripping my cock, I slapped the crown against her clit once, then fed it into her drenched opening. Her inner walls spasmed around my length, clamping down, holding tight. The groan that left my throat was like no sound I'd ever made before. It was feral and wild, writhing with lust. It was so fucking good that I had to do it again.

Pulling out, I slid right back in, admiring the way her cunt ate my cock. My gaze switched to her face, and I found her staring at me in wonder.

"You okay, Fallon?"

She nodded. "More than okay." She writhed her hips. "But please, fuck me. Fuck me hard. Make me forget that there was anyone else before you."

Just thinking about other men being where I was right now made me see fucking red. "I'll kill any other man who comes near you again, Filly. You hear me?"

She nodded, her eyes shuttering when I hit a spot deep inside her. Her inner walls clamped down for a moment before releasing me, and I began to thrust inside her. Deeper. Pushing further. Wanting to claim every last inch of her. If I was going to let her go after this, I needed to remember how she felt against me. I needed to know that she would think of me every time she took a step. I needed her …

Shutting my eyes tightly against the onslaught of all the things I wanted and never had, I focused on giving her everything. What I needed more though was a quick change in position. Yanking the pillow out from under her, I helped roll her over, then propped her hips up once more. I stroked her ass, landing a few blows that made her hips writhe.

With one final spank, I slid into her slick channel once more. She felt tighter this way, her legs pinned together beneath her. It added a whole new element of eroticism too. Her face was pressed to the mattress, but her blue eyes were on me. She looked lost in the sensations, floating away in some sort of subspace that I had never experienced in all my life. She looked free.

I massaged her ass, my fingers dipping between the crease of her cheeks and finding her tight hole. Pushing the tip of my thumb into her opening, I felt more than heard her surprise. Her whole body stiffened at the intrusion.

"Shh, it's okay," I told her, still rubbing, still fucking into her. "I won't take this tonight."

And the reality that I would never be able to take it hit me like a fucking freight train. After tonight, there would be no more Fallon. No more *us*. This was our one and only night to fuck, and the fact that she was bound right now tarnished it in some way.

I slid out of her and turned her around, quickly undoing the ties on the rope. She watched me warily, the question burning in her eyes. What was I doing? I was getting what I wanted, but I was also giving her what she needed.

Rubbing at her wrists, I brought one of her arms to my mouth and placed a gentle kiss to her skin where the rope had left an indentation. She gasped in surprise, and I hated that a kiss had been the thing to widen her eyes.

"What …? I thought …"

"I do, but I don't like seeing you bound like this."

Taking her by the ankles, I split her thighs wide, then sank into her once again. She reached out and grabbed me by my forearms, the sensation of being touched not making me recoil now. It made me come to life. An inferno of need and want, and all expectations burned to the ground.

She dug in her nails, urging me to fuck her harder, deeper. To mark her. I pulled her closer, my thrusts shallow to hit a spot inside her that I knew would have her coming undone.

And she did.

Beautifully.

When I was sure the last of her pleasure had ebbed away, I stood her up, still impaled on my dick, and took her to the ground. Spinning her over once again, I felt like a wild animal in rut, pressing her into the carpet, holding her in place with one hand on the back of her neck and the other on the small of her back. I plunged into her body without mercy. Fallon moaned, pushing back against me, trying to find more friction, and fuck, I wanted to get her there.

Dragging up her hips, I pounded into her, my body poised over hers to create more pressure, more thrust. Another position. This time against the wall. Her face pressed into the plaster, her hips out—her body a beautiful shape.

Wrapping a hand around her throat, I brought my lips to her ear, whispering, "I want to fill you with my cum. I want it to mark your skin. I want you to never clean it off. I just want you."

"Yes," she replied on a breathy whisper. "Take whatever you want from me, Orin. Take it all."

Her words sparked a change in me, and my hips took over, slamming into her, reaching the end of her body and drawing a cry from her lips. I bit the side of her neck, holding her flesh between my teeth as I came with a roar, emptying myself into her and claiming her as my own.

I let go of her neck, hanging my head and letting my breath barrel from me. Fallon was pinned between me and the wall, and I liked the way her body was slick with sweat. I stepped backward, reaching for her, but when she faced me, I recoiled …

Because tears were streaking down her cheeks.

23
FALLON

I WASN'T SURE WHY I WAS CRYING—I JUST KNEW I was. And by the look of horror on Orin's face, he was as alarmed by it as I was. He reached up a hand but dropped it before he could make contact. He looked magnificent, dripping with sweat. His body had worked hard to wring every last drop of pleasure from me, but the expression on his face sent a chill down my spine.

"Orin," I sniffled, hating that I was crying. I felt amazing. Better than amazing, so the tears made absolutely no sense to me. I had just been fucked into oblivion by a man who claimed he was a danger to me, but the way he treated my body—although roughly sometimes—didn't tell me that. He may have been filthy with his words, but he always made sure I was okay.

"Orin, talk to me." I wiped the tears away with the back of my hand.

He stepped back, still staring at me like he was regretting every single thing that happened over the last three-quarters of an hour when all I wanted was to do it all again.

"Please."

That one word seemed to break the spell. His dark eyes cleared and fixed on my face. "You should've used the safe word." Yanking his sweats back on, he stormed from the room, leaving me trembling, naked, and vulnerable. For a moment, all I could do was stand there until I shifted into action, snatched up one of his shirts, and slid it over my head. I yanked on the door and strode out into the hallway, wondering which way he'd gone. Farther down, a door slammed shut, and I walked in that direction.

As I rounded a corner, there were raised voices.

"I want her out of here." That was Orin's snarled voice. "I want her fucking gone."

I crept closer to find that the door hadn't closed properly. Keeping out of sight, I leaned against the wall and listened.

"What the fuck is up with you?" Finnan replied. There was a creak of leather and the *shhhkt* of a lighter. The smell of cigar smoke wafted out a moment later. "Did the bastard you tortured in the basement not bleed enough for you?"

"Fuck you, Finnan," Orin replied in a voice I'd never heard before. It was terrifyingly threatening. "Fallon. I want her gone. Away from me."

"Why? You yourself said she was in danger from the Bèar and now the Fiach clan. She has skills we can use."

"I don't care."

The leather creaked again, and I heard footsteps move around the room. Crystal hitting crystal sounded and then a splashing sound. "Have you fucked her? Is that why you want her gone?"

"That's none of your fucking business, Finnan, and you know it. Who I fuck and how doesn't concern you."

"I remember. You made it quite clear to my father when you joined the clan. No questions. Look the other way. The same went for the kills."

Orin was silent.

"Why is it that you cut out the tongues of your victims? Why is that the first thing you do?"

"You don't want to go there with me right now." I could hear the tension in his voice, imagine his hands curling into fists at his sides.

"Oh? I think I do. If you want Fallon to disappear, I could always give Velvet a new girl."

Velvet? That was the name of that horrible strip club the clan owned. Had Orin wanted me to go there? Was that ever an option? If it was, I'd played straight into his fucked-up plan by practically throwing myself at him.

A chair slid against the floor, then clattered to the ground. The next time Orin spoke, his voice was hard. Black. Savage.

"Talk about her like that again, and you'll be the next one to lose your tongue," he hissed.

Finnan's replying chuckle set the fine hairs on the back of my neck on end. "I see she's already gotten under your skin. Is that why you want her gone?"

"My reasons are my own."

There was a beat of silence before Finnan spoke again. "You want her gone. She's gone."

My fist came to my mouth as the effect of Orin's wishes

and Finnan's words struck home. I didn't want to hear anymore. I couldn't. Turning, I rushed back down the hall to the bedroom, where I stuffed a duffel bag with all the clothes I had. It was late. I had no phone. No money and no way out of here. It would be a cold day in fucking hell before I asked Orin for one single thing, so I tiptoed downstairs and to the front door, jerking to a stop at the sound of Keir's voice.

"Going somewhere?" he asked.

I peered at him through the doorway of the living room, finding him lounging on the couch with one arm draped over the back of the cushions. He had a beer in his other hand and wore sweats and a black t-shirt.

"I …" What the hell was I going to say? "I need to leave."

Keir's brows shot up, the ring through one of them catching the light. "It's nearly midnight, lass."

Shifting the bag higher onto my shoulder, I said, "I realize this."

He leaned his big body forward and placed the bottle on the table. "Does Orin know you're leaving?"

"Orin doesn't give a shit about me. I want to leave, and that's all there is to it."

"Okay, do you need a ride somewhere?"

I clutched at the handles more tightly. I had to remind myself that Keir had been nothing but nice to me all this time, and although I didn't trust him, I didn't think he'd try and hurt me intentionally.

He seemed to see all these thoughts flash across my face because he added, "How about you drive. I'll sit in the back, then whenever you get to wherever you want to be, I can return here with the car. Does that sound okay?"

Licking my lips nervously, I tried to think of another work-around but came up empty. I nodded. "Yes."

He smiled at me. "Okay. Let me grab some car keys, and we can go."

I watched him stand to his full height, then walk toward me. He held his hand out for my bag, which I clutched even more tightly. I thought he'd be offended by the rejection, but he smiled and walked past me to the entry hall.

There was a small locker on the wall. He reached in and pulled out a set of keys, dangling the metal ring on his index finger. "Are you ready?"

I nodded. With one final glance over my shoulder, I followed Keir out into the night and to the Rover parked at the front of the turning circle. After unlocking it, he handed me the keys without question and hopped into the rear seat. I stood there a moment, staring up at the compound before shoving my duffel onto the passenger seat and climbing into the driver's side.

The engine sounded like a gunshot in the still night, and as I peeled out of the driveway, something in the rearview mirror caught my attention.

It was Orin.

He was standing on the front doorstep looking pissed. I kept my eyes on him until he disappeared around the gate. Letting out a breath, I hit the accelerator, propelling us toward Galway.

"Where are we going?" Keir asked from the back.

My eyes cut to him, then back to the road. "I don't know. I don't think I can go home."

"No, you can't," he said thoughtfully. "There is one place you can go where you'll be safe."

"Where?"

"Back to Sloane's apartment. You went there, right?"

I had been there. It was safe, tucked away on the top floor, but wouldn't Orin find me there? Wouldn't he think to look? Or did he not care, and me disappearing on my own was the solution to all his problems.

"Do you have a key?"

"Yeah. You can stay there a couple of days until you figure things out."

Figure things out. I mulled those words over in my head until I wanted to scream. I thought I had figured things out, but Orin had to change all that. He didn't want me. After I'd given myself to him, he didn't want me, and it was that rejection that cut me so deeply.

I turned in the direction of the waterfront, finding the underground garage opening and descending into the depths. I had to stop when I reached a gate.

"There's a remote for the gate on your visor," Keir said. "The key is there too."

Flipping it down, the key slid out first and I caught it. I found the remote for the gate and clicked the button. It began to open slowly, leaving me anxious as I waited.

"Orin's going to go berserk, you know," Keir said.

My gaze flickered from the gate to his face in the back seat. "Not my problem."

"It might be your problem. He's in fucking love with you."

My eyes widened at that statement. "That's impossible. A

man like him doesn't love. How could he when he has no heart?"

Keir nodded like this wasn't news to him at all. "He hasn't told you about his past then?"

"No, and it's not my business to know about it."

"It might enlighten you on why he does what he does."

I pinned him through the mirror. "Why do you care whether I hear him out or not?"

He shrugged, giving me that smile again. "I've never seen him so protective of a woman. I think you'd be good for him if only he let himself trust."

The gate finally opened, and I drove through. "What do you know about his past?"

"A little."

"But you're not going to tell me."

"It's not my business to tell you. They're his secrets to keep."

And didn't that make me despise him even more. I had told him about the rape. I had opened up to him about everything, but he'd kept his mouth shut about his own dark past. I wanted to be angry, but then I remembered I didn't owe anything to Orin. I had saved his life, and he had saved mine. We were even now, and anything else wasn't important.

I pulled the car into a parking spot near an elevator and shut off the engine. Without looking back at Keir, I grabbed my duffel and got out. I stepped up to the elevator panel, pressed the up button, and then waited.

Behind me, Keir got out of the car.

"Will you tell him where I am?" I asked, even though I

hated myself for caring if he did.

"Not if you don't want me to."

His answer made me turn around and look at him. "Your loyalty would be to me?"

He shrugged. "He's been an arsehole. Why should I help him?"

The elevator car arrived, the doors opening with a quiet *whoosh*. I stepped inside and looked at Keir but stopped the doors from closing.

"I'd like to call my brother," I said, wondering why I was telling him at all.

He nodded and stepped toward me. Reaching into his pocket, he pulled out a phone and handed it to me.

I glanced at it, then back at him. "You're giving me your phone?"

"It's a burner," he replied with a shrug. Then he reached into his other pocket and pulled out a wad of cash. He handed it to me too. "So, you can feed yourself, lass."

Reaching out, I took the money, squeezing it tightly in my fist. "Thank you."

The elevator alarm began to ring, and I jerked my hand away. Keir slipped back into the car and turned on the engine. The elevator doors slid shut on him backing from the space and driving away.

24

ORIN

I HAVEN'T FELT THIS OUT OF CONTROL SINCE HER.

My rage was channeled differently this time, though, and it was directed squarely at me. Watching Fallon leave in that Rover felt like my soul was being ripped apart. After speaking to Finnan and being defiant in my need to send her away somewhere I wouldn't have to see her, I'd vacillated between wanting her gone forever and never letting her go.

The problem was I'd seen her tears. I'd fucking hurt her while we were together and that had been the one thing I hadn't wanted to happen.

Was I fucking surprised that she'd escaped the first chance she had?

No, but that didn't mean that her leaving still didn't hurt like a motherfucker.

After Finnan listened to my demands with a barely

disguised grin on his face, he told me what I had to do. After what happened in Westport, he wanted to know if any other strategic towns had been flipped by the Fiach Clan. I was supposed to be gone already—heading north—but I couldn't bring myself to leave without waiting a little longer.

Without holding out hope that Fallon would return.

I stopped pacing the living room when I heard a car pull up.

"Fallon." Her name was a whispered plea on my lips, and I raced outside. She had come back. She had changed …

"Where the fuck have you been?" I barked at Keir as he got out of the Rover.

He glanced at me briefly, then away. "Out."

My instincts started to blare in warning. "Out *where?*"

Walking slowly toward the door, he shoved his hands into the pockets of his sweats. "Just out."

"With Fallon? Where the fuck is she? Where did she go?" My monster bellowed inside me, and I grabbed Keir by the shirt and threw him against the entryway wall. Shoving my face close to his I demanded, "Where is she? Did you hurt her?"

Keir's expression looked sad. "I didn't fucking hurt her, Orin. Why would I hurt her?"

I'm not you.

They were the words he hadn't said, but I heard them loud and clear.

The darkness inside me was in a frenzy now. "Where. Is. She?"

He sighed, resigned, and completely unaware of how close

to losing it I really was. "She's safe, okay? She wasn't going to stay here so I made sure she went somewhere secure."

"Where. Is. She?"

"I can't tell you that."

My patience was running dangerously low. "Are you willing to fucking die to keep her location a secret?"

"Orin, man, threatening me with death only proves that you don't deserve her."

Pulling the Glock from the small of my back, I pressed it to the side of his head. When I spoke, my voice was a dangerous growl. "You will tell me where she is."

The bastard wasn't even spooked by his impending death.

"And then what? What will you do? Beg for her forgiveness? Excuse me for not believing that's fucking possible."

If Fallon wanted me to beg, I would have. If she wanted me to bleed for my sins, I would do that, too. I realized then that there wasn't anything I wouldn't do for her.

And now, I had lost her.

Reholstering my gun, I stalked back to my room and slammed the door. The only problem was everywhere I looked, all I could see was Fallon. She was there on the bed, on the wall I'd pressed her against, on the floor where I'd taken her like a fucking animal. Her ylang-ylang scent tainted the air, making every breath I drew in torturous to bear.

What the fuck was I thinking in sending her away?

The truth was, I wasn't thinking. I'd been terrified by the fact that she'd burrowed into my life so completely in such a short span of time that I had to exorcise her from my life before she hurt me—like everyone else had hurt me.

But this hollow feeling inside me felt like a chasm.

And the only way to fill it would be to get her back.

My anger boiled out of my room when I opened the door and stalked down the hall. Downstairs, I snatched the keys from the hook by the front door, walked outside, and got into the Rover. I would find Fallon if it was the last thing I did. And when I found her, I'd bring her home.

SIX HOURS LATER, THE SUN HAD RISEN ON GALWAY, and I was nowhere closer to finding Fallon. She was a ghost, disappearing into the ether and taking my cold black heart with her. How the fuck had I let it get this far? How the fuck had she gotten past all my defenses? I pulled up at the waterfront in Galway and sat there, staring out at the ocean. The fishing boats were coming in with their holds full of fish, the fishermen on the decks preparing lines and securing equipment.

Inside my pants pocket, my phone rang.

"What?" I demanded without looking at the screen.

It was Finnan.

"Where are you?"

"Galway."

"I told you to head north."

Fuck. "I'll leave after I take care of some personal business."

"Nothing is more important than the clan. I'll expect an update tonight."

He hung up before I could tell him to go and fuck himself.

A second later, my phone pinged with a message. I glanced down at the screen to find the name of three northern towns that Finnan wanted me to check out first. Castlebar. Charlestown. Tuam.

Gritting my teeth, I shifted the car into drive and headed north out of town.

It took me over an hour to get to Charlestown. Located on the County Mayo side of the border, it technically belonged to the Mac Tíre Clan, and it shouldn't have been compromised. Parking at the local pub, I stepped into the dark space and surveyed the patrons lingering there so early in the morning.

The bartender looked at me warily. "Can I help ya?" he asked, rubbing at a glass anxiously, his eyes darting to a younger man who was feeding fresh wood into the hearth on the opposite side of the room.

"You know who I am?" I asked, stepping closer.

"Aye. You're one of the Mac Tíre."

Reaching around to the small of my back, I grasped the grip of my Glock. "And do your loyalties, and those of the town, still lie with the wolf?"

The bartender put the glass down and fixed me with an intense stare. "Aye, my loyalties do, but Clan Fiach has been aiding the town the last few months. We thought the territories had shifted in ownership."

I ground my teeth together until my jaw hurt. "No," I replied, my voice low with barely contained anger. Fuck Finnan and his indecision. "No change."

The man's eyes darted to my bent arm. "We don't want no trouble here."

"You won't have any if you call Velvet in Galway the next time one of the Fiach Clan come in here. Speak to Mary."

He swallowed, his eyes darting back to the younger man. "Aye, I reckon I can do that."

Releasing my grip on the butt of the gun, I brought up my hand to show him I was unarmed, then stalked from the pub.

I got back in the car and drove southeast to Castlebar. After speaking to the locals, it was clear they hadn't been approached by Clan Fiach. The same could be said about Taum, but the fact that the border town of Charlestown was compromised did not bode well.

By the time I got back to Galway, the sun was setting on what had been a rare sunny day. My phone rang as I pulled into the parking lot beside the harbor, hoping to catch a glimpse of Fallon somewhere.

"What?"

"Anything?" Finnan asked.

I relayed what I'd found out.

"Fuck! That motherfucking, cocksucking bastard!"

I waited for Finnan to gather himself before asking, "What now?"

"I need to know about all the border towns. Go to every single fucking one and find out where their loyalties lie."

"I'll leave first thing in the morning."

"*Now*, Lynch. You leave fucking now!"

He hung up, and I threw my phone onto the seat beside me. It would take me a fucking week to go to each town and investigate. It wouldn't be as easy as it was today either. I didn't want to go. I wanted to fix things with Fallon, but

maybe a week would give her some time to cool off.
Maybe this was for the best.

25

FALLON

ONE WEEK LATER...

IT HAD BEEN A WEEK SINCE I'D SEEN ORIN.

A week since I'd seen anyone belonging to the clan, although I suspected someone was watching the apartment and following me whenever I left. Keir must've kept up his end of the bargain and not told Orin where I was, otherwise, I had no doubt he would've been hammering on the door and demanding I let him in.

I started going crazy just sitting around and waiting on the second day in the apartment, so I'd gone to college to see how much work I had missed. It had been close to two weeks since I'd last attended, and I had a lot of study to catch up on. Which was how I spent my days. Studying, and trying incredibly hard to ignore the gnawing ache that had set up behind my ribcage.

"Want to get a coffee?"

I blinked rapidly and turned my head in the direction of

whoever had spoken to me. The noise of the lecture hall came back to me in stereo, and I looked around the busy space.

"Fallon? Did you hear me? Want to get a coffee?" Molly smiled at me, brushing some of her black hair off her shoulders and behind her ear. She was a third-year student, but crossed enough paths socially that we'd hit it off. When I didn't answer right away, a frown marred her features. "Are you okay? You're not feeling unwell again, are you?"

Unwell.

That's what I'd told everyone when I showed up for classes after a two-week absence. It was the best I could do without revealing everything that had happened to me.

"Yes. No. I mean, I feel fine. Coffee. Coffee sounds good." I rose from my seat, stuffing the notepad and pen I'd had to buy before class into a bag. Thank God Keir had thought to give me some money, even though I still felt strange about taking it in the first place.

We left the college building and walked across the road to the café where most students went before and after class. We got a table near the back, and Molly joined the queue of students and professionals waiting to order.

Pulling out the burner Keir had given me, I saw there was a missed call from Grayson. Hitting the call button, I pressed the device to my ear and waited.

"Fallon."

It was just my name, but it instantly soothed my jangled nerves. "Grayson."

"How are you? Has that bastard Lynch tried to contact you again?"

I'd told my brother almost everything that had happened between us—everything except Orin and mine's physical relationship.

"Orin kept me safe, Grayson."

"And for that he has my thanks, but he's the fucking Reaper. All he knows how to do is kill. He must've had an ulterior motive."

We'd gone over this a dozen times already, but Grayson was always trying to find out what Orin's angle was. The truth was, there was no angle. We'd both developed feelings for the other that should've never been possible, but life-and-death situations certainly had a way of bringing two people together. He and Sloane would know.

"I don't want to talk about him anymore." He sighed. "How are classes? Did you miss a lot of work while you were with *him*?"

"Class was good. And yes, I did, but I can catch up. It'll distract me until you and Sloane get home."

"Thank fuck you could stay at the apartment," he muttered. "Have you been able to get to the house at all?"

"Orin seemed to think I couldn't. He said it wasn't safe. That Mannix King would have men watching the place."

"He's right. I don't want you going anywhere near that place again."

I bit my lip and flicked my gaze up to see how Molly was progressing in the line. "What about all our stuff? The photographs of ma and da?"

"I'll swing by the house when I get back and collect the sentimental things. Forget about everything else. Buy new clothes. The clan is taking care of you financially?"

"Keir gave me some money last week. It's starting to run low, though."

He grunted. "I'll call Keir and let him know you need some more."

"Thank you," I whispered. Molly was at the counter now, flirting with the barista taking her order.

"If you need me to come home early, I can you know."

Tears pooled behind my eyes. "I know."

"Just say the word. Sloane and I will be on the next flight back."

"No. I'm fine, Gray. Honestly. I just need to focus on my studies."

I heard the soft sound of Sloane's voice in the background, then Grayson's warm reply. To me, he said, "I have to go. We're having dinner with Sloane's mother and partner."

"Okay."

"Okay." He hesitated, then said, "I love you, Filly. Thank fuck you're safe."

"Love you, too."

I hung up the phone just as Molly returned to the table holding two steaming mugs of coffee. She placed one down in front of me, then took the seat opposite.

"So, tell me, who's the guy?"

My heart thudded, my mouth turning desert dry. "What guy?"

She actually rolled her eyes at me. "Please, Fallon. The guy you were just speaking to."

"Oh. No. That was my brother."

She sighed, her expression taking on a dreamy sort of look. "It's a shame he's married."

Molly, along with a couple of other friends, had met both Grayson and Sloane at the nightclub we went to a few months back. It had been my first time out where temptation was everywhere, but I hadn't felt compelled to have a drink or do drugs that night. Nor any other night since.

Molly took a draw from the top of her mug. "Is there any man in your life?"

"Is there in yours?" I shot back, enjoying the look of disgust arc over her face.

She was, for all intents and purposes, a permanent flirt. She never had a long-term relationship, happy to have flings instead. She claimed she didn't have time for anything more than that, but I could see that deep down she was a romantic who wanted a deeper connection with someone.

Molly smirked. "Touché, Fallon." Placing down her mug, she slumped down further into her seat. "Have you caught up with everything for school? I can help you if you need. I'm sure I can dig out my first-year notes."

"Oh, no, that's okay. I think I have everything under control now. I have a few more hours of study to make up though to be truly back on top of things."

"That flu must've really knocked you around."

I felt my smile wilt. That's what I'd told everyone. That I'd been sick with a flu that just didn't seem to end, but the reality was, my illness was something much more permanent. I was heartsick and couldn't see the end of my recovery.

Molly and I chatted until our coffee cups were drained and there was nothing left to say. I felt like a completely different person from the one I'd been before. I'd been through gunfire, car chases, infernos, and heartbreak. I *was* a different person now.

"Oh my God, who is that?" Molly whispered, and I looked at her before following her line of sight. Keir was standing just inside the door of the café in a pair of faded jeans and a black t-shirt that hugged his broad shoulders. He was scanning the busy space, but when his eyes latched onto mine, he started in our direction with an easy smile.

"Fallon," he said by way of greeting, his dark eyes flickering with interest to Molly. "And who's this?"

"I'm Molly," she said, introducing herself without shame. She stuck out her hand, and he took it, placing a kiss on the back. "And you are?"

"Keir. Pleased to meet you, Molly."

Keir honest-to-God winked at her before releasing her hand. When he returned his gaze to me, his smile was far less flirtatious and much more familial.

"Grayson called and said you needed something."

I needed something? Then I remembered. The money. "Ah, yes. I do."

"Great. Let me walk you back home, and I can get it for you."

Molly's eyes were wide as she watched me rise from my seat. "I'll see you tomorrow?"

"I guess you will." She turned her stunning ocean-blue eyes to Keir, batting her long lashes. "And I hope I get to see you around sometime soon."

"Aye, I'd like that," Keir replied, giving her a lazy grin. "See you, Molly."

After a brief wave, Keir and I were stepping free of the café and walking in the direction of the apartment.

"How much do you need, Fallon?" Keir asked, his regular persona slipping back into place.

"The same as before will be fine. I need to buy a few more clothes, but I can make it stretch."

Shoving a hand into his pocket, he pulled out another wad of cash and started to count the bills. If it was anyone else, I would've warned them that it was dangerous to be so open with the amount of money they were carrying. But Keir wasn't anyone. And Galway belonged to the Mac Tíre Clan.

I watched him count, gaping when he handed me double the amount he had given me last time. I shook my head. "This is too much."

"The clan takes care of their own, lass."

I stared at the notes in my hand. "At what cost though?" I had to ask the question. I couldn't keep staying rent-free in this apartment. I couldn't keep taking their money without giving anything in exchange.

"You're a smart woman, Fallon," Keir said. Reaching inside his jeans pocket, he pulled out a pack of cigarettes and a lighter. He didn't speak again until he'd lit a cigarette and taken a deep pull on the end.

Smoke curled around him as he said, "Finnan's given you two choices. Work at Velvet as a whore, or work for the clan as a medic."

"I'm not qualified yet." I had another three and a half years to go.

"It doesn't matter. Finnan saw what you did for Orin. He

knows that you're still studying, and he's willing to let you be the clan medic before you've finished college."

Swiping my tongue over my bottom lip, I asked, "I assume Grayson knows about this?"

"He will tonight when Finnan tells him."

We walked for a few more blocks in silence, the scent of cigarette smoke following us.

"There's no way out, is there?" I asked, suddenly feeling cold. I wrapped my arms around myself. I wasn't talking about making a choice between whoring and helping. I was talking about the fact that I had killed a man who belonged to another clan. There was no coming back from this.

I knew that being the medic was the far better option of the two I'd been faced with, but a small part of me wanted to see if there was another option. A third. Something that didn't involve me becoming a whore, or a member of a notorious crime syndicate.

"You killed a rival clan member," Keir reminded me. "The only way out now is death, I'm afraid." Bringing the cigarette to his lips, he inhaled, then let it out. The white smoke curled around him. "Want my advice?"

I nodded.

"Become the medic. You're too innocent to be a fucking whore for the clan. You have some real skills and you'll be an asset."

"What if I do something wrong and can't save someone?"

He shrugged. "The hospital is the last choice, but if you can mitigate against us needing to go, it would make Finnan a very happy man. He can only pay off so many hospital directors and staff to look the other way when one of us comes in with a life-threatening injury."

He stubbed out his spent cigarette on the bottom of his boot and pocketed the butt.

"Have you seen Orin?" I asked quietly, ashamed of myself for even wanting to know how he was doing.

"He's been up north handling some business for Finnan."

"Oh." My disappointment was a sharp jab under my ribs. "Right."

"I told him to stay away from you, though."

"And what did he say to that?"

"I believe his exact words were "*Are you willing to fucking die to keep her location a secret?*""

"Die?"

"He had a gun held to my head at the time." He shrugged.

I shook my head. "Jesus." Glancing up, I saw that we'd made it back to the apartment. "Thank you for walking me back."

"Anytime." He smiled. "My number is in the burner phone I gave you in case you ever need anything."

"Thank you."

With a nod, he crossed the street to where a black Rover was parked near the docks.

I turned and entered the building, drawing to an abrupt stop when a familiar voice came from just inside the doorway.

"That fucker better not have touched you."

The hairs on the back of my neck rose, and I turned to find Orin standing a few feet away, hidden from view of the street. His black eyes were fixed on my face, the expression of longing in them unmistakable.

My heart began to race, my body reacting to his nearness. "Orin, what are you doing here?"

26

ORIN

"ORIN, WHAT ARE YOU DOING HERE?" HER EYES had flashed with fear when she first realized I was here, but now her gaze had settled into cool contempt.

"I followed Keir. What were you doing with him?" My voice was low and threatening, but the monster inside me howled with relief at seeing her once more.

She chewed her bottom lip—a nervous gesture. "He came to give me some more money."

I felt the sharp point of a dagger stabbing into my chest at the reminder that I'd left her high and dry. "You don't need his money anymore. I'm here now."

She folded her arms across her chest. "Why are you doing this?"

"Because you're mine, Fallon." I took a step closer, and she inched back one. Fuck, the last thing I wanted was for her to be afraid of me.

She stared into my eyes with unflinching strength. "If I'm yours, why did you tell Finnan to get rid of me?"

I stiffened. Whatever she'd heard, she was treating it as gospel. "What do you think you heard?"

"I don't *think* I heard anything," she shot back, disdain dripping from every syllable. "You told Finnan you wanted me gone. To get rid of me, so I saved you all the fucking trouble and left on my own. Now, that's exactly what I want to be right now. *Alone.*"

"I'm not going anywhere."

She arched a brow at me. "You won't leave? Fine. I will." Fallon turned on her heel and left the apartment lobby.

And what did I do? I ran after her like the pussy-whipped asshole I was. To her back, I said, "Did you also hear me tell Finnan that I wanted you somewhere safe, and to have a security detail around you."

Her next step faltered, but she didn't slow. "It doesn't matter, Orin."

I ran a clawed hand through my hair, yanking at the strands. "It *does* fucking matter, Fallon." I'd caught up with her and grabbed her elbow, forcing her to stop. There were some curious looks from passersby, but none of them intervened.

Turning her around, I tipped her chin up so she had to look at me. "The reason I wanted you gone was because ..." I looked into her face with its fierce expression and tight jaw, but it was her eyes that were the giveaway.

There was fear in them.

The fear of rejection.

The fear that she wasn't good enough.

The fear that I might not want her.

I shouldn't have ever wanted something as pure as her in my life, but I was a selfish bastard.

"Fallon, talk to me."

"No."

She pulled out of my grasp, and I let her go, but that didn't mean I was giving up. "Filly, please."

That brought her to a stop on the sidewalk. She turned, her eyes narrowed with fury. "*Stop calling me that.*"

"No."

"I don't know why you're still doing this, still chasing me. You wanted me gone? I'm gone. You can go and fuck whatever woman you like now because you've obviously had your fill of me." Tears leaked from the corners of her eyes, and she wiped them away with a rough hand. "Now, leave me *the fuck* alone."

I made sure I had her attention because the next words I said, I wanted there to be no fucking misunderstandings. "You. Are. Mine." Grabbing her hand, I jerked her into the café we'd stopped in front of and dragged her through. I felt everyone's eyes on us as I towed her to the front counter.

"Bathroom," I barked.

The young woman behind the coffee machine pointed to a door in the back corner of the café. "Over there."

"Orin, let me go!" Fallon shouted. "Somebody, help me!" she yelled.

Hoisting her over my shoulder, I said, "Nobody is going to help you, Filly. They know who I am. They'll let me do whatever I please, and whatever I please right now is proving that you made the wrong decision."

She slammed her fists into the small of my back, and I

slapped her on the ass in warning. "Stop. Now." I used the same dominating tone as before, and just as I suspected it would, the sound of it made her pause. Only for a moment, but it was enough to let me know that things weren't completely lost between us.

The reprieve from getting punched in the kidneys was short-lived though. She began again, trying to wriggle her way free. I'd made it to the bathroom door, which turned out to be a room with a toilet, sink, and counter. I dropped her roughly onto the counter and locked the door behind us.

Her hair was wild around her face, her cheeks pink from the fight. Fuck, I wanted to taste her again, and as I let my gaze track down her body, I saw her nipples protruding from behind the flimsy fabric of her dress. I grabbed one between my thumb and forefinger, squeezing the aching bud until she gasped.

"You're mine, Fallon. There's nowhere you can go that I won't find you."

"Fuck you."

Darkly, I said, "I'd rather fuck you." I pulled her knees apart, and as desperately as she tried to shut them around my hand, I wouldn't let her. I kept them open with my hips while I shoved her dress up and pulled the panel of her soaked panties to the side. She made a small whimpering sound, and when I looked up, she slapped my face.

Once.

Twice.

Anger mixed with lust ignited in my blood. I grabbed her wrist before she could strike me a third time. With her other hand, she tried to slap me again, but I captured her just as easily as before. Securing both her wrists in one hand, I stretched her arms above her head and pinned them to the mirror. Her body arched toward me, pushing her breasts in to my face. Leaning forward, I bit one of them, relishing the hoarse cry that left her throat as I licked away the sting.

She squirmed on the counter, her hips rolling in that way that said she wanted my mouth somewhere else. I didn't trust her not to strike me again, though, so I undid my belt, binding her wrists, then securing a leather loop around the sconce light above the mirror. She pulled against the leather, but nothing moved.

Hooking my finger into the top of her dress, I pulled it down, revealing her lace bra and those nipples I liked to tease so much. Her chest was flushed, her breathing erratic. When I sucked one nipple into my mouth, she moaned. When I pinched the other, her moan turned into something more …

Submission.

"Stay still," I barked, pleased when she became statue-still. While I licked and sucked and bit at her breasts, I shoved my fingers under her mouth.

"Spit."

She spat onto my fingers, and I brought my now-soaked digits to her cunt, sliding them inside her. There was no resistance—nothing to stop me from claiming her pussy with a quick, hard finger fuck, and as I started to move inside her, biting her, teasing her, driving her higher, I waited for her inner walls to clench, for her body to give everything to me. I wanted it all. Her pleasure. Her trust.

Her fucking love. I was a sick bastard for even thinking I could have her and keep her safe, but I already knew I was selfish. I guessed I could add greedy to the list too.

"Please, sir," she mewled. "I'm close. So close."

Releasing her nipple, I leaned back, still pumping my fingers in and out of her. She was holding her body completely still even though I knew she wanted to writhe against the friction. I could see that in the way her legs trembled and her arms shook. She bit her bottom lip, drawing a groan from my throat.

Dropping to my knees, I latched onto her clit with my teeth and bore down. She cried out this time, her legs tightening around the side of my head. She thought she could stop me from tasting her when all she was doing was holding me right where I wanted to be. I sucked on her swollen bud, all the while pumping my fingers in and out of her hot, slick channel.

"Please, please, please …" she started to beg, her words like a litany in church. Only she was worshipping at the altar of the darkness inside me. "Please. Sir!"

Quickly, I yanked my fingers out of her pussy and shoved the zipper down on my jeans. My cock—hard and ready— slid into her, and she came. The feel of me inside her made her come so hard, made her cunt *squeeze* so hard, that I grunted and prayed I could hold back my own release.

I thrust into her heat, dropping my head into the crook of her neck and inhaling her ylang-ylang scent. Fuck, it drove me wild knowing I was making her writhe so violently that her body was overstimulating her pleasure. That I had been the one to do that. She fell—boneless—against me as I fucked into her, hitting a spot inside her that I knew I could reach from this angle.

"Yes, yes, yes," she whispered.

"Who do you belong to?" I grunted out, the sound of my balls hitting her pussy driving me to fucking distraction. "Who does this cunt belong to?"

"You," she moaned. "You. Always you, Orin."

I came with a roar, biting her on the neck, holding her flesh between my teeth as I emptied myself inside her. My orgasm rolled through me like a storm, each wave of hot pleasure joining the last until I wasn't sure I would ever stop marking her like this.

Not that I wanted to stop marking her like this.

I finally came down from the high of fucking my woman, unhooking her arms and unwrapping the belt. I massaged her wrists, kissing them where the chaffing had been the worst, then tipped her chin up so I could look into her face. Her eyes were heavy with pleasure. I stepped away, freeing my body from hers, but mourning the loss of her heat.

She slid from the counter and reached for the hand towel dispenser on the wall.

"No," I told her.

She stilled, peering at me. "You don't want me to clean up?"

Was I a bastard for making her leave my cum inside her and on the inside of her thighs? Yeah, I was, but I was a possessive bastard if nothing else, and I wanted her to walk around with it there—remembering how I'd possessed her body so completely.

"Leave it."

With a huff, she dropped her hand.

"Keep that attitude up and you'll have my handprint on your arse, too," I warned.

She shook her head, fixing up her dress. "This is the last time it's ever going to happen, Orin."

Her words may as well have been bullets. They tore through me, and I glanced down, expecting to see blood. "What do you mean *last time*? I plan on fucking you thoroughly every single morning and night."

"You can't just take what you want from me, Orin. You can't take it then disappear and leave me to pick up the goddamned pieces."

I leveled her with a hard stare. "That's easy. Come back with me, and I won't ever have to disappear."

She shook her head. "That's not the solution and you know it."

"What is the solution, then?"

Looking down, she brushed some imaginary lint from the skirt of her dress, then pinned me with a resolved stare. "Tell me the whole truth about you. All your secrets. All your lies. Then I might be able to move forward with you."

Tell her my truths? My past? My sins? I began shaking my head, knowing that if I told her everything in my past, it would guarantee that she wouldn't let me touch her ever again.

"I can't." I croaked the words out. "I can't do that."

Her expression fell, and she stepped around me. "Then do whatever you want, Orin, so long as it doesn't involve me anymore."

She unlocked the door and stepped out into the café.

I, however, stood there for a long time wondering whether she would be able to accept my past or whether she would abandon me just like all the other people I'd been foolish enough to care for had.

27
FALLON
THREE WEEKS LATER...

ORIN HAD BEEN AFRAID. I'D SEEN IT IN HIS EYES, but I needed to know the truth. At least then I might be able to understand why he pushed me away like he had. Whatever it was, it was unresolved, and I knew that if I forgave him, we would be stuck in this vicious cycle of fucking and building emotions, but as soon as he felt threatened by something I said or did, he would abandon me again.

My own ragged scars from my parents' deaths were enough for me to deal with without him casting me aside again too.

No matter how much I tried to forget about him, though, I couldn't escape the memories of the way he'd taken me in that café. Every touch, every sound, every moan and groan of pleasure was seared into my brain, and I was ashamed to admit that I'd taken those memories out of the box I'd shut them in more than once or twice. His complete domination over my body and my pleasure was so freeing, and it was only now—with self-reflection— that I saw the real reason I had cried that first time he'd taken me like he had.

When I was raped, I'd had no control over the situation. I hadn't been able to fight back or scream for help. I hadn't been able to do anything except lay there and have my body violated over and over again. I still remembered all their faces—the men who took something away from me that night. They weren't concerned with my pleasure or comfort. All they wanted was to take a little part of my soul with them and satisfy their own dark desires.

But Orin was different.

I hadn't realized it at the time, but when I was with him, those old fears hadn't surfaced. I hadn't thought about that event or those men—not once. Orin, although rough and demanding, never made me feel like I wasn't the center of his world. He never made me feel like I was nothing to him, and my pleasure was always at the forefront of his mind.

Being with him was *freeing*. I could trust him with my body, knowing he would treasure it. Sex—even the thought of having it—was always a trigger. I hadn't wanted to be intimate with someone for so very long …

Until him.

The events of almost two months ago seemed like ancient history.

There had been no more attempts on my life.

No times when I thought I was being watched by one of the rival clans, although I knew Orin still watched me. I never saw him, but I would often catch a hint of sandalwood on the air when leaving a class or feel him close by when I left a practical placement for one of my classes. He was everywhere, in the shadows I stared into, in the darkness of the night.

I was torn from my thoughts when the door to the apartment flew open and Keir walked in with Caolan. Caolan looked ashen as he wilted against the other man, and I assessed him quickly.

"Put him in the spare room," I ordered, pointing in the direction of the bedroom I had repurposed to hold the two gurneys the clan had appropriated when I accepted the role of medic. They acquired everything else I could've possibly needed too. First aid supplies. Linens. Infusion pumps. Ventilators. A defibrillator. A top-of-the-range autoclave, plus a whole lot more that had overflowed into storage shelves in the hallway and living room.

I still shook my head at the sheer number of drugs held in the locked cabinet on the wall just inside the door.

Keir grunted and changed directions, hoisting the other man up onto the edge of the bed. Once he had Caolan settled, I shoved him out of the way and started to triage. There were some nasty-looking wounds across his ribs and a small bullet hole near the top of his shoulder. They weren't life-threatening, but they would need to be treated before infection set in.

"Pass me that saline," I ordered Keir, holding my hand out for it without taking my eyes off Caolan's body. There was blood pooling at the small of his back, which meant there was another injury there I hadn't seen.

When Keir returned with the saline, I put it down and shoved my hands under Caolan's good shoulder. "Help me turn him. I need to see where that blood is coming from."

Keir took the brunt of the weight, shifting the other man over so I could get a clear look at the wound. There was a cut on the small of his back. It wasn't particularly big, but it was deep and bleeding openly.

I looked up at Keir from under my lashes. "Hold him steady."

He nodded, and I grabbed the saline to flush the wound. With the blood gone, I could see how jagged the wound was.

"How in the hell did this happen?"

"His car wrecked. I had to drag him out of there. He'd been impaled by some twisted metal."

Jagged metal. That would definitely do it. After cleaning the site the best I could, I patched him up with some gauze, then indicated for Keir to return Caolan to his back. Now that I wasn't afraid of him bleeding to death, I addressed the shoulder wound next. It was a clean through-and-through, somehow missing his clavicle and shooting straight through the muscular mass of his trapezius.

I cleaned that, patched it, then moved on to the last wound on his side. After irrigating it, I could see that it was road rash. "Jesus, what the hell kind of car wreck did he have?"

"There was a shoot-out. He must've taken that one in the shoulder and lost control."

"And where were you?"

"Ahead of him. We were picking up a shipment, but we'd taken two cars. When he didn't arrive a few minutes after

I did at the compound, I circled back and found him. The car had caught on fire. I barely got him out in time before it went up."

Caolan was a lucky bastard then. So many other things could've gone wrong. "Okay. Leave him here to rest for twenty-four hours. He'll be unhappy about it, but he'll be able to move around slowly after that."

I didn't notice it until then, but relief crossed Keir's face. He touched my shoulder lightly and said, "Thanks, Fallon."

I shook my head. "It's no problem. I'm going to wash up. Come out when you're ready, and I'll make you something to eat."

The grin he gave me transformed his face. "You going to feed me, Fallon?"

I didn't know why, but that sounded like he was flirting with me, and I wasn't quite ready for that. In fact, I didn't think I'd be ready for anything again with the way Orin still haunted my thoughts.

I ran my eyes over Caolan once more, then stepped from the room. In the bathroom, I washed my hands and then splashed some cold water onto my face. Staring at my reflection, I noticed the dark circles under my eyes were back, looking more bruised than before.

"Pull yourself together. Orin doesn't want you," I hissed to myself. "He's made that perfectly clear."

Although he'd been around, Orin hadn't approached me. I knew he needed time, but it had been three weeks since I'd last seen him, and each day he stayed away only confirmed that he wasn't willing to trust me with his past.

Yanking open the bathroom door, I strode into the kitchen

and started pulling things out to make an omelet. I was whisking the eggs when Keir emerged from the makeshift hospital room. He slumped onto a kitchen stool.

"Do you like eggs?" I asked.

"Sure," he replied, running a hand through his dark hair. "Sounds great."

I bit my lip and kept whisking. After I was done, I chopped up some veggies and ham, then began throwing things into the skillet. The scent of peppers and onions filled the kitchen.

"Have you spoken to him?"

I glanced over at Keir. "Who?"

"Orin. Have you spoken to him?"

I bit my lip recalling our last 'talk.' "If you consider getting holed up in a café bathroom as speaking, then yes."

His brows rose. "He locked you in a café bathroom?"

I could feel my cheeks flush, so I turned my face away. "He wanted to talk somewhere privately, and that was the only place close by."

"What did he say?"

Using the spatula, I shifted the vegetables around. "Say? Nothing I hadn't heard before."

"Did he apologize at least?"

"He apologized for some things, but the man is hardheaded and refuses to tell me everything about his past."

"From what I understand, it's a pretty dark place, Fallon. Maybe he's trying to protect you."

"It's not that." I turned to face him once more. "I told him everything. Every last detail of my past. The lows, then the lower lows that resulted from them. Not once did he tell me a thing about him, and if he wants me to trust him, how in the hell can I do that if I don't know him."

"You can trust Orin," he said simply. "He needs you, Fallon. I've not seen him so …"

"Pissed off?" I supplied.

"*Passionate.* I've not seen him this protective over someone else. Did you know he ordered everyone to not speak to you when you were first at the compound? He didn't want you getting overwhelmed by strangers. And now, we have shifts to keep an eye on you, but Orin is taking every single one of them. He's not slept. He doesn't eat. He's broodier than usual. What kind of man does all that if he doesn't give a fuck?"

I knew the answer to the question, but I couldn't voice it. Not with the glue holding my heart together still drying. I added the eggs to the skillet. "I don't know, Keir. He's so …" I couldn't find the words.

"In love with you," Keir supplied. "He's in love with you, but he's fucking terrified of that because it means he could lose you."

My heart stuttered against my ribs, the movement kindling the hope that had refused to be extinguished after the last time I saw him. "It doesn't matter anyway," I replied, still unable to look him in the eye. "He's not got the guts to come and tell me that himself, and until he does, this is where I'm going to stay."

I plated up the omelet, cutting it in half so we could share. Keir took his plate with a smile of thanks and began to eat. I ate mine too, carrying on a conversation with Keir, but my mind was somewhere else. Somewhere there were dark eyes, a commanding tone, and a man who claimed he was a monster.

28
ORIN

IT HAD BEEN FIVE FUCKING WEEKS OF TORTURE. Not the kind of torture that the fucker in front of me was currently experiencing but being away from Fallon had been my own source of torment. I hadn't seen her since she'd left me standing in the café bathroom, but I'd heard she'd taken on the role of medic for the clan and exceeded everyone's expectations.

Fallon was such a strong woman, and I didn't know why I didn't realize it before now. She may have been submissive in the bedroom for me, but outside of there, she was a fucking lioness ready to defend herself.

The guy in front of me moaned, and I fixed my cold, dead eyes on him.

It had only taken me a day to track down Owen Ward, but I spent at least two weeks learning his habits, watching him scuttle from his job at a fucking pub back home, then out again to score some pussy. The guy was a fucking broken record, and given that he always picked up a pro, I was willing to bet his dick would fall off the next time he stuck it in a filthy cunt.

And now, here we were. I'd bagged him walking home one night and brought him here to my little slice of heaven. The warehouse was cavernous, and the sounds of rats climbing the rafters and chewing the beams echoed around the space.

I made sure to give him my best smile. "You don't know who I am, but I know who you are, Owen Ward." With the tip of my knife, I peeled apart the sides of his collared shirt, spotting the Saint Patrick pendant on a silver necklace. Fallon said she remembered this—like the image had been branded into her memories with a hot iron. Sliding the metal beneath the silver chain, I yanked it off his neck and pocketed the medallion.

He moaned, unable to form coherent words since I'd cut his tongue out as soon as he'd regained consciousness. Blood dripped from his mouth, the ragged stump of flesh left behind flapping uselessly against the back of his teeth.

"Now, you may be wondering, *Why me? What have I done wrong?* Well, I'm going to tell you what you did wrong." I crouched in front of him so he could see my face clearly. "You touched something that belongs to me." His sky-blue eyes widened, and I nodded. "You and four of your buddies touched her, *used* her, and then left her. Do you know who I'm talking about?"

I could see the whites completely around his irises now, and the stark horror in them made the monster chuckle.

"I know the other four men have already died for their crimes, but it was you," I punctuated my statement by tapping on his bared sternum, "who should've been thrown into jail and gang raped daily. Do you think you would've liked that? I know Fallon didn't enjoy it very much."

Owen began to wrestle against his bonds, trying his best to free himself from the confinement. I let him do it, knowing that even if he did get free, there was no way he was walking out of there. I wouldn't let it happen.

As he struggled, I went to the workbench and grabbed the sledgehammer from its hook. The thing must've weighed at least twenty pounds and had enough force to break a grown man's thigh bone. I had no interest in breaking bone today though.

Walking back to face him, I showed him the thick iron head of the hammer, smiling when his eyes started to dart around the warehouse, looking for an escape he was never going to find. Today was about giving Fallon the justice she deserved.

I kicked at the chair he was sitting on, breaking one of the legs and splintering another. The wood gave way to his weight, and he collapsed backward onto the ground. The bottom of the chair fell out, and I grinned as the universe delivered on my plans.

While he struggled to get to his feet, I brought the knife to the edge of his jeans. As soon as he felt the kiss of steel against his ankle, he stopped moving. I ran the blade against the thick fabric, watching the seam split to reveal his calf, his knee, his thigh. I ran the steel all the way up to the waistband of the jeans, then removed them from his body. The fucker wasn't wearing anything underneath, but that only made my job easier.

"Don't move, Owen," I said to him. "I know you did this to Fallon while she was drugged and couldn't fight back, but today, we're going to do it my way."

His hoarse scream was muffled as I shoved the handle of the sledgehammer up his ass. Sodomy wasn't my thing, but I could see the poetic justice in this. I fucked him with the hammer until blood pooled on the floor beneath him, but I didn't stop. I continued until he passed out from the pain, then slapped his face to wake him up once more.

He blinked up at me, dazed for a moment until the pain hit him full force and his eyes began to water. I brought the bloody handle up for him to see, then discarded it like I'd discarded his tongue earlier. "How do you like being fucked against your wishes?"

I laughed darkly when he moaned, tears leaking from the corners of his eyes. My gaze darted to the large tattoo that spanned the width of his paunchy stomach. The ink depicted a gun with a bullet being fired from it, but his burgeoning waistline had stretched it—morphed it—so any menace it may have once held was now gone. Pulling out my knife, I placed the razor-sharp edge against the tip of the bullet. The steel was hungry for his blood, gliding through the first few layers of tissue effortlessly. He screamed, but he was too weak to move away as I filleted the flesh from his body.

With a grim smile, I held out the apron of skin for him to see. His blue eyes were bloodshot from his strained screaming, but I saw the flicker of relief that I was done.

"You think this is over?" I asked in a murderous voice. "You think I'm done with you?" I leaned in closer and whispered, "Not even fucking close."

I WAS CLEANING UP IN THE BATHROOM, WATCHING the pink water gurgle down the drain and waiting for the rush of endorphins I usually felt when I killed, but the sensation was conspicuously absent. I wasn't getting the sense of calm. I wasn't getting the powerful feeling of control. All I had was a sense of foreboding that Fallon wouldn't approve of all this if she knew.

Keir had spoken to me about opening up to Fallon about my dark past—not that the bastard knew a lot. He knew enough to know that I was not the kind of man you wanted to fuck with, but not the filthy debauched details of my childhood. Nobody did. Those secrets died with Ava when I shoved a blade through her heart.

But what if I could tell Fallon? What if I told her, and she didn't turn away from me in disgust? What if she could accept me for who I am and what I've done? I shook my head as soon as the thoughts coalesced. I couldn't do that. I didn't want to risk her looking at me any differently.

I wandered back into the main part of the warehouse, my distant gaze landing on the mass of meat and blood piled against the floor. Strips of skin were missing, muscle and bone exposed to the air. The whole cavernous space smelled of copper and spilled bowels, and as fucked up as that was, it brought me a sense of peace.

Drying off my hands on a rag, I leaned against the steel workbench where I had laid out my tools and pulled out my phone. I had to go away—to leave Fallon under Keir's watch—while I took care of business, but that didn't mean I didn't want to know what the fuck was going on while I was gone.

As soon as the call connected, I demanded, "Where is she?"

Keir let out a sigh. "In class."

"How is she?"

"Fine. Nothing is going to happen to the lass."

I ground my molars. Keir wasn't exactly my first choice to leave as lookout, but Fallon and he had formed a tentative bond in the time she was at Oranmore. If there were another man she trusted—even a little bit—it was him. I knew the bastard thought she was gorgeous, but Fallon was destined for only one man, and that fucker was me.

"So," he started, "Are you ready to pull your head out of your arse?"

"Fuck you, Keir." He didn't know how much was riding on this.

"I know it's not what you want to do, but, man, this girl? She's worth it, don't you think?" When I didn't reply, he continued, "Or maybe you don't say a fucking thing then I can have a crack with her."

Black spots appeared in front of my eyes as my anger morphed into an insatiable rage. "Stay away from her, Keir."

"Make me," he shot back, chuckling. The bastard had *chuckled* at me and hung up.

I PULLED UP TO THE CURB A BLOCK AWAY FROM Fallon's college, then hoofed it to Keir's location. He'd been holed up in a café across the street most of the time, and I would've felt like an asshole for making him do it, but he'd made that jab about Fallon, and now I wasn't feeling so contrite.

"You got a lot of fucking nerve," I snarled, making his head jerk up.

Keir took one look at me, then back at his computer screen. "You smell like smoke."

"Hazard of the job," I said, my jaw still tight. "Just like being armed every second of the day."

His dark eyes flickered to my face again, and he sighed. "Look, I'm sorry. I'm not interested in Fallon. I only said that so you'd *do* something instead of brooding and being a generally unpleasant person … well, *more* of an unpleasant person. You were not so chipper to start with."

He'd baited me? Fuck!

"Sit down before you scare away all the nice people," Keir told me, indicating the chair opposite him. I looked around the café to see that everyone was staring at me—probably wondering when I was going to start that murder spree I felt like having when I thought about Fallon with anyone else.

I sat, my attention on the building across the road.

"Relax. Class doesn't finish for another," he glanced at his watch, "ten minutes. Did you fucking drive fifty over the limit to get here in time?"

"Fuck you."

He held his hands up in surrender, a smile tugging at the corner of his mouth. "Hey, sorry I fucking asked." He dropped his hands and the smile faded, too. "You made the right choice."

"And what choice might that be?" I asked, my tone a warning for him to tread lightly here.

"You're going to tell her the truth. All of it."

I hated that he could read me that way. Nobody else had been able to—just Keir, and I wondered whether his own military training had involved interrogation.

I grunted, not willing to give him a verbal answer because I knew he'd fucking … ah, shit, there it was. That shit-eating grin that said he knew he was right, and I should praise him for it. Hyperintelligence was fucked.

With that smile still firmly in place, he shut the lid of his laptop and tapped the center of it with his index and second fingers. "For what it's worth, I think you're doing the right thing."

I glared at him.

He shrugged, completely unfazed by my outburst, and rose from his seat. "Good luck with her." He walked toward the door but stopped and added, "And don't hold back. On anything."

Before I could snarl at him, he was gone. I watched him walk past the café window, and when my eyes shifted back to the college building, I saw her. Fallon was wearing a pair of tight jeans that hugged her curves and a white sweater. Her blonde hair was unbound, and my dick grew hard just thinking about having it spread all over my pillow.

I bit the inside of my cheek to stop that freight train. I sat there, watching her until suddenly her head turned in my direction and my heart seized in my fucking chest. She held my gaze, biting her bottom lip as she thought through her options.

My dick was a length of steel in my pants, and I didn't give a fuck. Fallon was the woman I would always want. I reached into my pocket for the medallion, rubbing my thumb across its raised surface. I had to hope that my peace offering to her was well-received.

We were caught in the moment for a long time until finally, her shoulders set and her spine straightened. She started crossing the road, checking both ways more than once as she darted across the two lanes of traffic. I made myself stay completely still when she entered. I didn't want to scare her off. I didn't want her to take one look at me and run in the other direction because if she did, she would be taking my fucking black heart with her.

She took a seat in the chair Keir had vacated but said nothing.

Her blue eyes darted to my hand resting on the table, then returned to my face.

Inhaling deeply through her nose, she said, "What are you doing here, Orin?"

"I came to see you."

"Are you ready to talk to me? To tell me the truth?"

Was I? "Yes."

"Okay then." She glanced around, noting all the people still in the café. "We should go somewhere more private then."

Privacy. With Fallon. It had been something I'd been craving for weeks, but I promised myself I wouldn't see her until I avenged her. Rising from my seat, I followed her out onto the street, staying a couple of steps behind her as she weaved through the masses of people clogging up the sidewalks. The weather was warm for this time of the year, and everyone was out enjoying it.

We walked to the apartment, entering the front door and walking to the elevator. She said nothing as we rode up to the eighth floor, and I had to physically restrain myself from reaching for her. I couldn't touch her again until after she knew everything. Then, it would be up to her to decide whether she wanted me in her life—every fucked-up part of me.

Inside the apartment, she placed her bag on the counter and then filled up the kettle.

"Tea?" she asked.

"Sure," I replied absently. I didn't drink fucking tea.

I walked around the living room, looking at the metal shelving containing medical supplies while she busied herself in the kitchen. When she returned five minutes later, she held out a mug to me. I took it, then set it on the coffee table. Her gaze dropped to my steaming cup.

"You don't want my tea?"

I wanted more than her fucking tea, but I had to think this out carefully. "I want to talk to you more."

"Here I am," she replied softly, blowing across the top of her cup, and sending steam spiraling through the air at me. It smelled of the tea she was drinking and of ylang-ylang. Fuck, I'd missed that scent. "What did you want to talk about?"

I swallowed, wondering why I could look a man in the face while I shot him, but I couldn't stomach telling Fallon the truth. I tried to sit down, but when it was clear my frenetic energy wasn't having any of that, I jumped up and began to pace. Fallon watched me curiously.

"Orin, you're making me nervous," she said.

"Sorry," I bit out, running a hand through my hair.

She took a seat on the couch, resting back on the cushions like she had all fucking night to wait for me. I finally forced my legs to stop moving and stared at the woman who had stolen my heart without my permission. Without my awareness. Did I want it back? Fuck no. She could keep it. I wanted her to keep it. Forever. And I decided in that moment, that even if she didn't want to keep it, that would be okay. I would find a way to move on because all that mattered was her happiness.

Her safety.

And now that I'd taken care of that little Owen Ward problem, I could deliver on at least one of those promises.

Sucking in a deep breath, I dug a hand into my pocket and pulled out the Saint Patrick medallion. The silver pendant was dull in my palm, but I offered it to her. Sitting forward, she set her cup down and then looked at what I was offering her.

She frowned.

Picked up the chunk of silver to get a closer look, then dropped it like it had burned her.

"How did you get that?" She nudged the thing with her foot, too shaken to do anything else.

"It's for you," I said. "I took it from him. It's my trophy for the kill, but I took it for you."

Her eyes widened at the word *kill*. Could I blame her though. It wasn't every day that the man who obsesses over you kills another man because he hurt you—at least not in her world.

"You killed Owen?"

"Yes."

She stared at the medallion at her feet, then looked back up at me. "But how did you find him? Grayson looked everywhere."

Her brother's motivation was nothing on the all-consuming craving that I had harbored. "I found him."

"And you killed him for me?"

"Yes."

Couldn't she see there wasn't anything I wouldn't do for her? Nothing I wouldn't say. Nobody I wouldn't slay for her.

"He's dead?"

"He was when I left him. Unless he's the fucking anti-Christ, I think he's staying down."

She licked her bottom lip, and my cock stood at attention. "You did this. For me? To try and win me back?"

"No, Filly. I did it so you could finally feel safe again."

Tears welled in her eyes quickly, but she blinked them away. "I do feel safe, Orin. When I'm with you I feel like nothing, and nobody can touch me."

"They can't."

"But you killing the man who instigated my rape isn't going to be enough."

What the fuck else did she want from me then? "You want

my life, too? I've never been afraid to die, Fallon." I pulled the Glock from behind my back and held it to my head.

Fallon's eyes widened as she jumped up from the couch and dragged my arm down. "I don't want you to die, Orin. The only thing I want from you is the truth. *Your* truth." The tears were back, and she let them fall this time. "Good or bad, ugly or beautiful, I love you and want to know you completely, but I can't do that until I know who you were before you became who you are."

I hardly heard what she'd said, because all my mind could do was stay stuck on the words *I love you*. "You love me?"

She nodded, a tear dripping from her cheek. "I do. I love you even though I know I shouldn't, but ..." She gripped my hand, prying the gun from my fingers. She placed it on the table, then stared up into my face. "I need to hear it all. There is nothing you can say that will scare me away. I promise you that."

My heart slammed against my ribs in an attempt to get out—to get to her since she owned it now in any case. Could I tell her everything? Nobody—not one person knew the whole dirty truth of my childhood, but as I looked into her eyes, I realized that's exactly what I didn't want to do anymore. I wanted someone to share that burden with, and that someone was standing in front of me—unflinchingly.

I nodded, and she drew me down onto the couch. I rarely went back to those times in my head, but for her, I would. I would deep dive back into the blackness, and hopefully, she would be the one to pull me out once I was done almost drowning.

"I'm an orphan." My voice cracked over the words. "I was

in the orphanage until I was ten. Nobody wanted me. But then, a day after my tenth birthday a couple adopted me. They couldn't have children of their own. Originally, they were going to adopt a baby, but my adoptive mother told me later that as soon as she saw me, she knew I was the one that needed their love."

Fallon reached out and took my hand, squeezing it, lending me strength.

Taking in a shuddering breath, I continued, "The first couple of years living with them had been great, but when I was twelve and a half, they both died in a freak car accident involving a tractor. It was winter, and the road was slick with ice. They didn't stand a chance.

"I fell into the foster system then. I was too old to be adopted, but a nice family who was already fostering another kid took me in. Blakely was the other kid."

"The woman who took us in that first night?"

I nodded. "I keep tabs on her now that I know where she is again. I thought I'd found my forever home. For years, things were perfect. I was doing well in school. I played rugby. My foster parents came to all the matches, too. It was the happiest I'd ever been … until my foster mother, Dee, was told she had relapsed. Her ovarian cancer was back and more aggressive than before. Within four months, she was dead. My foster father fell apart. Started to drink, and after a welfare check, it was decided that Blakely and I would be placed with other families. We wanted to stay together, but the family that agreed to take me in only wanted me and not her. She went to live somewhere in the south of the country while I stayed around Galway.

"The couple who took me in only wanted a boy because they were part of a child sex ring. I …" My breath halted in my throat, my thoughts frozen on that time.

"You don't have to … if you don't want to," Fallon said, tears dripping from her eyes.

I stared at her beautiful face and knew I had no choice. Whether I lost her for telling her the truth or lost her for not telling her, the floodgates had been opened, and I was powerless to stop the tide.

"The woman, Ava, would drug me. When I woke up, I'd be tied down, and she would be on top of me, getting me hard with her mouth. I remember the first time I woke up, I didn't know what was happening. I'd never felt the sensation before. There was a noise, and I turned my head to see that a camera had been set up on a tripod. There was a red light blinking, and I remembered counting it while the woman sat on my cock and took my virginity from me."

There was a sob, and I caught Fallon balling her hand over her mouth. She mouthed the words *I'm so sorry* to me, and as much as I wanted to hold her, I restrained myself. What if, after she learned of everything, she didn't want me to touch her again?

I cleared my throat. "Her husband sat on the other side of the camera with his cock out, masturbating to the scene. It went on like this for years, and although I tried to either stay awake so I couldn't be drugged or run away, they were always there. I was still attending school though since that was the only place I could truly relax. One day, the coach of the rugby team approached me and asked about the bruises on my arse. He'd seen them while we were showering after training. I broke down and told him everything. About a week later, the cops arrived and raided the house. I slipped out while no one was watching me, but I hung around to watch them both being hauled away."

"What happened to them?"

"A couple of years in prison for him, and seven years for her."

"That's so wrong."

I nodded. "So there I was, sixteen and without a home for the fourth time in my life. I had no interest in going back into the foster system, so I lied about my age and joined the army. I was tall for my age, and since I'd played rugby on and off for years, I'd filled out. It was about six months into training when my sergeant noticed how good a shot I was. I went through expedited training to be a marksman. For the first time in my life, I felt powerful.

"I discharged when I was twenty-two and started freelancing in wet work, but not before I hunted down Ava and her husband and put a fucking bullet through their skulls. His kill was quick. I dragged out Ava's, hurting her as much as she had hurt me. I thought killing her would bring me my greatest joy, but it was over too quickly, and afterward, I was left feeling … empty."

I glanced up at Fallon, whose big blue eyes were wide.

"Is this too much for you?"

She shook her head. "No." Looking out the window, she said, "But it's late. We should eat."

Fuck, she was right. It was fully dark outside, and I had no idea where the time had gone. I followed her into the kitchen where she was getting out pots and pans. She filled up one pot and put it on the burner.

"Is pasta okay for you?" she asked.

"Fine."

Jerking her chin in the direction of the counter, she said, "Sit down. Let me look after you for a while."

Unable to come up with a reason why I shouldn't, I sat, watching her move confidently through the kitchen. Now that the story had started, I found I wanted to continue it. I sensed that this break was less for me and more for her, and I couldn't blame her. The shit I'd gone through was fucked up. Getting lost in the rhythm of Fallon, it wasn't long before she placed a bowl of pasta in front of me with a chunky tomato sauce.

Wordlessly, she took her seat beside me, and we ate in silence. When I was done, she took my bowl and hers to the sink where she rinsed them and stacked them in the dishwasher. Afterward, she took my hand and led me down to the bedroom. She left me standing in the doorway while she threw back the quilt and slipped between the sheets.

"Come and lay with me?" she asked in a deceptively small voice.

I couldn't deny her a damn thing, so I shut off the light and approached the bed. She sighed when I was settled beside her, then inched her way closer to my chest. She rested her cheek on my pec, her arm draped lightly over my stomach.

"Is this okay?" she asked. "I want to comfort you, but now I understand why you don't like to be touched."

"It's fine," I croaked, slamming down the emotion threatening to clog my throat. It was more than fucking fine. It was perfect. I curled my arm around her back, my hand resting on her hip.

"Why do you cut your victims' tongues out?" she asked into the darkness.

Somehow, not being able to see her face made it easier to talk. "I can't stand the screaming. Ava screamed a lot when I was torturing her. It triggers me now, I guess."

"And your preferences for sex? Having submissive partners, having them restrained? All of that is tied to *her*?"

"Yes." I rubbed my free hand over my face. "It's fucked up, Filly, but it's the only way I can fuck anyone now."

"Hmmm," she replied. "How did you come to join the clan?"

"Kellen, Finnan's da, learned of my reputation as a freelancer. He offered me a permanent position in the clan as Reaper and promised that I wouldn't have to share any of my secrets about my proclivities in the bedroom. There is nobody—not one person—who knows the full truth of what happened and why I am the way I am … except, now, for you. I want you to know so that you'll be better able to understand me, and hopefully see why I overreact. I see in you something that I couldn't protect in me …" I drifted off, running my hand along her hip. My cock began to stir, but I was sure Fallon was unaware of it.

"If you still need to tie me up when we fuck, I'll understand." The words she spoke were unexpected, but the meaning wasn't lost on me.

"What?" I asked, needing to be sure.

"I love you, Orin. Every scar. Every dark thought that lurks through your mind. Every part that makes up you. I love you. If you can take me when I've been ruined by other men, then I can accept you when you've only tried to survive what life has thrown at you."

I could barely breathe. "Does this mean that you forgive me?"

"Yes. I wanted the truth, and you gave it to me."

I let out a breath I hadn't known I was holding and pulled her in more tightly to my body. She ran her hands down my chest, tracing over the tattoo covering my sternum, then lower along my abdomen. My cock jerked at the contact.

"You're playing a dangerous game, Filly," I told her, my dark tone no match for the moon outside.

"Maybe I want to play it with you."

29

FALLON

THE HEAT COMING OFF ORIN'S BODY MADE ME hotter than I'd ever been, but I loved the feeling of him under my fingertips. I traced the ridges of his abs, knowing that if I brushed a little lower, I would feel another hardness straining to get out. Now that I knew his truth, I understood him better and hoped that he understood me too. We had both been taken advantage of, only he had had the guts to take his vengeance and thrive, whereas I had turned to substance abuse to recover from my ordeal.

I let out a disbelieving laugh.

"What is it?" Orin asked.

"It has literally taken me years of therapy to finally see that my turning to drugs was just another coping mechanism for the assault."

"Sometimes I wonder whether therapy would've helped me or whether this darkness inside is my coping mechanism. Do you think people are pre-programmed to be whatever they become, or whether they have a choice?"

"Nobody should have to go through what you did, and if you came out the other side a little banged up, that's not your fault either."

I let my hand rest on his stomach, feeling it rise and fall with his breath. His thumb was still sweeping over my hip but was slowly moving lower onto my ass.

"Fallon, I've missed you."

"I've missed you too."

He moved without warning, picking me up and depositing me on his lap. I froze in position, waiting for him to decide that this was too much, that there was too much contact, but as his hips surged and his cock rubbed against my core, I let out a contented sigh.

He gripped the tops of my thighs. "I might stumble every once and again, but I know you'll be there to pick me up."

Tears welled in my eyes for the hundredth time that night, and I dashed them away with the back of my hand. "Are you sure this is okay?"

"More than okay," he rumbled. "Fallon, with you, I can trust again. I love you." With one strong hand around the back of my neck, he pulled my head to his, taking my mouth in a savage kiss. I clutched at his shoulders, digging in my fingers until he made that sexy growling sound I liked so much.

"I need you naked," he said, breaking the kiss and sucking on the side of my neck. "Please, tell me I can have you again."

I grinned into the darkness. "Yes, sir."

He growled and tore the sweater from my upper body. His hands immediately found my breasts. He cupped them both, rasping his thumbs along my nipples and drawing pleasured moans from my throat. He sat up, his abdominals flexing with the movement. I ran my nails down his torso, reveling in the fact that I could touch him without making him recoil. That he loved me like I loved him.

"Are you attached to those jeans?" he asked against my neck.

"No. Why—"

I yelped when I was suddenly on my back again. A moment later, the lamp on my side table turned on, and I blinked up at Orin. His dark eyes were wild with lust, his gaze taking in my breasts and stomach. With a grunt, he tore the button from my pants and shoved the zipper out of the way. Lifting my hips, I let him take the jeans and panties from my body, suddenly breathless when his tongue touched my pussy.

The first contact made me writhe.

The second stroke of his tongue made me wish he hadn't taken so fucking long to come back to me.

The third? Well, I was in heaven.

He ate at my pussy like a man possessed, sliding one digit into my channel to tease my flesh before feeding me another. My back arched off the bed when he crooked one of his fingers inside me, hitting something deep inside that left me breathless.

"You're getting close, aren't you, Fallon?" His words were a harsh puff of air against the inside of my thighs. "You want to come, my little whore?"

"Yes!" I clawed at the sheets, feeling my orgasm barreling toward me, knowing there was no way to stop it.

"Don't come until I say you can."

I squeezed my eyes shut and muttered the words he wanted to hear. "Yes, sir."

"Good girl," he praised. "That's good."

He pumped his digits into me, driving my pleasure higher and higher until I was sure I wouldn't be able to take any more. The sound of him plunging into my wetness only added to the eroticism of the scene, and when he reached up and squeezed one of my nipples, I nearly blacked out from the anticipated pleasure.

"I want to hear you beg," he told me. "When it becomes so much, so strong, that you have to beg me to let you have your release. Beg me for it."

"Please. Please, please, please," I mumbled, mostly incoherently because it was taking everything in me to not come, to not be a bad girl.

In one swift movement, he removed his fingers and slammed into me until our pelvises were locked, our hips connected so intimately that I had no idea where my body ended and his began. I came the instant he was fully seated inside me, writhing and bucking against his body. Orin remained motionless above me, watching me with hooded eyes as I ground myself over and over on his cock in the hopes of maintaining the friction I needed.

The only indication that he was suffering with the amount of pleasure coursing around us right now was the slight tick in his jaw. Other than that, he looked like he was unflappable in the face of this storm.

When I finally came down, my breathing was erratic, my pulse tachy. And Orin had a look of wonder on his face.

"Did my little whore enjoy that?" he asked.

I nodded, unsure why this form of degradation play did it for me in the bedroom. Maybe it wasn't the words themselves that turned me on. Rather it was the man and the way he said it. Like he'd kill anyone who attempted to say something similar to me.

I offered him my hands, holding them in front of me with my wrists crossed. He stared at them for a moment, his gaze bouncing between my face and what I was offering. Eventually, he shook his head.

"I don't like seeing you bound, Fallon. I never want to restrict you like that again."

Slowly, I looped my arms around his chest and stroked the hair at his nape. "You trust me that much?"

Leaning down, he captured my mouth in a fierce kiss, then said, "I trust you with my life."

EPILOGUE

ORIN
THREE WEEKS LATER...

WAKING UP ALONE IN BED USED TO BE THE norm. I'd thought that's exactly what I wanted to be: alone. After all, touching people made my fucking skin crawl. It still did, if I was being honest, but waking up with Fallon wrapped around me was the best fucking thing in the world. Lifting my hand, I gently ran my fingers through her blonde hair, rubbing it between my thumb and index finger. The scent of her shampoo rose to greet me, making another part of my body rise to the occasion, too.

She made a small, happy sound and lifted her head to look at me. "Good morning." She covered her mouth with a yawn.

"Morning, Filly." I brushed my hand over the horse-head-shaped birthmark on her shoulder, then leaned down to kiss it. A shiver ran through her body, and my cock stirred a little more. Running my teeth up to her neck, her shivers intensified, but before I could take her mouth in a kiss, she stopped me.

"We're going to be late," she reminded me.

"Fuck your brother," I mumbled, only half meaning it. Fallon was it for me, and I knew Grayson was a huge part of her life. "I want to keep you all to myself."

She laughed, but the sound quickly turned into a moan when I lifted her up and latched onto one of her nipples. My tongue lapped at the taut flesh, driving her to distraction just like I'd intended. Grayson and Sloane were returning to Ireland from their extended honeymoon to the States. Fallon wanted to meet them at Knock Airport.

She dug her fingers into my shoulders, drawing blood. Like I gave a fuck, though. I loved it when Fallon lost herself in my touch. My hands, which I'd thought were only good for killing, could also give pleasure and I intended on lavishing my woman with that pleasure every single damned day.

Switching to the other breast, I wore Fallon down until she was rubbing up against my stomach and chest, looking for the friction she so desperately needed.

Releasing her nipple with a bite, I said, "Slide down and impale yourself on my hard cock."

She did, moaning when she pushed the blunt head into her drenched center and took me all the way down. It was my turn to groan this time. The feeling of her inner walls clenching tightly around my shaft was one of my favorite things in the whole fucking world. Fallon sat atop me for a moment, looking down at me. She traced her fingers over the tattoos on my chest and torso, lingering over the Mac Tíre in the center. Folding herself down, she kissed the top of the wolf's head, and I gripped the tops of her thighs.

"Move for me."

Sitting up, her hips began to roll at my command, my gaze fixed on the spot where our bodies met. Nobody else's pussy held my cock like hers. Nobody felt like her, either. She was tight and warm and gloved my erection like she was made for me. Fallon smoothed out the roughness of my edges. Although I had to keep those edges as sharp as motherfucking glass for everyone else in my life, I knew I would never hurt her. How could I when she owned me body and soul?

I watched in fascination as a flush crept across her chest and up her neck as her pleasure built. Her bared breasts swayed with her movements, her unbound hair wild around her face. She was a goddess, and my fingers tightened unintentionally—as if trying to keep her with me. Always.

"Orin," she said, and the plaintive sound of her moan made me want to give her every damn thing I had.

"Brace your arms on the bed beside my head. I'm going to pound that pretty cunt of yours until you scream."

She followed my command, planting her hands, and I lifted her slightly higher so she was hovering over my cock. With my knees bent and one powerful thrust, I entered her again, hitting her more sharply inside. Fallon gasped, her fingers tightening around the sheets.

"Yesss," she hissed, dropping her mouth to mine.

I continued to slam into her, owning her like she owned me.

"Does my whore like it?"

She bit her lip, and a fresh wave of arousal soaked me. I

would never dream of saying these words to her outside the bedroom, but when we were together, and she was taking my cock so beautifully, Fallon embraced the names. She got so fucking turned on by it, and there wasn't anything I wouldn't do for her.

"Who does this cunt belong to?"

"You, sir," she replied as I pushed a breath out of her. "You. Always you."

My returning grin was fierce as I turned her around and yanked her pussy down to my mouth. My tongue slid through her folds while I pressed my hips up, urging her to take my cock down her throat. She swallowed my length, taking me down to the base.

"Can you taste yourself on me?" I asked, taking her clit between my teeth and worrying at it.

She gasped, "Yes."

I shoved my hips up, making her gag on my length. "Yes, *what?*"

When I eased back, she whispered in a wanton moan, "Sir. Yes, sir."

With a feral smile pulling at my lips, I pressed into her again, tunneling my tongue into her opening and tasting how fucking turned on she was. She flooded my tastebuds, and I swallowed her down, feeling her presence filling in the cracks in my soul.

Stroking her clit, I brought her to the edge as she brought me to the edge.

"Orin, I'm … I'm …"

She didn't need to finish the sentence because I knew she was coming. Her ylang-ylang taste flooded my mouth, and I greedily sucked it all down. My own orgasm came without warning. One moment I thought I could do this for-fucking-ever, then I was overwhelmed with sensation. I hummed against her pussy, and that was all the warning she got before I spilled down her throat.

Fallon swallowed down every last drop, taking her time to clean my cock for me once I was done. I continued to stroke through her folds, enjoying the way her thighs quivered when I reached her sensitive clit.

Shifting her carefully to the side, she rested her head on my thigh and looked up at me. Her gaze was languid with the remnants of her orgasm, and I liked seeing her like that. It was a private moment between us, and I fucking rejoiced in the fact that no other man would see her this way.

"We should shower," she murmured.

My cock perked up. "Okay."

She eyed my semihard dick and shook her head. "Alone. We need to go otherwise Grayson and Sloane will be left waiting."

I knew she was right, but that didn't mean I wanted to leave this moment with her. Eventually, she rolled from the bed, and I watched her pad into the en suite bathroom. We were staying at the apartment in town. I'd moved in the very next day, glad to be away from the compound, from the room I'd used to sleep and fuck in.

Fallon's phone—the one I had set her up with—beeped from the nightstand. A quick glance at the text made me frown. Grayson's plane had already landed. Fuck. Knocking on the bathroom door, I heard Fallon's chuckle.

"Couldn't keep away could you?"

Opening the door, I stuck my head in and locked eyes on the woman who had brought me to my knees. It took a lot of willpower to look away from her wet body and say, "Grayson's flight came in early."

Her eyes widened. "Shit. Okay." She turned off the faucets and dragged a towel around her body. "You get in while I get dressed."

Stalking inside the bathroom, I wrapped my hand around the front of her throat and backed her against the bathroom counter. "Are you sure we have to go?" I flexed my hips, making sure she felt my hard cock straining to get inside her pussy again.

"You're insatiable," she replied, breathless.

"Only for you." I kissed her softly, releasing my fingers and stepping into the shower. Fallon stood and watched me for a moment before disappearing.

When I emerged a few minutes later with a towel wrapped around my waist, Fallon was fixing her hair in the mirror. She spoke to me through the reflection.

"Ready to leave in five?"

"Yeah." I dropped the towel, not bothering to hide my smirk when I saw her eyes drop to my waist.

FALLON

WHEN WE ARRIVED AT KNOCK AIRPORT, GRAYSON and Sloane had been waiting for almost forty minutes for us to arrive. I wasn't sure how he was going to react to mine and Orin's relationship, but I had to hope he took it well enough.

At least we were in a public place.

He couldn't make too much of a scene here.

Orin's fingers tightened around my own as we got closer to the café they said they were waiting at.

"It's going to be okay."

I looked up at him and gave him a weak smile. "How do you know?"

"I just know."

Blowing out a breath in the hopes of expelling all the nervous energy fluttering around in my body, I fixed my gaze on the sign for the café and straightened my spine. I could do this. I was a grown woman. I didn't need my brother's approval, but that didn't mean I didn't want it. I wanted him to be okay with this.

I spotted Sloane's platinum-blonde hair first. She had her back to us, talking animatedly to Grayson whose blue gaze suddenly fixed on my face. A smile broke out when he saw me, but it vanished when he saw who was standing next to me. He rose from his seat abruptly, knocking his mug and spilling coffee onto the table.

Sloane glanced around to see what had set him off, and when she saw me with Orin, she smiled.

"What the fuck is he doing here?" Grayson demanded, his booming voice silencing everyone around us.

I tightened my grip on Orin's hand and closed the distance between us. "He's here with me, Gray."

My brother wasn't looking at me though. His eyes were focused on the man beside me. Orin's expression had settled into cool indifference—like this was a common, everyday occurrence.

"I don't want him anywhere near you."

"Well, that's too bad," Orin drawled back. "Because I'm not going anywhere."

Grayson turned his ire on me. "Don't feel obligated to be with him, Fallon. He doesn't give a shit about anyone but himself."

"That's not true, Gray. He loves me—"

Grayson snorted. "Please, the only thing the Reaper loves is the kill."

I felt Orin tense beside me. "You shouldn't fucking interrupt her," he told Grayson, all civility stripped from his tone.

"Don't tell me how to speak to my own goddamned sister," he barked back, stepping up into Orin's personal space.

Orin let go of my hand.

"Grayson," Sloane called, getting to her feet.

I took one look at her, then stared at my brother, whose features had softened completely. He walked to Sloane's side, wrapping a possessive arm around her waist while laying his other hand on the small swell of her belly.

Pure joy bubbled up from inside me, and I pulled them both into a hug. "Why the hell didn't you tell me?" I demanded, touching the bump in Sloane's abdomen. "How far along are you?"

Sloane covered my hand with hers and smiled at me with tears in her eyes. "We wanted to tell you in person, but then our one-month honeymoon turned into two ..." She sighed. "I've just reached five months. In another five, you're going to be an aunt."

"I think you mean the *best* aunt," I replied, wrapping my arms around both of them. Grayson stiffened, and I felt a wall of heat hit my back. Grayson looked up, and his expression turned black. Not so subtly, he pushed Sloane behind him, but she wasn't having any of it. Stepping around him, she approached Orin with her hand out. He stared at her a moment before sliding his palm against hers.

"I'm Sloane. I've not officially met you, but I've heard about you, Orin. It's nice to meet you."

"Nice to meet you too," he grumbled in reply, looking a little shocked. Grayson hovered behind her, glaring at the other man.

I blew out a breath. "Look, Grayson, if you're going to keep murdering Orin with your eyes, things are going to get tedious. We're family. I choose him. We love each other. Get used to it."

He blinked at me, momentarily shocked. "You love him?"

I nodded.

"Why?"

Orin's gaze flickered to mine before I returned my eyes to my brother. "Because, besides you, he's the best man I've ever known."

Grayson's jaw bulged. "He's fifteen years older than you."

"I don't care."

"Yeah? Well, I fucking care, Fallon. I don't condone this relationship."

I shook my head. I didn't need his permission to love Orin. I didn't even need his support, although that would've been nice. "I'm sorry you feel that way, but he's the man I want."

Turning, I stepped into the line of Orin's body, feeling

his arms wrap around me. He dropped a kiss to my head. "Come on. They must be wanting to get home."

We started out of the airport, Orin, me, and Sloane ahead of Grayson, who had been relegated to bringing the luggage.

Looping her arm through mine, Sloane said under her breath, "He'll come around. He just needs to get used to the idea."

I cast a look over my shoulder at my brother. By the looks of things, he wouldn't be coming around for a long time yet.

EPILOGUE

KEIR

I FISTED THE WOMAN'S DARK HAIR AND PULLED, arching her neck back as she rode my cock. What was her name again?

Tilly?

Milly?

Molly.

Her name was Molly. Honestly, I didn't give a fuck about what her name was. After watching Orin chase after Fallon—the woman I was pretending Molly was right now—I knew I had to find another pussy to sink into.

Fallon was everything I wanted in a woman. Smart. Brave. Not afraid to ask for help when she needed it. When Orin had been gone, I had been able to pretend for a little while that she was my woman, and not Orin's. I honestly didn't fucking see what she saw in him. He was a terse, icy bastard who would sooner shoot you than save you. Fallon was in danger of being eaten alive by him if she wasn't careful.

"Yes, just like that," Molly moaned, dropping her head between my collarbone and jaw. She was riding my dick like a pro, bouncing on top of me and curling her hands through my hair. She held me closer, her hot breath escaping into my t-shirt and fanning across my hot skin.

"Yes, yes, yes," she muttered.

Cinching hard fingers around her waist, I helped lift her more fully off my cock so that when she came back down again, I entered her harder and deeper. Her black hair had spilled over her shoulder, and I fisted it once more to keep it away.

"You like that?" I asked, flexing my hips even harder into her slick pussy. Her inner walls started to tremble with the need for release.

"Yes!"

I pressed even harder against her, my balls slapping her ass. Reaching between our bodies, I rubbed at her clit, pressing my thumb against the tight bundle of nerves and waiting for her responding moan.

She wasn't Fallon, but she would do to work my frustrations out.

Flipping her over abruptly, I pressed her into the folded-down back seats of the Rover and pinned her there—her ass in the air. With one hand pressed to the back of her neck and the other tight around her hip, I fucked into her body, trying to get the images of Orin and Fallon together to desert me.

I fucked her roughly, taking my pleasure without any

regard for her own. This wasn't like me though. I made sure my partners were satisfied, but knowing Orin was probably sinking balls-deep into *my* girl right now was making me see fucking red. Tightening my grip on her hip, I pressed her chest down, forcing her face into the leather.

Her breaths were harsh, misting the fabric beneath her mouth—each exhalation forced violently from her body. Between us, her arousal slipped and slicked our bodies. She was enjoying the brutality of my frustrations, and I knew it was wrong. I should stop. I should pull out of her body and take her home.

But then I thought about Fallon again, and my agitation and rage came back tenfold.

Molly's inner walls began to quiver around my length, and I reached around to play with her clit. The sooner she came, the sooner I could get her the hell out of here and go back to the compound.

"I'm coming," she started to whisper, her voice getting louder and louder with each thrust, each passing second, each drive into her body. She spasmed around me, her slick channel milking my cock.

I came with a loud groan, still pumping into her body, still holding her down. Once my orgasm subsided, I was left with a sheen of guilt and regret covering me. I had used Molly to sate a dark desire to have a woman who wasn't the least bit interested in me.

Releasing her, I helped her sit up. She had red marks along the front of her neck and on her hip, but the look of bliss on her face erased any guilt for being too rough with her. With a sleepy smile, she started to pull on her skirt and bra.

I was still fully clothed, save for my cock hanging out of my unzipped pants.

I didn't usually fuck women I barely knew in the back of the clan's Rovers.

I was just overcome with an insane amount of jealousy that I knew of only one way to dispense it.

"That was …" Molly started.

"I know. Great," I replied. The words were hollow, but I slapped a smile on my face like I'd fucking enjoyed it. "Thanks."

"For the orgasm? You're welcome." She smiled back at me as she pulled her shirt back on. "Thanks for mine, too."

"Can I drive you somewhere?" I asked, hoping to fuck she said no. I had no desire to spend any more time with her than I already had.

"I'm fine. I don't live too far from here anyway."

An awkward sort of silence fell over the car, and I cleared my throat. After zipping my cock back into my pants, I pulled on the rear door latch and stepped out to wait for Molly to follow.

Reaching into my pocket, I found my packet of cigarettes and took one out. I had quit smoking years ago, only taking the filthy habit up again recently. I could only blame that on the blonde-haired woman who had appeared at the clan's compound. I patted my other pockets for a lighter, cursing when I realized it wasn't there.

"Have you seen my purse?" Molly called from inside the darkened interior.

"It was in the front," I replied, my gaze sweeping the surroundings. The harbor was quiet as an impending storm looked like it was rolling in, leaving the streets sparse.

After a few minutes, Molly emerged with flushed cheeks. "Thanks again," she said, then started up the road in the direction of the café I'd first met her at with Fallon a few weeks back.

Raking a hand through my hair, I got into the driver's seat and turned over the engine. It came to life with a roar, and when I looked down to see if I'd left my lighter in the front somewhere, my gaze snagged on something small and gold sitting in the center console. It hadn't been there before—I was sure of it.

I reached for the object, bringing it closer to my face to inspect it.

It was a bullet.

And etched into its side was a name.

Finnan.

"Jesus *fuck*."

ACKNOWLEDGEMENTS

I don't often write acknowledgments. Whether it's because writing is such a solitary journey on its own or whether I never really felt like I had unwavering support from someone, but on this book, I felt like I did.

Firstly, I must thank Leila for being the best beta reader and friend an author can have. Your encouragement, comments, notes, and suggestions have all made this book what it is.

Next, this book couldn't have been written without a little shove from the universe, and from a suggestion that I needed to start getting up at 5 a.m. again to start getting all the words. So, to Nina Levine and all the girls in the *Stupid AM Writing Club*, I thank you for your support and words of encouragement. Getting back into word sprints was the best thing I could've done, and I can't wait to tackle many more projects with these wonderful human beings around me.

To my awesome Dolls—my street team. Every single one of you is an integral part of my books' success. Without your sharing your love of my work, creating amazing edits, and generally shouting about how fantastic my books are, I wouldn't have much, so *thank you*!

To my family for letting me explore my dark fantasies through stories. Writing may not be the most lucrative career, but it's certainly the one that makes my soul feel full.

And lastly, to you, for taking a chance on me. Whether this is your first Kally Ash book or your fifth, thank you for falling in love with my morally gray men and the women who bring them to their knees.

THE REAPER

MAC TÍRE MAFIA

USA TODAY BESTSELLING AUTHOR

KALLY ASH

www.ingramcontent.com/pod-product-compliance
Lightning Source LLC
Chambersburg PA
CBHW030800200726
48285CB00013B/327